Little Reminders of Who I Am

Little Reminders of Who I Am
Copyright © 2020
Jeff S. Bray

ISBN: 978-1-952474-14-9
Cover art by Carolyn Bray at Colorful Creations by Carolyn
Cover design by David Warren

Published by WordCrafts Press
Cody, Wyoming 82414
www.wordcrafts.net

Little Reminders
of Who I Am

Jeff S. Bray

WordCrafts Press

To those who desire a second chance at life and love.
May God leave you the little reminders that will lead you home.

PROLOGUE

So, what do you think, Carter?" the visitor asked as he sat on the park bench.

"I haven't done this for a while," said Carter. His worn tweed trench coat was buttoned and scrunched up. He removed his hat and ran his fingers through his white hair and replaced it. His hat matched his coat; old and worn, much like the stubble on his chin.

His friend looked him over. *Must have been a matching set, one day, back when tweed was fashionable,* he thought.

"Carter," he began. "I am here with the explicit instructions of sending you on this task."

Carter thought for a moment, opened his mouth to speak but stopped himself, doubt evident on his face.

"She will relate to you. And only you," he said.

"I just don't know. He knows I don't like assignments like this. It is far too difficult when things—get complicated," defended Carter.

His friend was silent. He had heard the story and knew Carter's struggle. No one likes a failed assignment.

The visitor finally spoke, "Consider this. Maybe that is the reason why He chose you for this assignment?"

Carter looked into his visitor's crystal blue eyes. They seemed to glow through the darkness of the park that surrounded them. He broke the stare by glancing at his watch. It was getting late, and he wanted to get some sleep.

"Can I think about it?" Carter asked as he stood, knowing what the answer would be. There was no 'thinking about it' when it came to assignments. You do as you are asked. He knew he was going to take the job, his visitor knew he was going to take it, and most certainly the One who sent him knew he was going to take it.

"You know how this works," the visitor said as if reading his mind.

"Yes, I guess I do," Carter said. He adjusted his coat. It was still summer, but the evenings were beginning to hint at the chill of fall. He looked at the shoebox his visitor had brought. "Is that part of it?"

"Yes, it contains all you need." The visitor handed the box to Carter, who opened it.

"There are quite a few items in here. How long do I have?"

"A little over two months," the visitor explained. "First contact will be the day after tomorrow. Then you can work your assignment as you see fit. But understand, time is limited here."

Carter took a deep breath and released it. He closed the box and gazed into the distance. The traffic was light, typical for a Wednesday evening. The breeze picked up again, causing the brim of his hat to raise. *Two months. Not a lot of time at all.*

"So, what do you think?" Carter's visitor asked once again.

"Okay, Gabriel. I'll do it."

Davies Deli was not your typical sandwich shop. Not normal in that it used real bread instead of submarine rolls. It was the complete opposite of chain restaurants like Subway and Quizno's, but that is what made it unique. To Aaron, what made it extra special was Deborah. Deborah was Mr. and Mrs. Davies, daughter. She worked behind the counter and was the reason Aaron had been a faithful patron for the last couple of weeks.

He first noticed her when she visited mom and pop on Fridays. She helped them with accounting and payroll. But after the regular counter person, Josh, quit, she was asked to cover shifts until a replacement was hired, that was two weeks ago. Now her brown ponytail and deep hazel eyes were a regular sight.

The deli intrigued him. It resembled an old-fashioned 60s soda shop, right down to the circular cushioned stools. Aaron pretty much had 'his spot' at the end of the long ceramic tiled counter up next to the dessert case. After two and a half weeks, he was convinced that the seat knew him well. It seemed to hug him every time he took his place. He was even more convinced that he had become attracted to

Deborah. Now he just needed the summon up the courage to tell her.

Aaron was a straightforward person. He would tell it like it is and was not afraid to back down from a challenge. Yet, he wasn't without tact; he knew how and when to express himself without offending the person he was speaking to. People considered him friendly and easy to approach. However, things were different with Deborah. His tongue refused to work whenever he tried to speak to her. He had made a few attempts at conversation, but they often ended after, "Hello." He had made it to, "How are you?" once, but that was it. Yeah, Aaron had it bad. He was like a teenager with a crush.

Aaron couldn't understand his struggle. Words were his life; he wrote for a living as a columnist for the *Houston Gazette*. The Gazette was a periodical for locals and tourists that gave them information of what was happening within the city of Houston. His column, *Flavors of Houston*, was a popular review column on local eateries. Aaron would visit small restaurants, usually family-owned, sample their food, and then write a review of his experience.

Now the one thing that Aaron was known for was the very thing that defeated him. When he was around Deborah, his mouth wouldn't work, and his mind would go completely blank. He couldn't even write a proper review. He was supposed to have turned in his review of Davies Deli two weeks ago. But he had nothing, nada, zilch. He loved the place, but he couldn't find two words to save his life. She had his mind clouded that badly.

After the second week of fumbling with the words, he'd had enough. He had to do something. After a drawn-out discussion with the mirror in his apartment, he decided today was the day. He had to just do it. He was going to ask her out.

Aaron was in his office completing a blog about an Italian restaurant he had visited a couple of nights previously. He did not particularly enjoy himself. The staff was rude, and the food was bland. Not to mention he had waited over half an hour for a seat in a not-that-crowded of a restaurant. He was known for what he did, but mainly by name only. Not too many people could recognize his face, so being Aaron Stephenson—Food Columnist, did not help him get a table that evening. It was the first time he found it challenging to find a positive perspective on a place, but Nathan had wanted this review for weeks now.

Nathan picked up on his negative vibe and asked him about it. "So, how's the Andretti's piece going, Aaron?"

"I think it's as good as it's gonna get," Aaron admitted. "I'll have it to you by lunch."

"Was it really that bad?" Nathan asked.

"Let's just say, I have been treated better," said Aaron.

"Is that it?" Nathan said as he turned to leave Aaron's desk.

"Yes, no," Aaron smirked, tipping his hand. He did not really want to talk about a poor dining experience.

Nathan obliged and sat down.

"You know Davies Deli over on Davenport?"

"Yes. Daren and Angela Davies have owned that place for years."

"Well, I went in a couple of weeks ago to write a review. Great place. Great food. Excellent service."

"So, what is the problem?" Nathan asked.

"Did you know they have a daughter? She does their accounting."

"I think I have heard something about her. It's been a while, though, but yeah, I guess I knew. What about her?"

Aaron smiled. His thoughts swam over her face, her smile, her ponytail bouncing as she raced to feed hungry patrons.

"Uh oh, I know that look," said Nathan. He knew his friend. He had seen that look in his eyes before. "You like her?" Which was more of a statement than a question.

"Nate, she is amazing." Aaron beamed.

"Have you gone out yet?"

Aaron looked to the ground, then out the window. Fall was coming; he could see the last leaves on the tree outside clinging on for dear life. "Not exactly. In fact, I haven't said much more than a 'hello' to her."

"But you are a writer, Aaron. Words are supposed to come naturally to someone like you."

"Yeah, they should, but not with Deborah. I cannot seem to get my mouth to work right."

"Yep, you have it bad," said Nathan. "So, what are you going to do about it?"

"Today's the day. I am going to head over there for lunch again. But today will be different."

"Again? How many times have you been there?"

Aaron blushed, "Every weekday, for the past two weeks."

Nathan's jaw dropped. "I was wrong. You don't have it bad. You're in love."

"Nate, I don't even know her that well. All I know about her is that she has brown hair that she always wears in a ponytail with a nylon band that always matches her shirt. She has hazel eyes that sparkle a thousand different colors, and she has a giving heart for her parents and for those who visit the shop. Other than that, I am clueless about who Deborah Davies is."

"But you would like to know," said Nathan.

"I *need* to know," corrected Aaron.

"So, what are you going to do?"

"I will find out when I get there." Aaron looked up at the clock. It was still early; 9:30. "As soon as I get this Andretti's piece complete, I am heading over there, and I am not leaving without a date, or at least a phone number."

Pop, by any chance, did you pay Josh his final paycheck?" Deborah asked as she entered the kitchen. She was holding a spreadsheet with a puzzled look on her face.

Darren Davies didn't look up from his broom. "Oh, yes. I meant to tell you. He came in not too long after his last day. Said he needed it for moving expenses."

"Did you give him cash?" Deborah asked.

"Yes, he seemed to be in a rush. I didn't want him to have to wait until payday?"

"Pop, you can't do that," Deborah explained. "Taxes need to be taken out. Every cent needs to be accounted for."

"Oh. I'm sorry, DeeDee," he said. DeeDee was his nickname for her since she was two. It had come from them trying to teach her Debbie, but all she could say was DeeDee, so it stuck, for him anyway. "I was just trying to help."

Deborah smiled, then looked around. "Pop, please, not here. It's okay, I can fix it. But just let me know before you think about doing that again. Where's Mom?"

"She is just opening up," he pointed toward the front of the restaurant. Deborah followed his finger into the dining area. Mom was hanging up a sign in the front window about the daily special—Meatloaf Sandwich.

"People really seem to like that, don't they," Deborah commented.

"I know, right?" said Mom as she stepped down from a stool. "We always sell out. And it's almost time to get started." She headed through the swinging doors and into the kitchen.

Mom and Pop were always trying new things. Many of their sandwich concoctions made her initially twitch, but they seemed to have a knack of making the unpleasant sounding taste astounding. Last month Pop had created a Supreme Pizza sandwich, which was also a great success.

"I'll be ready," Deborah said with a smile. She headed back to the office, but a figure stood with his back toward her near the office door. He wore an old brown tweed coat and matching cap.

"Can I help you, sir?" Deborah asked the man. *Did Mom already open up?* she wondered.

The man turned and faced her. "I'm sorry, I'm afraid I am a bit turned around. Where is the men's room?" he asked.

Debora pointed behind her. "It's around the corner, past the display case."

"Thank you," he said through an awkward smile. His grey eyes sparkled with recognition. He passed her and followed her directions.

Deborah watched him as he walked around to the back of the dining area, where the restrooms were. She shook her head and walked back into the office, sat at the desk, and covered her eyes a moment. The gentle throb that had edged at her the last six months reminded her she was not feeling well.

"So, how are you feeling today Dee—I mean Deborah?" dad said correctly as he entered the office.

Deborah lowered her hands. "Okay, I guess. Still feeling drained. But I can get around."

"Mom says you should take a break. She thinks you are working too hard, especially since Josh left."

"I'm fine, Pop. Really, I am. If I keep moving, I am better off. Taking a break, I would just get agitated. I need to be moving around."

"That's what I told her, but she is still concerned. So please, for her, try and take it easy. You don't have to do everything. Let Erica help you. That's why we have her. Miguel can help too."

"I know, and I will. We just need to start seeing applicants soon, so we can replace Josh."

"We had Josh for years. It will be hard to replace him."

"Yes, I know. But it's been two weeks already. You need to replace him so that I can get back to my job. I will help you find someone. We can begin on Monday."

Pop looked out at his wife, now wiping down the counter, then back at her. He cleared his throat. "DeeDee, would you join Mom and me at church on Sunday?"

Deborah sighed. It was the same thing every Friday. Usually, he would wait until the end of the day to ask, but today it came early. "Pop, we have been over this. You know Sunday is the only day I can relax. A day for me. I don't want to waste time at a place I don't want to be, around people I don't want to be around, learning about things I no longer believe in."

Her dad showed the sadness he felt. "I just thought..."

"Pop, I'm sorry. I don't know, maybe someday," Deborah lied. But she could not find any other way to end the subject.

That answer seemed to suffice, so Pop turned and left to finish his opening duties. Deborah went back to the books. She was trying to find where she left off. She found the negative amount and reconciled it through what her dad had paid Josh and balanced out the ledger. She was caught up on payroll up to clock-in that morning. She closed the program and sat back in the chair. It gave a squeak of age typical of older chairs. This one had definitely seen better days, but Pop liked it, and to be honest, it was rather comfortable. "*Why change something if it still works,*" her dad would say. Which is probably why he had not hired anyone new to replace Josh, and why he kept on asking her to church on Sundays.

Before Josh made his departure, she only saw her parents on Friday. She would come into the deli during her afternoon break to do the paperwork, make sure Josh and Erica would get paid on time, and balance the books for the week. Then she'd sit and make small talk over a Reuben and a cherry Coke until she needed to head back to her office across town. Inevitably Pop would ask her about church on Sunday. Each week it became more difficult to come up with reasons not to go. This disappointed both of them, but they kept it to themselves.

Today, she had not expected the question so soon. Normally, she would have all day to prepare her response of the week. She meant no disrespect; she was just caught off guard. She didn't want to go, but she did not want to hurt their feelings, either. She just wanted them to understand her point of view.

Deborah closed her eyes. Her head was spinning again, but that was normal these days. She took a deep breath and released it slowly, just as she was instructed to. It helped, so she opened her eyes and surveyed the room. Bookshelves were filled, and tables stacked high with cookbooks surrounded the office as old photographs lined the walls. They were mostly of Mom and Pop in various poses around the shop—shaking hands with mayors and other people of varying importance who had visit the deli.

There were also snapshots of her grandparents, the original owners; only back then, it was a bakery, she thought. There was even a couple of photos of her. In one she was in a white dress standing next to Pop. It was taken when her grandparents handed over the family business to them. In the other she was with Grandmom. They were both covered in flour. Grandmom was looking over her shoulder and had her hands on Deborah's, pressing a cookie cutter into dough. The photo made her smile.

Deborah would always remember the tradition that the photo froze in time. This place was sacred—a staple of her childhood— filled with the memories of fresh bread, cakes, and most of all cookies. While she could recall the sounds of mixers and rollers and the taste of warm chocolate, the cross cookies she and Grandmom made on Saturday mornings stood out above them all.

Even if she didn't have the photo on the wall as a memento, she could remember the feeling of the warm lemon flavor on her tongue and the way the sugar just melted away. She smiled and looked past the photo. She was not sure why that tradition was no longer followed; Mom was great at baking. She just assumed the recipe was lost or maybe buried somewhere in these stacks. Right on cue, as if it jumped from the back of her mind and into reality, she saw a set of silver objects resting on top of a stack of Grandmom's cookbooks. They shimmered in the light coming in from the window.

Deborah got up and walked to the shelf. The glow was two cookie cutters, both in the shape of a cross.

How did these get here? Deborah asked herself. She had been in this office for months doing her parents' books and never noticed them sitting there before. She picked them up, and the little girl in her instantly remembered pressing them into the fresh dough as she giggled. She could clearly hear Grandmom's voice retelling the story of Jesus and the cross. She had forgotten about the stories. It was something the girl in the photo couldn't tell you through a freeze frame. But there they were again, clear as day, every word. Every story she had now been convinced was not real. Deborah quickly put the cookie cutters down. As she shook her head she whispered, "Such fairy tales."

Deborah walked into the restroom adjacent to the office. She faced the mirror that was over a small sink. The truth was that she didn't feel well at all. Drained was just part of what she had been experiencing. Pop knew about the ringing in her ears, the headaches, and her being tired all the time, but she didn't tell him about the dizziness or nausea. Maybe Mom was right—she needed a break. But her parents needed her right now. And how many times had they sacrificed their health for her wellbeing? Now it was her turn to be there for them.

She turned on the faucet, which squeaked almost as much as the chair. She splashed lukewarm water on her face, ran her wet fingers through her hair, took the green nylon scrunchie from her wrist, and put her hair up. The Friday lunch rush was about to begin.

The Houston Gazette newsroom was small, the size of a high school classroom. Its freelancers and columnists were assigned desks along the walls, separated by partitions that gave a little bit of privacy, but not much. Each of the four staff writer had an office down a hallway. Aaron's office was at the end of that hall across from Nathan's. It was his second month being off the floor. He was enjoying the privacy.

Seclusion aside, Aaron had to face it, the Andretti piece was as good as it was going to get. He ended up watering down his experience to Andretti's: A great place to visit on a budget. He knocked on Nate's door to face the music. No answer. The band would have to play after lunch, so he headed out the door. Typically on Fridays, everything was winding down, the only ones working would be the sports department getting ready to head out to the local high schools for football, baseball, or softball depending on the season. But all of that was on hold. The North Heights Festival was about to begin. Everyone was getting ready, even though it was still a week away. Assignments were being finalized, pencils sharpened, and tablets were being charged.

Aaron's assignment was centered around the eateries that

would set up shop through the Food Court area. One of the perks of being a staff writer was that he had an expense account. In his position as Food Columnist, he rarely paid for a meal. And if he spent more than his allotment, he could write it off at the end of the year. This would be his first time covering a festival, and he was excited. Carnival food was the unhealthiest food of all, and he loved every bit of it. He smiled as he got in his car. *Maybe Deborah would like carnival food too.*

Through his travels, Aaron got to know Houston streets well. Many of the establishments he visited were off the beaten path, so he became familiar with back roads. He discovered most of the best places to eat were not in the popular strip malls. They were around the corner, down the road, or at the end of a cul-de-sac. On the main highway, it would take half an hour to get to Davies Deli from the office. But due to his homework, he could make the same trip in less than 20 minutes. And today he was on a mission.

Aaron pulled up to the somewhat lonely building just off the main road leading to the interstate in just under 17—a new record. The building was isolated from everything else, but it was far from forgotten. Vehicles surrounded the rectangular structure and spilled on the road down to where the residential community began to the south and the businesses to the north.

The building itself was unassuming. In no way did the outside prepare a patron for what was waiting for them on the inside. The building was a double-wide trailer converted into a restaurant. It had new brown two toned Hardie-siding and a fairly new metal roof. He knew it had a strong history and must have been through several facelifts over the years to look as new as it did; he wondered if it was even the original structure.

Aaron saw a sign near the door announcing the special of the day, Meatloaf Sandwich. He opened the door, and the smell of fresh meatloaf hit him; he instantly knew what he would have today. The dining area was as full as the parking lot suggested. Nearly all the booths were full. Erica had her hands full taking trays to waiting tables, and Miguel was quick bussing the empties to make way for the next onslaught of hungry guests. There were three spots available around the counter, including his regular spot at the end. Peach cobbler was the dessert special judging by the way the dessert case was set up.

He sat and didn't even pick up a menu. He looked around but didn't see Deborah. Aaron wondered if she was there. Maybe he had missed her. Up till now, he felt reasonably confident, but his nerves took a vacation when he finally saw her. Well, not her face. She was behind the serving window in the kitchen. He could see a ponytail with a green scrunchie. She was helping Mr. Davies. He watched her hair dance as she went back and forth, obviously in a rush. It was busy, and people were waiting.

She saw Aaron and gave a quick smile of recognition, then a roll of the eyes as she blew a stray hair upward that came loose from her ponytail. Her face was slightly beaded with sweat. She looked tired.

"Either Erica or I will be with you soon, Aaron."

She remembered my name. So far, so good. He smiled.

He continued to watch her make her way back and forth from the kitchen to the service window and then to the waiting tables. After 15 minutes or so the place slowly began to clear out of the half-hour lunch crowd. Those with an hour lunch lingered, sipping on iced teas or Davies' famous homemade lemonade. Some were sampling the peach cobbler, giving nods of approval after each bite.

Erica had brought him an iced tea, already in a to-go cup. *They know their stuff.* Aaron took a sip, unsweetened with lemon. *They really know their stuff.* Aaron pulled out his notepad for his review and took note.

"Okay, Mr. Stevenson, what can I get for you today?" It was Mr. Davies.

"Hello, Mr. Davies," Aaron said. He smiled and jested, "Sorry, business is so slow."

"I know, it is a sad situation. Perhaps we should place an advertisement locally," said Mr. Davies with a wink.

"Yeah, I don't know about that rag, there are some obnoxious people who work there," Aaron continued.

"True, but even obnoxious people need to eat."

"Yes, indeed. Well, this crazy guy would like the meatloaf sandwich. I smelled it when I walked in. Now I can't get it out of my head."

"Excellent choice. I spent most of the morning cooking it, so it is fresh," Mr. Davies said with a prideful smile. "I'll get the order to the missus, and we'll have it out in a jiffy."

With that, Davies walked to the window and shouted out some numbers—cook shorthand for all Aaron could tell. Maybe it was the language that had been spoken with the family, recited for generations. It made him feel at home, comfortable. He definitely liked this place.

Not five minutes later, he had a fresh refill of tea and a basket that was filled with a steaming pile of French fries and his sandwich. It was loaded with a thick slice of meat with caramelized onion topped with a sweet tomato glaze. On the side was more sauce for dipping. It was an amazing meal. He took his time with it, noticing very little around him. The room began to empty until there was just a trickle of booths occupied. Erica caught up with the tables, and he noticed Deborah as she sat in the office.

Deborah saw him looking, and he turned away. His nerves were doing cartwheels again. He looked away so long that he failed to notice that she had gotten up and walked over to where he was. "How did you enjoy the meatloaf?"

For a moment, he thought his tongue was broken. So, he smiled weakly and pushed his empty basket away from him.

"Pop makes it from a recipe that Grandpop used to make, not in the restaurant though. Back then it was a bakery. It was Pop's idea to make it into a sandwich. His ideas usually turn out pretty well."

"It was wonderful. The best I've had?" Aaron finally said. But it came out more like a question.

"You don't sound too sure,"

"No. Yes, it was great. Thank you." Aaron looked around. Unsure of what to say next. He saw the display case again.

"Peach cobbler for you?" she asked.

"No, I couldn't."

"You sure? I made it myself. Another recipe from the bakery days. My Grandmom's. I have played with it, so it's not exactly like hers, but I've had no complaints."

"You talked me into it," Aaron said with a newfound courage.

"Great." Deborah grabbed a ceramic bowl from under the counter and scooped a healthy portion of cobbler into it. Then placed it in the microwave behind her. "It's best when warm. Not too hot, it makes the apples mushy."

She opened up a container of vanilla ice cream and prepared a scoop. When the microwave beeped, she carefully added the ice cream and sprinkled a dash of what appeared to be cinnamon on top and set it in front of him.

"Let me know what you think," Deborah walked away to ring another customer up at the register.

Aaron was not sure what her Grandmom's tasted like, but what he was tasting he was confident would beat it in any competition. He knew food. This was made with fresh peaches, not canned. You can always tell when cooks cheat their way through dishes. And it was not cinnamon that she sprinkled on top; it was nutmeg. Even the cobbler had a hint of the underused spice. Aaron could tell it was meticulously made, and it was spectacular. He thought back to what Nathan had said about being in love. This only added to her mystery, and his curiosity of getting to know her better only grew.

Aaron was full from the sandwich, but he didn't care. The cobbler was so good he finished every bite. He would worry about the stomachache later. Deborah returned after a visit with Erica and a trip to the kitchen. "Well, paperboy, how was it?"

"Life-altering," Aaron said.

"Wow. I was aiming for 'tastes great,' but I'll take it."

"Nutmeg, right?" he asked.

"You could tell?" Deborah began, then realized. "Of course, it's your job to know that." She took the empty bowl and placed it in a bus tray under the counter. "On the house."

"No, I couldn't," Aaron said. "I can't accept anything free. Especially in a place, I plan to review. It promotes bias."

"Fair enough," she said.

"Plus, the paper pays for it anyhow," Aaron explained with a wink. "Haven't paid for a meal for months."

"Really?" she asked. "Well, you'll have to treat me sometime."

Aaron couldn't tell if she was teasing or serious. He received it as a server teasing with a customer. *Flirting with the customer, a guaranteed tip generator.* He left her comment alone. He handed her his receipt and his company credit card and headed over to the register.

Erica came up to him with a curious smile. "Refill your tea for the road?"

"Yes, thank you, Erica," said Aaron handing her his cup, his eyes still on Deborah.

She returned, and Aaron signed the receipt. Erica handed him his tea with the same smile, then left to tend to a customer who was waving her over.

"You're in here quite a bit. Do you have one of our reward cards?" Deborah asked.

"You have those?"

"Yes, it was something Pop wanted to do to compete with the chains. He wanted a regular crowd. He read somewhere that rewards were a good way of keeping customers coming back."

"That's smart."

"So, how many sandwiches have you eaten here?"

"Not too many," Aaron said. "I only discovered this place a couple of weeks ago. Well, the Wednesday before last. I've had lunch here every day since then."

"That's loyalty. You should have gotten a card. Every six you get a free sandwich. You would have had two free meals by now."

"Will thirteen be enough to ask you on a date?" Aaron

blurted. His face immediately went red, not entirely sure where the question came from.

Deborah smiled; her hazel eyes glimmered for a second. Then she looked to the ground and took a breath, and her smile faded. "I'm not sure about that. I am busy between work and what I do here. I just don't think it would be a very good idea." She turned around and quickly headed into the office. Then she closed the door.

Aaron looked around. Erica was close by cleaning a table as the last few from the lunch rush were finishing their meals. She was pretending not to have heard his failed attempt. He looked up and saw a pair of old eyes peering through the kitchen window. Mr. Davies. *Had he heard him crash and burn too?* Without a word, Aaron got up and left, leaving his tea behind.

What was that all about?" Pop asked.

"What?" Deborah replied.

"You. You just let him go."

"Who?"

"Mr. Stevenson, from the paper," said Pop. "You just let him leave. You should let him take you out."

"Oh, Pop, I don't need or want a relationship right now. I am way too busy."

"Relationship? Who said anything about a relationship? He just asked you on a date?"

"Who asked who on a date?" Mom said, coming out of the kitchen.

"Mr. Stephenson asked DeeDee out," Pop explained.

"Who?" Mom asked.

"The Aaron boy, he sits over next to the display case during lunch. He works over at the paper."

"Oh, the tall young man. He has brown hair and brown eyes."

"Yes, that's him. He asked Debbie out. And she said 'no.'"

"I didn't say 'no' Pop. And his eyes aren't brown; they are green."

"Aha," said Pop, pointing at her. "So, you do like him. Like him enough to know what his eye color is."

"I never said I didn't like him. Yes, he is attractive, but I am not looking for a relationship."

Pop threw his arms up in the air, "Here we go again with the relationship."

Deborah sighed.

"It is just a date, and you need to get out more. You are working too hard, Dee." Pop sat on the chair beside the desk. "All I am saying is to think about it, huh?"

Deborah looked up at her mom as if to ask for some help. She only saw eyes that apparently agreed with Pop. "It would do you good to get out, Deborah," she said, and then smiled. "You never know—he may be your knight in shining armor."

Debora sighed. She looked over at the cookie cutters again. *Such fairy tales*, she thought.

"What was that all about?" Aaron asked himself.

He sat in his jeep for a moment in silence. It was still warm out, so he turned on the engine to get the AC going. He shook his head, *Rookie mistake, Aar,* he thought. It was a phrase he had heard often growing up, one of his dad's favorites for when he blew it. It was a phrase he hated.

Aaron looked back at the restaurant. He took a deep breath and let it out. Thank God it was Friday. He wouldn't have to come back until Monday, if at all. With that type of embarrassment, he should cut his losses and find another lunch spot. *There is a Subway on the other side of town*, he considered.

Aaron backed out and headed back toward the office. No date, no phone number. He was sure Nate would not let him forget about it for a while.

To his luck, Nathan was nowhere to be found. His secretary,

Janice, said that he got a hot tip and headed out the door about an hour ago.

"Thanks, Janice," said Aaron with much relief. "I'll be in my office. I need to put the final touches on the Andretti piece. When you see him, let him know I'll make the deadline."

Aaron shut his door. It was a small office, but it served its purpose. *How much space does a food columnist need anyhow? A desk and a keyboard should suffice.* But he managed to make his tiny space work better than office spaces twice the size. Nathan always joked about it. He would say that Harry Potter's pantry closet was larger than his office. But that didn't bother Aaron.

He did have the desk and keyboard, his trusted laptop. The small desk also contained a worn-out thesaurus, a Bedford Book for Writers, and a half-full jar of Tums. While the job of food critic had its perks, it did carry its share of drawbacks. He touched his chest, *Andretti's—never again*, he thought.

Aaron also had a two-tiered bookshelf in the corner. On top was a 12-cup Mr. Coffee maker, a couple of mugs, and a decanter of sugar, even though he took his coffee black. He prepped the coffee pot and sat in his chair, which was probably older than he was. It creaked under stress, but held, as it always did, perhaps as it always had since it was built when things were made to last.

He pushed a button on his laptop, and it whirred to life. He leaned in for the facial recognition and his home screen popped up. Dozens of icons appeared. Aaron found the one he was searching for and double-tapped his mouse pad – "Andretti's a Great Place for the Family on a Budget."

He didn't even give it another look. Just as he told Nate, it was as good as it was ever going to get. Opening up his browser to the paper's webmail account, he typed a quick message and sent it to Nate.

Not two minutes later, he could hear mumbled voices in the hall; Nate and Janice. One voice, the male, came closer. Aaron heard a quick 'tap, tap,' and the door opened.

"So, does she have a friend?" Nate asked with a sly grin on his face.

"Who?"

"Deborah Davies? You were supposed to ask her out. Or did you forget, like the Andretti piece?"

"For one, the Andretti piece is in your Inbox. And two, you are a happily married man, Nate."

"I could always be happier," he laughed. The truth is that he was happily married. Nate and Sarah's marriage was worthy of emulation. They had been married 20 years. They still took the time to sneak a kiss, and they still said, 'I love you,' when getting off the phone.

"We didn't get that far," Aaron said, then lied, "she became preoccupied, and I didn't get to ask. It was busy."

"Well, there is always next time," Nate replied. "I'll go get the Andretti piece over to editing so we can get in Tuesday's edition."

Aaron sighed. He was grateful to be done with it. Andretti's was probably the hardest review he had done for *Flavors of Houston* in the three years he had written the column. And that said a lot given some the dives he has been in. In most cases there had been at least one saving grace. When a restaurant failed in one area, they would most likely make it up in other areas. Some would have great customer service, others would offer generous portioning, and some had a reasonable price range. That made Aaron's job a bit easier—find the positive and he never had to focus on the negative and hurt the livelihood of an establishment.

He thought about Davies Deli. He would eventually have to get back to writing the review of them. Even though he had been to the restaurant nearly every day for two weeks now, he had yet to take his notes and write a word about the restaurant itself. Aaron knew he would have to get over his emotional roadblocks and just write the piece.

This thought reminded him of his utter failure not two hours ago. *I don't think it would be a good idea,* she had said—*not a good idea.*

Aaron clicked on the mouse, and his screen lit up. He needed to check his calendar to see who was next on the list. It was a seafood restaurant on the north side of town. He had heard good things about it. Nate and his wife had been there a couple of times. His brother had laid the new parking lot last year after the old one became too small to handle the customer flow. It doubled the occupancy but tripled the business.

Aaron's first step before he visited a restaurant was to see what had been written about it before. Food critics, Google Reviews, and even local paper reports were important. He did not want to write a carbon copy of what others have said. It was the one thing that made his column unique. He would approach it from the angle that the others had left out.

Google Reviewers all gave it four or five stars. Great food, friendly waitstaff, reasonable prices were all highlighted. Typical for a restaurant review. There were a couple of twos and threes. Aaron paid extra attention to the fours. They tended to be the most honest, even threes in some cases. Fives were either close relatives of the owners or from those who expected their review to be seen by the establishment and possibly receive a gift for the review.

The twos were usually customers expecting to be treated like the only ones in the place, or those who had the standards of a five-star restaurant—most two ratings centered around rude or inattentive wait staff. But Aaron was sure if you looked at the specifics you would find that the patron who complained was visiting at lunch rush with only 30 minutes, 10 of which they used on the commute. So, any delay would be inexcusable to them—they were the only customer in their minds that mattered.

The threes and fours were generally a fair balance: the goods and the bads. Threes were usually on account of wrong orders, or a truly rude server. Aaron knew the industry well. He had been a cook for five years before and during his college days. He saw how waitstaff was treated and witnessed a server having a bad day. Unfortunately, that spilled over to customer interaction. But customers didn't care that their server had a sick five-year-old or whether a server was struggling personally.

Fours were the genuine deal. Customers who enjoyed everything but found one tiny flaw. Maybe the server did not automatically fill their tea glass when it was low, or there was a spot on a fork. Small things. Things that with minor changes could get a five. But Aaron did not like fives. *No restaurant is perfect; there is always room for improvement.* That being said, he did not like a review that pointed out the improvement factor. It was an afterthought, not the spotlight.

The Houston Gazette was targeted to businesses in and around the Houston area, so he primarily focused on lunch menus. Occasionally he would venture out and review a dinner menu because business elites had to have a nightlife too. The Chimney Rock Sea House was in Southwest Houston almost to Missouri City, just across Bray's Bayou. Their hours began around happy hour and closed around midnight. Great for those city folk heading out to the suburbs like Southton or Sugarland.

Aaron had reviewed many sites and got a good feeling for the place. He looked at the time. *Almost happy hour.* But he wasn't hungry. That meatloaf sandwich was pretty heavy, and his nerves were shot. Maybe a quick drink would help him loosen up. He could people-watch and witness the preparation for the rush. One telltale sign that a place was on top of it; how much rushing around is done right before the busiest hours.

Aaron printed out the directions and highlights from the reviews he saw. He shut down his laptop, packed it up, and turned out the lights. All in a day's work.

Chapter
FIVE

T hank you, Clarence," said Deborah, escorting the last customer of the day out the door. "See you on Monday." Clarence Taylor was a regular. He always came in at 2:00 and stayed until closing. Deborah was almost convinced he had a secret crush on her mom. He would always sit at the same booth next to the kitchen door and glow if she made an appearance.

Deborah locked the door and turned back to Erica. She was wiping down the last table where Clarence had sat. As she finished, she brushed her blonde hair from her face and exhaled, nodding in approval. She liked Erica. She was a hard worker, and it was not easy to find a good waitress, especially among the college crowd. Erica wasn't like the others—she was determined. She was attending the University of Houston and majoring in English; she wanted to be a teacher.

"Looks good," Deborah encouraged. "Thank you for all your hard work, Erica. It is a pleasure to work with you. I just want you to know you are appreciated. Mom and Pop have been struggling since Josh left. Thank you for all you to do fill in the gap, I know they appreciate it. Between what you and Miguel do, I don't think they could handle it."

Erica smiled, "I do my best. But I tell ya, it's not as easy as I thought it would be."

Deborah smiled. She knew it all too well. She has been working off and on as a waitress for years. It is much more than taking orders and delivering food. "Believe me. I get it. Pop should have your check before you clock out. When you see Miguel, let him know."

As she headed back to the office she could hear Pop banging pots and pans together and mom yelling to him, "Why do you have to be so loud, Poppa?" It made her smile. She loved to hear her parents together. She envied their love, wanting to experience for herself what it was like to grow old with someone. Deborah did not want to believe what the doctors said. She was not convinced their diagnosis was accurate.

In reality, there was no actual diagnosis. The doctors were as puzzled about her fatigue and lethargy as she was. She had every test thinkable, but no real reason why she could be fine one moment then completely drained the next. The tinnitus, they said, was a common thing, that many people suffer from ringing of the ears. In her case, ear—her left ear to be exact—so they were not concerned by it. But the fatigue confounded them. Today was a good day. She still had energy, and she had been on her feet most of the day.

Fridays at the deli were the worst, usually. People were getting paid, money to burn, so they would spend a little more and tip a little better. Great for servers in a way, but it kept her and Erica on their toes and encouraged them to give excellent customer service. Yet, it made her miss the comfort of the stillness of her office.

Deborah had been a human resource director for an

insurance company after she graduated college a couple of years ago. But when Josh quit, her parents convinced her to 'get back into the family business.' So, she took a leave of absence to help them adjust to losing Josh and assist them in hiring his replacement.

What was only supposed to be a two-week leave looked like it might end up being a full resignation. Truth be told, she didn't believe that Pop wanted to replace Josh now that she was there. And with her unknown condition, he most likely felt safer to have her close by his side. But Deborah's plans did not include working the counter of a sandwich shop. She was not her parents. She only wished that they could understand that.

Josh understood that his time at Davies Deli was temporary, so did Erica. Houston being a college town, Mom and Pop had been through several servers, mainly those who needed the job to pay college expenses. But for Deborah, expectations were a bit higher. It took a year before she finally agreed to do the books.

She struggled because she could only see it as her parents trying to lasso her back into the family business. Her being the only child pretty much signified that she would be the one to assume the reigns when her parents could no longer run the deli. They had groomed her every chance they had, but instead of giving her a passion for the business, it turned her off. Now, for her, it was comparable to having a root canal without anesthesia.

The one bright side to her job was that she was getting to use her administrative degree. She was able to help her parents save money on an actual accountant. At least in that sense, it helped alleviate her guilt over the lack of interest in owning a restaurant. And although she wouldn't admit it out loud, she did enjoy interacting with the customers.

In Human Resources, people are your job. New hires, benefits, evaluations, and the unfortunate termination were all people centered. If she didn't like interacting with people, then her job would not be enjoyable. Waitressing was also about people. You met new people, had your regulars, and you dealt with good ones and bad ones. *Good ones*, she thought, *like Aaron.* She was not happy with herself for how she reacted to him asking her out.

Deborah knew Aaron's intentions were honorable; she just did not need her parents to tell her what she already knew—another area where they seemed to take great pleasure in interfering. They would be married for 35 years come December. It was their dream to pair up their only daughter with a good man with a stable, reputable job. After all, they married young, so why shouldn't she?

Right now, it seemed that Aaron Stephenson was on their radar as the match for her. *You just let him leave,* she could hear Pop say again. And that is precisely what she did. She looked up at the cookie cutters again, then out the window, *I wonder what he is doing now?*

"I've been waiting for a table for a half an hour now," said the upset man in the lobby of the Chimney Rock Seafood House. He spoke a little more loudly than he probably should have given that, what Aaron assumed was his date, was behind him with an embarrassed look on her face.

He could not make out what the maître d' said, but he assumed it was an emphatic apology and the assurance he would be seated soon. He grabbed the arm of a waitress passing him and spoke into her ear. She rushed off back into the dining area, presumably to bus a table and get the couple the seating they were waiting for. Aaron scribbled a note in his journal.

Aaron had been sitting at the bar area for just under two hours. He had sipped through a few iced teas and sampled a couple of the appetizers. He thought he might have been recognized because the food was brought to him fairly quickly and was meticulously plated. *No one is this good,* he thought. It could have been another reason for the quiet tone of the maître d' and the rush job of the waitress. He took more notes.

Happy hour had not been as expected. It was much slower and not as many patrons as he anticipated. But it was Friday, and office hours were often extended an hour to help those getting ready for the weekend, especially the bankers. The angry guy in the lobby may have well been a banker. He had that 'all business' look about him. He was still huffing when the waitress led him back to a freshly cleaned table.

Now it was past 6:00, and the place was filling up. The gentleman tending bar kept his glass full, another tip off that he was noticed—not that he minded. Brian, his name tag read, came for another refill, but Aaron waved him off. "What's on tap?" Aaron asked.

"Several brands. What are you looking for?" Brian asked with a smile.

"Blue Moon?" Aaron asked, almost sure of a no. Not many restaurants carried Blue Moon on tap.

"Certainly, sir. With or without an orange wedge?"

"With, of course."

Brian knew his stuff.

"Coming right up," Brian said and turned to take another order from his neighbor, a man in his 50s nursing his third whiskey. Aaron took more notes.

Aaron watched patrons come and go. They all had the same expressions most people have visiting a restaurant: the overindulgence of food and beverage, the giddiness of a first date, and the obvious relief of night away from their kids were all common. Aaron had a game where he would try to guess how long a couple had been dating by how they interacted with each other. Angry guy in the lobby was most certainly less than a month, judging by his date's response to his overreaction. His neighbor, he figured either recently widowed or unwillingly divorced. He had that 'nobody knows the trouble I've seen' look in his eyes.

Atmosphere was a critical aspect of rating a restaurant. And unfortunately, some of that was beyond the owner's control. All it took was one customer in a bad mood to ruin the evening for those sitting close to them. More likely what would happen to the patrons who sat around the angry guy from the lobby, but Aaron was seasoned enough to understand this. His rating would not reflect one angry customer, but in how the staff reacted to the situation. So far, Chimney Rock had performed exemplary. Aaron scribbled once again.

Brian had returned with a chilled mug of Blue Moon with a nice head on it and a generous wedge of orange. He placed it on a cocktail napkin in front of Aaron. "Will you be eating, sir?"

"Yes," said Aaron. He had read over the menu thoroughly and knew exactly what he wanted. "I'll take the grilled salmon and shrimp. Dirty rice and asparagus for the sides."

"I'll put it in. Let me know if you need anything else."

Brian walked over to a computer screen and typed in his order. Aaron could just see the kitchen staff leaping to battle stations as the ticket printed. They were ready to make the most perfect salmon filet that they had ever made. *One of the perks*, he told himself as he sipped his beer.

"So, what do you think so far, Aaron?" A familiar voice asked from behind him.

She was short with just as equal short dark brown hair and eyes. She pushed up her glasses and smiled.

"Hey, Jessica," Aaron welcomed. "So far, so good. I think they recognized me, so I am getting superb service. Not that I am complaining." Aaron looked around, "You here alone?"

"No, I'm here with daddy," she said, pointing to the restroom. "We're just waiting on a table."

"Well, let them see you are talking to me, and you'll get a prime table," Aaron laughed. Not that he was anything. Jessica's dad was the owner of the *Houston Gazette*. He could get a seat in a heartbeat, but he was not the type of person to allow his status to gain himself special treatment. He was a gentle, quiet man. The 6'5" figure appeared, almost having to duck to get from the hallway leading to the back.

"Hello, Mr. Stephenson," Eli Lorrie extended his hand. Aaron stood and shook it.

"Hey, boss," Aaron was still a good six inches shorter. "Checking up on the staff?"

Eli smirked, "Not exactly. Didn't realize you'd be here this evening." He asked the same question Jessica had asked. He repeated his thoughts. "Been here long?"

"Just a few hours. I wanted to get a feel for the transition period. Maybe that is what gave me away. That and my notebook." Aaron pointed to the composition book he always took notes in. It had become a habit he could not break. Nothing digital for notes, everything handwritten.

"Lorrie, party of two?" the maître d' announced.

"That's us," Eli said to Jessica. "Well, keep up the good work, Stephenson." Then he walked toward the podium.

"So, Nate tells me you got a girlfriend." Jessica smiled like she knew a big secret.

"What? Who?" Aaron defended.

"Deborah Davies, over at the deli. I know all about it. Nate told me how you have a crush on her and asked her out."

"A crush? What, are we in high school?" he said, a little upset at the invasion of privacy.

"Hey, I'm just relaying what Nate said," she laughed.

"Yes, I am interested, but no, I haven't asked her out yet," he lied, not wanting to face further ridicule.

"Well, you should. I've been there several times. She's a great match for you."

"I'm not sure I am ever going back," he said, picking up his beer and taking a sip.

"Uh, oh. What happened?"

Aaron looked at her. Maybe a woman's perspective would be beneficial. "Ok, I tried to ask her out. When I did, she made an excuse and went into her office and closed the door."

"Hmm," she said, searching for an appropriate response. "What excuse did she make?"

"She said she was busy and didn't think it would be a good idea." Aaron took another sip. This draw a bit longer.

Jessica pursed her lips in thought, then asked, "Where were her eyes?"

"Her eyes?"

"Yes, where was she looking when she gave her the excuse," she asked with an authoritative scowl.

Aaron thought back. He told her about the glow, the smile, and then it vanishes just as quickly.

"So, she was looking at the ground?"

"Yes, I suppose so," Aaron agreed.

"See, that is a good sign. If she were not interested, then she would have been looking you in the eye when she said those things. The smile was the giveaway. You should ask her again."

"You think?" Arron seemed to brighten up.

"I know so," Jessica said.

Eli reappeared. "They won't hold the table forever, Angel."

"Really, Aaron. I mean it. Ask her," she said and left with her dad, back toward the area where the angry man from the lobby was sitting.

Aaron turned just as his plate landed in front of him. Brian had a grin on his face. "Your salmon, sir. Let me know if you will need anything else, or a beer top off."

Aaron smiled back and picked up his fork. The real test of properly cooked fish was that there would be no knife needed. And just as he expected—a perfectly cooked salmon filet. He opened his notebook and put his thoughts to paper.

Chapter
SIX

Saturday was slow at the deli, and Pop was beginning to experiment with something new that he was not ready to show anyone just yet, so Mom let both Deborah and Erica leave a couple of hours early. Deborah spent the evening channel surfing, when she came across a documentary on baking. The deli being once a bakery she paused. They were discussing the origin of the term *baker's dozen*. She learned that loaves were once sold by weight instead of quantity. If 12 loaves were underweight, then a baker would face severe consequences. So, they began including a 13th loaf to be sure that it would be enough.

'Is thirteen enough to ask you on a date?' echoed in her mind again. She couldn't help but smile.

Sunday morning was spent with a cup of coffee and a book. It was far more attractive than sitting on a hard pew, listening to a man speak about how sinful everyone else was. She did feel bad, but she had no intention of accepting her Pop's invitation to church. She had only one day of rest, and Sunday was that day. It was the only day she did not have to put on a mask and pretend everything was okay. Six days a week were spent making everyone else happy and covering up the ache she had inside. She could not let on how bad she felt, too many people were counting on her. Sunday was the day she could rest in not feeling well.

A light rain was beginning to fall on Monday as Deborah made her way out to her car. She glanced across the street onto the walker's path that ran along the creek. A man in a dark tweed trench coat sat on a park bench. He was looking off into the distance as if waiting for someone. Deborah felt that he looked familiar but couldn't place him. As she started her engine, the man looked in her direction. His white hair and stubble peering out from under his hat triggered her memory—*the man from the restaurant.*

Usually a strange man would have her going in the opposite direction, but the look of him somehow softened her heart. She couldn't explain it, but he seemed harmless. The rain could have been a reason as well, but she pulled up to near where he was sitting.

"Excuse me, sir?" Deborah asked after lowering her passenger side window. "Are you okay?"

The man looked up, but not so much with recognition.

"It's going to get heavier than this mist. Can I give you a ride somewhere?"

That got his attention. He looked over at her and smiled.

"That would be very kind," the man said, his beard parting in a generous smile revealing a perfect set of teeth. *Not very common for a homeless man,* Deborah though.

As the man stood Deborah could see he had something tucked into his coat, something he was protecting. He pulled it out as he approached her car, it was a shoebox. She leaned over and opened the door for him.

"Are you sure I won't be an imposition?"

"Not at all," said Deborah. "Get in before you're soaked."

The man sat and buckled his seatbelt, setting the shoebox on his lap. He smiled but said nothing.

"So, where to?" Deborah asked.

"The library will be fine," the man said. "It's on the way to the deli."

Deborah was shocked for a moment. "How did you know where I am going?"

"I remember you. You work in the deli on the other side of town. I saw you in there yesterday. You helped me find the facilities," he explained.

"How did you end up over here?" Deborah asked, wondering if he followed her.

"Coincidence, I suppose," he explained. He remained silent for a while.

After a couple of turns, he broke the silence. "So, how are you feeling, DeeDee."

Once again, Deborah was astonished at what he knew. "Where did you hear that name?"

"Your dad calls you DeeDee. I am sorry, is that a father/daughter thing? My apologies."

"My name is Deborah," Deborah said defiantly.

"Understood. Again, my apologies, Deborah."

"It's okay. And yes, only my Pop calls me DeeDee. It is a name that I really don't care for. My dad is the only one who still sees me as the little girl that would sit on his lap and listen to stories. I'm 25 now. I would like for him to see me as the adult I am now, not the little girl from back then," Deborah said, a little embarrassed at how much personal information she just revealed to a stranger.

"Dads will be dads," the stranger admitted. "Fathers are like that, always seeing their children as children. But they will always accept them: good and bad, right or wrong, young or older. It's through a father's eyes that children have eternal youth. You should be grateful for a love like that, Deborah. It means he loves you."

Deborah chewed on the man's words for a moment. Then she said, "Yes, sir. I suppose it does. It doesn't mean I have to like it though."

The man laughed. "I'm sorry. Where are my manners? My name is Carter." He extended his hand, and she shook it.

"Pleasure to meet you, Carter," Deborah said, making the final turn toward the library. Traffic was heavy as it always was on a Monday. The mist, now a steady rain didn't help. "So, what's at the library?"

"Ah, the question is, what's *not* at the library?" Carter theorized. "Books, stories, and history. I love a good story—happy stories, sad stories, true stories, made-up stories, anything and everything. Life is not life without a good story. I have a story. You have a story. It is what makes us who we are. And we need to tell people about our stories. Without telling our stories, we are just books sitting on a shelf."

"Me? I am too young to have a story," Deborah said, more to interject into the conversation.

"Everyone has a story. You stated that your father has called you DeeDee since you were little. Now there is a story there."

Deborah smiled. Yes, there was a story. She could recall her parents laughter with her struggling to say her given name. The cute confused ramblings of a toddler.

"See, you remember," said the man as if reading her thoughts. "I can see your eyes dancing. That means you recall why your Pop chose to call you DeeDee. You have a story; it's just that youth keeps you from realizing it. And with little girls, stories usually revolve around their daddies."

Deborah again felt the weight of what Carter was saying. It must have shown.

"What?" Carter said with a hopeful smile.

Deborah smiled.

"Seriously, I want to hear it," Carter said.

"My Pop and I used to take walks on the beach. He would call it our Daddy-Daughter Date. We would grab hot dogs near the shore and eat them on a bench, sand and all. Then we would walk as far as we could. He would hold my hand, and we'd pick up shells. We even found a sand dollar once, but with the moves, I lost it a long—"

A loud car horn snapped Deborah out of her memory; the light had turned green. She pulled through the intersection and into the library drop-off lane. She parked behind a cab near the entrance.

"Well, here we are," said Carter.

"Yes, well, it was a pleasure meeting you, Carter."

"Yes, it was. I enjoyed our talk," Carter said. He tucked his shoebox under his coat again and leaned back into the car before shutting the door. "Remember, Deborah, fathers are always there. No matter how far we get from them, they still love us. Even when it seems they only want their own good, they have our best in heart."

Carter shut the door and hastily walked up the steps and out of the rain. Deborah pulled back into traffic and drove the rest of the way to her parents' deli a few miles away.

As she parked her car behind the restaurant, Carter's words wouldn't leave her. Deborah didn't doubt that her father loved her. Maybe she was too hard on him. Hard about the job, about men, perhaps even a little about church. She parked and checked the visor mirror to make sure her face was in place, adjusted her purple hairband, and exhaled—another day.

As she went to raise the visor, something on the back seat caught her eye. Deborah looked harder but still couldn't tell what it was. She turned and reached back and picked up the item on the seat. Her eyes, face, and heart fell into shock. It was a sand dollar. In disbelief, she flipped it over and on the back were the letters, "P" and "D." The P was for Pop; the D was for DeeDee. It was the sand dollar that she and her dad had found on the gulf shore over 17 years ago.

Monday morning arrived a bit differently for Aaron. He had no mysterious visitor outside his studio apartment, and the squall line had passed through. He started his jeep, this time firing up the heat, the front had brought the first chill of fall with it. Sunday's sermon was echoing in his mind. It was a challenge to make a difference in someone's life through encouragement. He was determined to accept the task and would be on the lookout for someone in need of words affirmation. That was the main thing he enjoyed about Pastor Mike's sermons; they ignited something inside that would spur you on to action.

Aaron enjoyed church but did not attend as much as he felt he should. However, yesterday he was up early, so he went. It was like he never missed a Sunday; always greeted with hugs and handshakes. Another reason why he loved the place.

"Good Morning, Aaron. Good to see you!" and "How was your week?" were standard greetings. Everyone knew what he did for a living, so many would comment on his latest review, either in agreement or taking exception to his point of view—mainly out of a bad experience they had had, which would always make him laugh.

Aaron did not mind talking with people. In fact, he enjoyed hearing other points of view, but it would never cloud his judgment nor change his mind. He was fully aware that you can't fully judge anything based on other people's impressions. It was a science, more than a one-time experience, negative or positive. It was one of the reasons he would show up early to study a place, to gain perspective. He even had studied Church on the Bayou.

After relocating, he needed a church he could grow old in. He had only been in one church, the church he was born into, the church he attended until he moved to Houston a few years ago. The last thing his sister told him before he drove off was to be sure to find a good church; it was the first thing he made an effort to do.

But with his meticulous nature, he had attended many first services. Until last year when he stumbled across Pastor Mike at a food-tasting event he was covering. The pastor had a well-loved barbeque sauce, and it impressed Aaron enough to get his vote. Pastor did not place but did well with making sure folks would attend the next church cookout, and this included Aaron. From there, it became natural to attend.

From his first service, he was hooked; the manner in which Pastor Mike spoke drew him in. The compassion he exuded was infectious, as was the welcoming spirit of the congregation. He felt like he had been there much longer than the few hours he had been. With his profound preaching style, there was always a challenge that came with a sermon. "This week God wants to challenge us to," was how he would close his sermons.

Yesterday it was, "This week God wants to challenge us to take the words of I Thessalonians 5:11 to heart. Have an open spirit as you face your Monday. Be on the lookout for a soul in need of encouragement. Then pray about the difference you can make, and be faithful to follow through and be a light in the middle of someone's darkness. And keep this one final thought in mind. You may be the only person who can make a difference. You could be the one God's handpicked to speak life into their life."

Aaron was ready. He looked into his rearview mirror, brushed a stray lock of hair into place, took a deep breath, and exhaled—another day. He backed out of his assigned space for apartment number 502 and headed to the office.

Chapter
SEVEN

Deborah spent the morning and much of the afternoon in a fog of confusion. *Where did the sand dollar come from?* She showed it to Pop, and while the moment was nostalgic for both of them, he had no clue as to how it ended up in the back seat of Deborah's car, and she believed him. She could always tell when Pop was being less than truthful. She had experience in that department. She would always turn to Pop when childish curiosity prompted adult questions. He had a tell that would reveal if what he was saying was the truth. She looked him in the eye and asked him. He said he had no idea; he was telling the truth. And mom wouldn't know too much about the shell since it was a father-daughter thing.

She considered all possibilities; her donation of clothing the previous week, but she had used her trunk for the boxes and bags she took to the shelter; she picked up some dry-cleaning recently, but that was before she began working at the deli; she had no other passenger in her car except that morning's visitor. But how could Carter have put it there? He was just a vagrant whom she gave a ride to the library. *He did have that shoebox with him,* she reasoned. *But how could he...*

"DeeDee, you okay?" Pop asked from behind the pass-through between the kitchen and the servers' area.

Deborah snapped out of her daze and grabbed the two baskets in front of her, placing them on a tray. "Yes, I'm fine Pop."

"Still thinking about the sand dollar?" he asked, placing the third basket that completed her order.

"I just don't understand how it got there. I thought I lost that thing years ago."

"Well, I'm glad you found it. Good memories," he said with a fatherly smile.

Deborah returned the sentiment. "Yes, it was a great day." She added the basket to the tray and delivered it to a trio of bankers she knew from the building she worked in.

She was so phased that she did not notice that Aaron was sitting at the counter, in his normal spot. He was eating a Reuben today, the special. Erica must have helped him, which relaxed her; she was not yet ready for a confrontation over how they left things on Friday. She skirted her way around the dining area, checking on the thinning crowd. She topped off a couple of to-go drinks, took payments from an elderly couple and a four-top, then made her way into the kitchen and out of view. She sat in the employee eating area next to the kitchen.

"So, are you going to avoid him every time he comes in now?" It was Erica.

"Not you too," she said with a frown. The last thing she needed was for everyone to gang up on her about her love life.

"Sorry," Erica raised her hands in defense. "It just looked like you two were hitting it off on Friday. It's obvious he likes you. So, what's the deal? You don't like him?"

Deborah did not want to have the relationship third-degree,

but answered anyway, "It has nothing to do whether I like him or not. I am just not in a position to be thinking about a relationship right now. Not with how busy I am helping Mom and Pop and trying to keep my job with the agency. It's just too much to throw another iron in the fire."

"How do you know he is looking for a relationship?" Erica asked. "Maybe he just wants to take you out?"

"You sound like Pop," said Deborah. But it was true. She was overthinking the whole thing. All Aaron asked was if he could take her out. She smiled as she remembered how he fumbled with his words and how cheesy the line was. *"Is thirteen enough to ask you out on a date?"* She again had to laugh.

"Aha!" Pop said, coming around the corner with a spatula in hand. He pointed it in her direction. "I've seen that look before. You are thinking about the Aaron boy."

Erica smiled, grabbed a busser's bin, "I'm going to help Miguel," she said ducking out into the dining room.

"So, what if I was," Deborah said.

"Then you need to talk to him," Pop said, sitting across from her. "You left him hanging in the wind last time you saw him. And you have not been by his seat all afternoon."

"Pop, I did not even know he was here until just now," she said. "Plus, I wouldn't know what to say to him."

"You can begin with, 'Hello. Yes, I'll go out with you.'"

Deborah shook her head, "No, I may have hurt his feelings, and I am embarrassed by how I reacted."

"Good, you should tell him that." Pop said.

"Tell him-who what?" Mom came out of the dishwashing area.

"The Aaron boy. Deborah is going to talk to him."

"Oh, good. You should go out with him, Deb," said Mom.

Erica came back into the kitchen with a grin on her face, "You know, I can hear every word you guys are saying out there?"

Deborah shot a surprised look, "I doubt that. The vent-a-hood is too loud."

"I dunno about that, but I could hear you when I was by the door." Erica paused, set down the bin, and stared at Deborah. "And he's asking to see you."

"Who?"

"Who else?" Erica pointed with her thumb over her shoulder. "You better not keep him waiting too long. We are still looking for his review in the *Gazette*. Don't want to get a poor review of customer service."

"Well, go!" said Pop heading back to the kitchen.

Mom patted her on the shoulder and went back to washing dishes.

Deborah took a deep breath and exhaled; *Okay, here we go.* She stood up and fixed her hair a bit. When she pushed against the swinging door, she couldn't see where he was sitting; it was hidden by the dessert display. She could hear his fingers tapping against the countertop, a sign of nervousness. *Could he be just as anxious as I am?*

He was wearing a tan, leather jacket, and his keys and to-go tea were already in his hands. His green eyes lit up when he saw her. He smiled. She smiled. The silence went on for what seemed like forever until both spoke at the same time. Both quickly stopped.

"Sorry," Aaron said. "You first."

"I'm sorry for the way I reacted on Friday," she looked away from his gaze. Yes, she was embarrassed.

"And I am sorry for being presumptuous and making you uncomfortable," he quickly followed.

"No, you don't have to apologize. Yes, I was uncomfortable, but not for the reason you are suggesting."

"Oh?" he said, his tone brightening.

"You were not rude. If anything, I was. And I owe you an explanation," she said still avoiding eye contact. "As well as an answer."

She looked up and met his stare. He had a furrow in his brow, but a smile on his face. "And?"

"Yes." The only word she could utter.

"Yes?" Aaron echoed.

"Yes, thirteen is enough."

His smile doubled in size, and she could swear he jumped a little inside.

"Really?" Aaron asked.

"Really." It was her turn to echo. "And yes, I would like to go out with you. When did you have in mind?"

He paused for a moment like he was mulling over the possibilities.

"Well, how would this Friday sound? I have to head up to Dallas tomorrow for a conference and won't return until Thursday."

"That will work. This should be my last week here, and I will be free this weekend."

"Oh, really?" he replied with a disappointed tone.

"Yes, this is just temporary until Pop finds a replacement for Josh, the guy who left a few weeks ago. Pop is making a final decision this week."

"Well, I will miss seeing your smiling face," he said. "And trying to guess what color you'd be wearing. Your color coordination talents are spectacular."

She smiled, not everyone noticed her efforts to match her top with her scrunchie.

"So, where will we be going?"

"Well, that is the interesting part."

"How's that?"

He smiled and looked at his watch. He glanced over his shoulder as Clarence walked into the deli. "You'll see on Friday. It's a surprise." He nodded over to the older gentleman sitting down. "I'll let you get back to your customers. See you on Friday." He raised his teacup as a goodbye and headed to the door.

She watched him walk out the door and speak to Clarence, "Have the Reuben, it is amazing." It made her giggle.

She felt a hand on her shoulder. "See, was that so hard?"

"Pop," Deborah said.

"You made an old man happy," Pop said, still with a spatula in hand. "I just want you to be happy, DeeDee."

She let this one slide. "I know Pop. But I am happy. I don't need a man in my life to be happier. I have you and mom for that."

"True, but sometimes a hug from a father is not enough. Sometimes you just need more." He headed back into the kitchen; Erica had hung a ticket she had taken from Clarence. And yes, he ordered the Reuben.

Aaron could feel the electricity flowing through his body. It carried him back to his jeep, then to the paper, past Jessica, and into his office. He did not see or hear anything. He floated in a dreamy state, and completely missed Nate knocking on his door.

"What happened to you?" he asked.

Aaron smiled.

"You look like a man who has a date."

"It's the strangest thing. I didn't say a word," Aaron stood and paced his small office. "She seemed to avoid me all afternoon. Then she just appeared, said yes, and we are going out on Friday."

"What about Dallas?"

"I'll be back by then. I'm driving straight back Thursday night. Not that it matters; it's only a three-hour drive. I need to be back for the County Fair on Friday."

"And *that* is your date?" Nate asked with a tone of doubt.

"Sure, why not? It will be fun." Suddenly Aaron wasn't so sure.

"Does she like carnivals? Or carnival food?"

"You sure do know how to bring a guy down."

Nate laughed. "You're right. Sorry. I'm sure you two will have a great time."

"Thank you." Aaron sat behind his desk and woke his sleeping laptop. "Now, if you'll excuse me, I have a review to write."

"Davies Deli?"

"Yes, I have meant to write it for weeks. Now seems like the perfect time."

"Just don't let your infatuation cloud your review."

"Not at all, you know me better than that. It was the Reuben today that pushed me over the edge. Best I've ever had."

"Just making sure." Nate turned to leave the office. "Oh, by the way, the reason I stopped by. You may need to redo the Andretti piece. The big man felt it lacked perspective. He would like you to make another visit."

"Are you kidding me?"

"I wish I were. Sorry." Nate said, handing him his printed story back. "He highlighted a few things and made some notes."

Aaron took them but did not read them. He placed them in his "to-do" bin.

"Boss also said for this week, to rerun the Bubba's Ribs piece from March. He ate there on Saturday and enjoyed himself. He wanted to add it to your list, but I mentioned that you had reviewed it already. Perfect timing, I guess."

"So, this is not a rush job then?"

"Look at it this way," Nate said with a sly smile. "You can take Deborah."

"Nuh-uh," Aaron said, shaking his head. "I *want* a second date."

"Okay, Romeo, do it your way. Best of luck to you. Just watch out for that tilt-a-whirl." Nate laughed and shut the door behind him.

Aaron laughed and shook his head. *Now to get to work.* He turned to his screen and opened a blank page—and just stared. Lost in thought. He smiled. For once, he could not think of a word to write.

Chapter

EIGHT

Tuesday morning was just a normal morning. No vagabonds on benches across the driveway. Just her routine ride to the deli to get ready for the lunch rush. Today's special would be a Chicken Caesar Salad Sandwich. It was an attempt to appeal to the growing vegetarian population in Houston. But Pop did not understand that if you put a chicken in the meal, it was no longer vegetarian.

But it's a salad? he would justify.

The thought made her laugh and lose focus on driving. She almost ran a red light. She slammed on the brakes and she swore.

She was near the library at the same light as the day before. Deborah looked up at the multi-story building. She wondered if Carter was in there and what types of books he liked to read—*if he could read.* Immediately she felt bad. It was rude to assume a person's ability from their appearance. For all she knew, he held a PhD in Literature and read Plato or Socrates. The sound of a horn, again, snapped her out of her daze, and she proceeded through the intersection, embarrassed.

Ten minutes later she was at the deli. Deborah parked in her usual spot and shut off the engine. As part of her routine, she took a deep breath in and exhaled—*in with the good, out with the bad.* As she exhaled, a wave of dizziness hit her. A sudden sharp pain just behind her left eye drew her hand to her temple. The world spun and reached her stomach. Deborah quickly opened the door and released her breakfast onto the concrete below. She sat there for a moment, coherent but shaken. The pain relented and the merry-go-round in her head slowed and let her off the ride.

Deborah sipped at her water mug and regained her composure. Afraid to attempt another deep breath, she settled for a few shorter breaths that her doctor had taught her the last time this occurred. Deborah thought about it for a moment. It had been nearly five weeks since her last episode. The worst part was the doctors were clueless as to what was wrong. Her symptoms were consistent with epilepsy, except she was not having full-blown seizures. The medication was supposed to help, and it did, but occasionally one would slip by.

After about 15 minutes, she felt right as rain, like it had never happened. Without thinking, she inhaled, exhaled; nothing happened. *Another day,* she finally admitted to herself, completing her morning prep. She walked into the deli with no intention of telling her parents about her episode. No sense in worrying them. They had enough concerns on their shoulders. Just a few more days and Pop would have a new expediter, and she could finally get some rest.

On Tuesday evening, Aaron was in his hotel room and unpacked, ready for the late welcome reception for the food critics conference he was attending. Although it was just a shade over 200 miles, the weather in Dallas was dramatically cooler than Houston. Those Northers never made it fully to Houston. The city was far too close to the Gulf to have such an impact on temperatures as landlocked Dallas experienced. He was glad he packed his heavy coat.

Aaron did not like attending these conferences. He did not see himself on the level of a 'food critic.' To him, the term reflected negativity. He was the type of person that would always try and find the good, even in the middle of the bad, just as he had done with Andretti's. Critic. Critical. Words that reeked of arrogance and superiority. His sister, Sally, had once told him that if he did not have anything nice to say, then don't say anything at all. For some reason it stuck with him. And what a great profession he chose to be the judge of a business that was often someone's livelihood. But *critic*? He hated the label.

This is where Aaron wanted to be unique. The world was filled with critics who complained about everything from a two-minute wait for a table to a spot on a fork. Aaron tried a different approach. He looked past the small things; small things could be explained. A delay could mean a staff member called in sick and a small spot on a fork didn't mean you would become violently ill if you ate with it. The small stuff was insignificant. But some of these men and women he was about to shake hands with reveled in finding those small things instead of appreciating the good things all eateries have to offer.

There was an outdoor passageway between the hotel lobby and the conference center. That brief minute chilled Aaron to the bone, even through his jacket. Once inside he shook off the cold and followed the sign leading him to the correct room. The hall was about half full. Most faces were unfamiliar—some he had only seen through their column photo or a television interview. Being only a couple of years in the business, he was relatively obscure; no one to seek out in a crowded room with such well-knowns.

He scanned the room and immediately knew where the most notable of his kind sat. There was a crowd gathered around him like chickens around a pile of feed. Ethan Chadwick was local to Dallas and was known for his flamboyant nature. A review by *Ethan Eats* was the springboard to success or the kiss of death to any restaurant. If there ever was a *critic*, it was Ethan Chadwick. There were even rumors a few places had to shut down after his visit because of such a bad review that no one ever came back in.

"Aaron," a voice called out from his left.

Aaron turned to see a vaguely familiar face, but he could not place his name. He smiled nonetheless as if he was a long-lost buddy. They grasped hands and shook firmly.

"Hey, it's good to see you," Aaron said, reaching back into his mind and pulling out nothing. "It's been too long."

"Yes," the burly man nodded. "Since Memphis. What a conference that was." He pointed over to Ethan's table. "At which you-know-who over there could not bear to show his face. Said that '*Memphis was a tired ole city with nothing worth his while,*' if I remember the quote adequately."

"What can you say, some people just don't get it," Aaron answered.

"No, they don't." The man paused a bit, then waved over to the opposite end of the room. "Well, I got to get going. Good to see you again, Aaron."

They shook hands again, and he was off. Aaron was still blank. He looked over the room again. Ethan's table erupted in a chorus of laughter. Aaron shook his head and headed back to his room.

The phone in the office rang and startled Mr. Davies, who was in the kitchen working on a new creation to add to the menu. It was his habit to experiment and try new things—a habit he picked up from his mom. Mr. Davies scampered as quickly as a near 60-year-old man could and got to the phone. He gave a breathy greeting as he looked at the clock; 9:12 PM.

"Mr. Davies?" the caller asked.

"Yes, this is Darren Davies. It's a bit late, what can I do for you?"

"I'm sorry to bother. I was hoping Deborah would be there."

"Mr. Stephenson?"

"Yes, it's me. Please call me Aaron."

Mom entered the office, "Pop, who in tarnation would be calling at this hour and here?"

Pop cupped the receiver and said to her, "It's the Aaron boy. He wants to talk to DeeDee."

Aaron chuckled, he could hear every word and told himself he would have to remember the name, 'DeeDee.'

"Well, she's not here," said mom.

"I know that, precious. You think I should give him her number?" Pop asked.

Mom thought about it a moment. It was not like they were giving it to a stranger, and they were going to be going out finally. She saw no harm in it and told Pop to give it to him.

Pop relayed the number and then extended a warning, "You know, Mr. Aaron, that's my little girl?"

"Yes, sir. Yes, I do," Aaron said, a bit nervous at Mr. Davies' tone.

"I don't care what you say about my place here, you hurt her, and we will have words. I like you Mr. Aaron, but please be careful with her. My DeeDee is…" He paused for a moment as if searching for the right word. Then continued, "… delicate. Like a flower. You understand?"

"Yes, sir. I appreciate your trust in me. I really want to get to know your daughter. She fascinates me. I have nothing but good intentions."

"Well, good then. We should have no problems. I'm glad you called Mr. Aaron. Now you go. Go give my DeeDee a call."

"I will, and thanks again. I will see you soon."

"Yes, and before I let you go, tell me, what are your thoughts about a Spaghetti Sub?"

Aaron considered it a moment, "Sir, I will be first in line for it."

Pop smiled, hung up, and got back to work.

Aaron dialed the number he was given.

Deborah was still a bit shaken by the morning episode. Although the rest of the day went well, it weighed on her mind. She could not understand how one moment she could feel perfectly fine and then, in an instant, feel completely miserable. Then perfectly fine again minutes later. She could not understand even more that the doctors said she was fine. She was not completely convinced with their conclusion of it possibly being epilepsy, but she kept on taking the medication. Popping her second prescribed pill of the day, she looked at the clock: 8:45 PM.

She figured Aaron would be in Dallas by now. Not having spoken to him before he left, she was not sure exactly what his trip was for. Deborah kicked herself for not giving him her number so he could call her—not that she would know what to say. She hated to be on the phone anyhow. It was a teenager activity filled with awkward pauses and miscommunication. She always preferred face to face conversation, so she could read the other person's face. Much like the way she could read Pop. His voice would say one thing, but his eyes and facial expressions would reflect another—his tell. The only tell she received from Aaron was that she could see that he was attracted to her. That was genuine. And that intrigued her.

After another surf through the endless nothingness, she shut the TV off and headed to her room. Deborah's apartment was small, even by city living standards. Any smaller and it would be considered a studio. The only thing she believed that kept her building from labeling her apartment as such was the wall that separated the living area from the bedroom. But it was hers. She spent the time, and money, to decorate it to reflect her style, which meant throw pillows, knickknacks, and abstract art.

The bedroom itself was much plainer. No one would really see the room, so it was simple and served its purpose, to sleep. The only electronic devices in there were an alarm clock and her phone charger. It was a little after 9:00, and she was ready for sleep. That was the advantage to the medication; its primary side effect was drowsiness. So, it was rather easy for her to sleep when she needed to.

Deborah went through her pre-bedtime routine of washing her face, brushing her teeth, and putting lotion on her arms and legs. It was something she had done since high school. Without it, she couldn't get to sleep, no matter how tired she was; even with her good night pills, it wasn't happening. Her ritual complete, she snuggled under the covers of her queen-sized bed. Then the phone rang.

Chapter
NINE

I'm sorry," said Aaron. "Did I wake you?"

"I'm in bed, but I wasn't asleep. Tough day." Deborah explained.

"Should I call you tomorrow, then?"

"No, it's okay," she paused and corrected, "I mean, it's okay. I can talk." Her face was cringing. She did not like a phone conversation. "How are you? I guess you made it to Dallas okay."

"Yes, I don't like these things. Mingling is not my thing, and half of these guys are stuffed shirts anyhow. How was your day?"

She thought about saying something but held back. It was not his concern. "It was okay. Not too busy. Another terrific Tuesday in the books."

Aaron chuckled under his breath. One of the ladies at his church would say 'terrific Tuesday.' Although Mrs. Thompson sounded like she meant it, for Deborah, it was slightly sarcastic. "So, what was the special of the day?"

"The Chicken Caesar Salad Sandwich," she said. "Same as always."

"Sorry I missed it; best in town."

There was a moment of silence. Deborah *really* did not like phone conversations. "So, who are you mingling with?"

"Other foodies. Critics from other parts of Texas. It is a smaller gathering than the national one we have in February up in Nashville, but there are still a quite a few people."

"And you talk about food?" Deborah asked.

"In a way. It is more of a 'look at the places I have reviewed' and 'see what periodical picked up my blog' type of setting. Personally, I hate it."

"So, why go?"

"Nate, my boss. He insists on me coming up here. He says it's for the sake of the paper. But it is expense-free, and whatever I do spend is reimbursable."

"Sounds like fun."

"Eh, it gets me out of the routine. But half the time, people are boasting about their accomplishments, and the other half they are teaching you the wrong way of rating a restaurant."

"How is it wrong?"

"I don't understand this group sometimes. Their idea of training is not right; they *want* you to go in and find what is wrong with a place. It is more about the negatives of a visit than what the critic enjoyed. I don't know. Maybe I am the one missing the boat. To me, a critic should be impartial and fair. I mean, there is always something good about an eatery, no matter how bad the visit is. That is what *I* do, I try and look for the good and convey that to my readers.

"For instance, I don't care for lettuce. But does that mean I should go in and rip Davies Deli for using lettuce on their BBLT? Of course not. I would, however, make sure to point out that Davies Deli put the extra B in the BLT by doubling the portion of bacon that normal eateries use. A critic should not be critical about a place. No matter how bad it is."

"I see," Deborah said to convey she was listening.

"Have you ever been to Andretti's?" Aaron asked.

"No, I do not think so. That's the place on the west side, right?"

"Yeah, that's the place. Well, it was by far the worst place I have ever been in—ever. And I have been doing this for three years. But did I bash the place? Did I thumb my nose and publish a list of their faults?"

"I would have to say, no," Deborah said.

Aaron laughed. "I'm sorry, I don't mean to bore you."

"I'm not bored at all. I am interested in what you do. I couldn't imagine a free meal ticket anywhere I wanted to go. It's part of the reason I agreed to go out with you."

Deborah paused a moment, waiting for a laugh, but received more awkward silence. She really, really hated phone conversations. But the silence was broken with a hearty laugh. She discovered that she loved his laugh.

"Well, I'm glad you feel that way. I have to go back to Andretti's for a second visit. My publisher felt my first submission, 'lacked perspective,' and wants a rewrite. Perhaps you are the additional perspective I need."

"Is that where we are going on Friday?" she asked with the teenage first date tingles welling inside her stomach.

"No, Andretti's will be our second date," he said.

"You're asking me out on a second date before the first?"

"I suppose," he said. "Creepy?"

Deborah smiled, "How do you know you will want a second date? What if your review of me is not what you expected?"

"Not possible. I look forward to Friday. It'll be an experience.

I just hope I'm granted a second date after you see what I have planned."

"Which is?"

"Nuh-uh. It's still a surprise. You'll have to wait until then."

She giggled; more giddiness. Then it occurred to her, "How did you get my number? I never gave it to you."

"I took a chance and called the deli. Your dad answered and was gracious enough to give it to me. It came with a stern warning that I should keep your honor intact, but I assured him my intentions were pure. I was surprised he was there this late."

"Yes, when he is feeling creative, he will stay late and experiment, just like Grandmom would."

"Spaghetti Sub?" he asked half-mocking.

"Is that what he's working on now?"

"I suppose. He asked my professional thoughts on the concept."

"What did you tell him?"

He thought a moment, "I told him if you were holding the basket, then I would be first in line."

"You did not," Deborah called him out.

"Okay, maybe I didn't go that far. But you holding the basket may have been brought up." More laughter. "Well, I have taken up enough of your time. I know you are ready for bed and will let you get some sleep. I'm about to hit the sack myself; long day tomorrow."

"Yes," she said. "So, you can learn how to spot crooked sandwich baskets and send our faithful back to Subway."

"Your baskets are crooked?" said Aaron surprised.

Deborah laughed, "Yes, Mom found them through a distributor who was practically giving them away because of the defect. It's minor, but enough that the original purchaser made a stink about it. You can't tell because of the liner we use."

"Well, I will make a note of that for my next visit. Could affect my perspective of the whole deal."

"You are finally writing a review on Mom and Pop?" Deborah asked.

"I am trying to. But it's difficult to write this one. Maybe you are clouding my clarity. I can't seem to find the right words."

"But you're a writer," she said.

"I know, right?" Aaron paused, "Well, I will talk with you later. Good night, Deborah, or should I say, DeeDee?"

"Sorry, only Pop can call me that," she replied, but was amazed at how it made her feel to hear him use the name.

"I figured as much. Good night."

"Good night."

Deborah plugged in her phone, set her alarms, and turned out the light.

Aaron, just over 200 miles away, did the same.

Both fell asleep with the other on their minds.

"So, how's the assignment going?" asked Gabriel.

Carter smiled, knowing that Gabriel knew precisely what was happening. He had the insight with the big guy. It was He who sent Gabriel on the errand of giving him this assignment.

"I feel we are making progress. I understand that the time here is limited, but I also know that His timing is always perfect, so I am not concerned."

"True." Gabriel hesitated, not entirely sure how Carter was emotionally. He did not like to see his fellow workers suffer an assignment that went terribly wrong. Not that it was Carter's fault, even he did not know the final choice a person would make. His boss was sometimes reluctant to share every detail, but as Carter just stated, He knew what was best. Gabriel continued, "She is about to become involved with a man named Aaron Stephenson."

"Yes," Carter nodded his head in recollection. "I have seen him around the deli. Quite a bit, actually. I figured she was the reason that kept him coming around."

"Well, she may have some doubts about pursuing the relationship. She may even confide in you about it. God has worked on her heart to soften it toward him. He has plans for them. But you know how it goes—one of His children can easily get sidetracked by the enemy when they are confused about who He is."

Again, Carter nodded. "I look forward to the opportunity."

"And the next item?" Gabriel pointed his head at the shoebox that rested the bench next to Carter.

"Soon. Saturday sometime. It's a fairly simple drop. This one is much easier to place than the last one. She almost saw me in the car."

"You may have an opportunity before then. Keep your ears open. He will let you know."

Carter shivered at the thought. He still felt he let God down by not saving that poor young man. He was ashamed and had rarely spoken to Him since, at least not directly. All his communication came through Gabriel and others of his kind.

"I will keep my eyes and ears open. Good to see you again, Gabe."

With a flash, Gabriel disappeared into the night. Carter

reached into the small paper bag on his lap and scattered seed on the ground. The few remaining pigeons scampered for the free meal.

The following morning, Aaron, too, was enjoying a free meal, the complimentary breakfast that came with the hotel stay. He always enjoyed hotel breakfast bars. But his critic's eye was always open. One of the downsides of the profession, never really enjoying a meal for what it was worth. The syrup was cold, the butter was a brick, and the menu said they offered lox for the bagels, but he could not find it, nor bring himself to ask about it; he didn't like lox anyhow.

He slowly ate his meal, not wanting to finish. Finishing meant he would have to make his way across the cold breeze-way to the conference center for the first of several dry and uninformative meetings. *Why do I always let Nate talk me into this?* he thought, munching on a piece of rye toast. His first session was "The Science of the Little Things," hosted by none other than Ethan Chadwick. Not the way he would like to spend the next hour and a half, but as he read once, "It is wise to study the ways of one's adversary," or maybe it was a movie quote. Either way, he would treat the class as what *not* to do.

To Aaron's advantage when he arrived at the session, the room was small and practically full; he was able to find a corner to tuck away in and remain obscure. He still wanted to fit in and not get hard looks, so he opened the binder the venue provided and pretended to take notes. What he did was scribble out a letter to Deborah.

Hey Deborah.

Right now, I am pretending to take notes from one of the stuffed-shirts I mentioned to you. It is hard to sit through a session with someone who can be so negative. I don't understand how people can be that way. They do not understand they are messing with someone's livelihood. The stuff he writes publicly has put people out of business. Hardworking mom and pop shops like yours. Open one day, doing exceptionally well, and then visited by the great Ethan Chadwick, then gone after a whisper of three pickles on his plate instead of four. I guess I will never comprehend their thought process. Never mentioning a word about food or that a server did a good job.

Speaking of a good job, Professor Chadwick is telling us that there is no such thing as excellent service, that there is always something to be improved, and that we must find it and bring it to light. That it is our responsibility to our readers. Sheesh, such ignorance. Well, he is about to wrap up, guess I will too. Not that you will ever read this. But for what it's worth, I am glad I met you and that thirteen was enough. I cannot wait to see you on Friday. I just pray you are not scared away by what I have planned. I would love to make it to our second date and for many more beyond that.

Yours truly, Aaron.

"Are there any questions?" Ethan Chadwick asked the crowd.

Nearly three-quarters of the hands went up. Aaron's were raised, only they were raised to push open the door to exit the room. He had an hour before the next session; time to explore the neighborhood.

It was incredible how much difference 250 miles could make on temperature. Houston had a relatively decent climate. However, since it was closer to the Gulf, the moisture tended to hang around more than it would inland, giving the city a constant muggy feeling. Nothing compared to further east, but just enough that Aaron could tell the air in Dallas was thinner and cooler.

The front that had blown through Houston a few days ago still had Dallas gripped in a bitter chill. It was too early for lunch, and he did not have enough time to eat if it were. He settled for a walk around the block. Mostly to wake himself up from Ethan's laborious rant on what Aaron was doing wrong. He came across just a couple of eateries. One advertised Vietnamese Cuisine and the other was a sandwich shop, not that different from Davies. It advertised the lunch special, just as the menu board did back home. *Thanksgiving Day Sandwich served with Sweet Potato Fries*. Aaron took note. He would have to tell Mr. Davies about this.

Other than the two restaurants, the only places around were a dentist, two law offices, and a UPS Store. Aaron finally found a coffee shop around the next corner. It was still packed with patrons seeking their morning dose of caffeine. The aroma was alluring, so he stepped in.

The bell sounded, but nobody took notice. They were lost in conversation, their newspaper, or scrolling their phones. The clerk at the counter finished a lady's mochaccino order and gave him a hearty smile. "What can I get ya?"

"Small coffee, black," Aaron said.

"Dark, medium, or light roast?

"Dark. The stronger, the better," Aaron wanted to prepare for the rest of his day.

"Sugar, cream?"

"No, black will be fine."

The guy shot a quizzical look but punched a few buttons on the register. "That'll be $4.32."

"For a small?"

"Yes, sir. Would you like the medium? It will be an extra $1.08."

"No, a small will be fine, thank you." Aaron gave his name, paid with a $5, and dropped the change into the tip jar that was conveniently placed next to the register.

Aaron eyed the place in his normal fashion. It was very much like every other coffee house he had been in. Cups for sale; bagged coffee, both whole bean and ground; gift cards for purchase; and various coffees themed signs and decorations. There was a menu board behind the counter on the upper wall. It was supposed to have a chalkboard written look into it, but it was not very well done.

What would Ethan say? Aaron mused. *While the décor is convincing, how can a person order from such an atrocious looking menu board? The ghastly appearance makes each drink seem appalling.*

Aaron laughed. It must have been out loud because a guy

with his nose in the daily paper looked up and gave him a grunt. He lowered his head in apology and found a seat next to the window that looked out over the busying street. Taxis, couriers, and businessfolk all made their way around the city, all having a destination. All having plans, meetings, and deals to close. Aaron just had a day filled with dos and don'ts of evaluating his profession.

"Ronnie?" the barista called. Aaron continued to stare out the window. He called again. No one responded. Aaron looked over to see the guy staring right at him with his eyebrows raised.

Aaron returned the look. "Aaron?"

"Black coffee, no cream, no sugar?"

"That would be me," Aaron said, heading over to the counter.

The barista handed him his coffee with a roll of his eyes like it was his fault that they got his name wrong. He took the coffee then glanced at his watch—time to head back.

"Thank you," Aaron said as he made his way to the door. The bell rang, and he was back out on the chilly street. Ten minutes later, he had an empty cup and was back in the lobby of the convention hall. "Trusting Your Palate" was next on the agenda. Dr. Sara Lewis gave the session. *Never heard of her*, Aaron thought. That was the case with most of the people at conventions he attended. She must be someone because the hall was just as full for her as was for Ethan. And again, Aaron sulked in the back corner, out of sight out of mind.

Darren Davies noticed there was something different about his daughter from the moment she stepped into the deli.

For one, she was smiling, and two, there was an urgency, a purpose to all she was doing this morning. He pointed it out to Mom. She smiled and patted Pop on the shoulder—her way of telling him to accept it, that it was a good thing. He shook her off and approached his daughter.

"Everything okay, DeeDee?" Pop asked.

Deborah smiled. "Yes, of course. Why would anything be wrong?"

"No, I don't mean anything wrong. You look unusually happy today, that's all."

Her smile grew. She knew he meant the best, but her love life was not his business. "I am fine, Pop," she said and kissed him on his stubbly cheek.

He looked back through the pass-through window at Mom who was watching their exchange. He shrugged his shoulders and went back into the kitchen.

Deborah felt like she was walking on air. She would glide from table to table, taking orders and expediting her and Erica's orders. She did not care that it was busier than usual. She didn't care that her feet hurt; she didn't notice any of it. For the first time in a long time, she was happy.

She was so focused on how she felt she did not notice that Carter walked in and sat where Aaron usually sat. Erica had taken his order, and she did not see him until he was halfway finished with his corned beef.

"Carter? I didn't see you come in. How are you?" She set the empty tray down.

"Fine, thank you, Deborah. How are you feeling today? Better than the last time I saw you I expect," he said as if he knew a secret.

"As a matter of fact, yes. I am feeling better, thank you,"

she replied. "How was the corned beef? We don't get many orders for that."

"It is an acquired taste," he said. "Or if you have been around as long as I have, you learn to appreciate a meal wherever you can get it."

Deborah frowned for a second, considering his condition. She wondered what it would be like with nowhere to go, no job, and nothing to do but wander between places. She noticed his cup of coffee was low. "Can I get you a refill?"

"Certainly, Dee—Deborah," he corrected. "Sorry, it just seems so perfectly fitting given your demeanor this morning."

She smiled again and looked at his empty basket. "Interest you in a bowl of peach cobbler? Best in the county."

He looked at the display case, then back to her.

"On the house," she assured him.

"You talked me into it. Beautiful *and* courteous, splendid combination."

"You got it," she winked and went to serve him.

A few minutes later, she returned with nearly a double portion; she felt for the older man. She placed it in front of him, and her mind went back to the sand dollar.

"Can I ask you a question, Carter?"

Carter swallowed a mouth full of peaches and dabbed his mouth, "Certainly."

"That morning, when I gave you a ride to the library," she paused to watch his reaction. His expression did not waver. "Did you happen to see a sand dollar in my car anywhere?"

His white eyebrows furrowed in thought. He looked down for a second, then back up to her, "No, I'm sorry, I can't say that I did."

Discouraged, and doubting his honesty a bit, she deflated, "Okay. Weird."

"Why? What happened?" Carter inquired.

"It's nothing," she said.

"Please, I would like to hear about it." He set down his spoon and met her eyes. "You had started to tell me about your father and a sand dollar. Does it have to do with your story?"

She sighed. "In a way. That morning, after I dropped you off and came to work, I found a sand dollar on the backseat of my car. The strange thing is that, like I had started to tell you, I thought I had lost it years ago."

"I see," Carter said.

"My dad and I, when I was 10, were walking on the beach when we found it. It was the first sand dollar I had ever seen that was in one piece. So, we kept it. When we got home, we both put our initials on the back."

Carter smiled at her transparency. "You love your father—or Pop rather."

Deborah glowed. "Yes, that day was an amazing day. Not that I love him any less today, but those days were simpler." She blew the lock of hair from her face. "I don't know. Maybe I was younger and naïve. I love my dad, but now it just seems like he wants to pass me on to another man. He says he wants me to be happy, but he doesn't understand that I *am* happy."

"Dads can be like that. Doing things for their kids that they feel are best. He knows he will not always be around and wants to be sure you are taken care of. And who knows, maybe time with a man like Aaron will be a good thing."

"How do you..." Deborah asked.

"I overheard you and Erica. Sorry," Carter admitted. "And I am sure he means well, Deborah."

"Yes, I know. But it can be overwhelming, given the situation." She paused, knowing she had said too much.

"And what situation would that be?" he asked, furrowing his brows again—sincere interest on his face.

"Nothing, sorry I mentioned it." She definitely did not want to talk about it. "I better get back to work. Thank you for listening, Carter."

"Thank you for talking with me," Carter said, scooping another bite. "And thank you for the cobbler. It was wonderful."

Deborah smiled and left him to finish.

Carter watched her leave. It was the part of the job he liked the least, leaving someone hanging. He knew there was a higher purpose. God always had grander things planned. Things that even he could not see clearly. He was being obedient. And praying for a better outcome than what had turned out with Jeremy. He shuddered. Then he finished his cobbler, paid for his meal, and left the deli.

Aaron was watching the clock, eager for 1 PM, the end of the final session of this arduous conference. He reminded himself to thank Nate personally for this painstaking three days. It was now Thursday, and he wanted to make it back to Houston before closing time.

Of course, Ethan was giving the closing remarks and was using every last moment to express how important he was, and of how little importance all the other attendees were. Crazy enough, he would receive round after round of applause after each pause. He sounded like a politician touting campaign promises to his constituents. And more people were drinking his Kool-Aid and wanting seconds. All it did for Aaron was to make him nauseous.

After his third, "in closing," Arron got up and headed for the parking lot. He had already checked out and had his bags in his vehicle. He was back on I-45 for the three-and-a-half-hour drive. It was about lunchtime, but he passed every fast-food chain. His heart and mind were set on Houston and some hometown cooking. With any luck, he would get into town an hour before Davies closed. Thursday was fried chicken sandwich day. He smiled just thinking about it. Or was it scrunchied brown hair and hazel eyes? Either way, he could not wait to make it back home.

Chapter

ELEVEN

It was well after 7:00 when Aaron pulled into his parking space. He was angered, disappointed, and very hungry. He had made good time until he hit Madisonville. Then a four-car pileup with a jackknifed semi blocked the entire highway. He failed to notice the red taillights until it was too late to make the last exit before the backup began.

The sign in the distance informed him that the next exit was in two and three-quarter miles. But he would not make it to that exit for another hour and a half; everything was at a standstill. It was so bad that motorists were getting out of their cars and conversing with each other. Even the breakdown lane was filled with overanxious drivers who were eager to get where they were going. They too were not going anywhere.

Once he was past the incident, he found himself grateful he didn't cover breaking news. He said a quick prayer for those involved and made the rest of his trek without further incident. However, it had deterred him enough to miss eating at Davies and seeing Deborah.

Aaron entered his apartment, and though it was relatively clean, the faint smell of staleness filled the room. He emptied his pockets on the entryway table and turned on the lights. After placing his suitcase on the bed, and a nature call, he sat in his recliner and turned on the television. The Rockets season had yet to start, but Thursday Night Football was about to come on. He had little interest in the sport—another area he would dread writing for—so he flipped stations. After a half-hour of surfing through nothing much, he remembered he was hungry.

He planned to call Deborah, but first things first; his growling stomach. While it was not the anticipated fried chicken sandwich, a Salisbury steak Hungry Man hit the spot. He sat back into his chair, ate, and relaxed every mile off his body. Aaron was generally happy about his life, yet he always felt that something was missing. It usually occurred to him when he arrived home to the emptiness of his small apartment.

After tossing the meal carcass, he picked up his phone and sat back down. Just as he hit the off button on the remote, his phone rang. He did not recognize the number right away, he had yet to save and assign it; it was Deborah.

"I was expecting to see you today," Deborah said. She cringed with the disappointment she let slip into her voice.

"Yeah, so was I," he answered. "I had every intention of coming by, but a jackknifed rig had other plans. I was caught behind it for longer than I wanted to be. I just got in not too long ago."

"I stayed an extra few minutes, just in case," she said, hoping she didn't sound too desperate.

"I'm sorry, Deborah, I should have called."

"It's okay," she said. After a long pause, she asked, "So, where are you taking me tomorrow?"

"Nuh-uh, told you, it's a surprise," he laughed. "You'll see tomorrow."

"Not even a hint?" Deborah asked, trying to get some idea of what she should wear.

"It's unconventional. Not somewhere you would think people would go on a first date."

"Well, just as long as it's not an amusement park," she replied with a laugh.

There was silence. A really long silence.

"Aaron?" she said.

More silence.

"Oh, man. It's the carnival, isn't it?" She really hated phone conversations.

"Maybe?" Aaron said.

"Oh, gosh. I am so sorry. That is not what I meant. No, anywhere is great. I was just teasing."

More silence.

"Aaron?"

"I'm here."

"You okay?"

"Yes," Aaron said. "Guess I didn't do too well."

"No, I was just teasing," she said with a defeated sigh. "This is why I don't like talking on the phone. It is nerve-wracking. I get nervous and try too hard to lighten the mood. I have nothing against carnivals. I love them, actually. I was just trying to be silly. Guess I'm the one who failed."

She heard him laugh, "Deborah, It's okay. We can do something else."

"No, if that is what you had planned, I want to go,"

she said, trying to fix things. "It's cute. What made you pick that?"

"Actually, to be honest, it's a working date. I'm supposed to go over and review the different food vendors. Nate's idea, he's my boss."

"Sounds fun."

"Really?" he asked.

"Yes. I think it will be fun. I would love to see you in action." Which was the truth. She found what he did fascinating. And beneficial. Who wouldn't love a free meal ticket to any restaurant in the county?

"Okay. Yes, the pre-centennial carnival is out in Magnolia Park, up northwest of town. Your insight will help me write a well-rounded article."

"I look forward to it."

"Good," he said. "What time will you finish at the deli? I know it's Friday, and you need to finish the week's books."

"Shouldn't take me too long. I only have to log Erica and Miguel. Payroll is usually pretty quick. Plus, I can head into the office early if I need to. So, sixish."

"Sounds good. The action doesn't happen until after sunset anyhow. Do you need time to get ready?"

"You can come by my place around 7:00. I should be ready," she grinned, feeling like a teen again.

"Seven then. I look forward to it," he said.

"Will I see you tomorrow for lunch?"

"Still not sure. I have to complete this week's entry for La Cabaña. The conference set me behind a bit. If I can escape the office, I may make it over there. If not, I will see you at 7:00."

"Oh, okay," she replied. "Well, I hope you can get away."

"Me too."

They said good night and hung up. Deborah went to her closet. *What to wear?*

"You understand what you need to do?" the heavenly being asked.

"Yes, Gabriel. I understand. I just do not see how this will help," Carter responded.

"You'll see. All it takes is a simple movement, and it can change the course of the entire evening. Trust Him, you'll see."

"I do trust Him. I just don't understand."

"Are we ever meant to fully understand how He works?" Gabriel asked matter-of-factly.

"I suppose not. I will see that it gets done."

"After this, you can deliver the next item."

"Yes, I will place it in time."

"Thank you, Carter. You are doing an exceptional job. The Lord is pleased."

Carter smiled. "Thank you, Gabe. That means a lot."

Once again, a flash of light took his visitor away. Carter looked into the shoebox. Just a couple more items, and one Phillips head screwdriver. He took it in his hand and tried to understand how the simple tool could make such a difference. As Gabriel had said, he was anxious to see what God would do with it.

Friday was busier than usual, the extra workers in town saw to that. Between the carnival in town, two medical conventions, and a business expo close by, Deborah hardly noticed the time flying by. She didn't even have the time to slip into the office to begin her weekly paperwork. She wondered how it would affect the time she could leave to get ready for her date. She smiled at the thought. Both Mom and Pop could tell she was happy and anxious, but to their credit, they kept it to themselves.

Erica, on the other hand, was more than willing to mention the change in Deborah's demeanor. "So," she began with a toothy grin, "tonight's the big night?"

Deborah didn't like people knowing her business, but she couldn't help but smile. Erica had been there when Aaron asked her, so it wasn't like it was a big secret. "Yes, he's picking me up at 7:00."

"Where is he taking you?" Erica pried.

Deborah broke into a laugh, half amusement, half embarrassed, "You know the carnival over in Magnolia Park?"

"You're kidding?" This time, Erica was laughing.

"Nope. He has to evaluate the food stands for a piece he is writing."

"Interesting," Erica said.

"What? It'll be fun." Deborah said, half sure, half trying to convince herself.

"If you're a teenager. I'm closer to that age than you are, and I know I wouldn't be too interested in going."

"Well, thanks," Deborah said.

"Hey, I wish you two the best. Just watch out for the tilt-a-whirl," she giggled.

"No, food is okay. I draw the line at rides that spin you around till you puke. I get enough of that walking around here on a 10-hour shift."

Erica did not respond to that remark. It was well known about Deborah's dizzy spells, but no one ever talked about it, especially Deborah. Erica was caught off guard at her willingness to kid regarding her condition.

Deborah noticed Erica's uneasiness. "Sorry, I know I shouldn't joke about it. I'm fine. I was just working too hard. It hasn't happened in a long time," she lied.

Erica gave a half-smile and went to a customer who had waived her over.

Deborah looked up at the clock. It seemed to slow down. The once-crazy lunch crowd had dwindled to just a few lingerers, one, of course, was Clarence. He was sipping at a bowl of pea soup. It was his favorite, probably because Mom made it.

She grabbed a bottle of cleaning spray and a rag and began to clean up the empty booths. After returning a half-dozen of them to their ready-to-be-seated condition, she excused herself to the office to get back on track with the weekend paperwork. "If you need anything Erica, shout. I will keep the door open."

"I can handle Clarence. I'll be sure to keep him away from Mom," she winked and headed over to him to refill his coffee.

Deborah clicked on the ancient computer on her desk. Then she went to get herself a cup of coffee; the relic took forever to get going. She could feel the watchful eyes of Pop staring at the back of her head. She paid no attention and filled her cup, two sugars, and one cream, just perfect. Upon returning, the little blue spinning circle told her the system was still booting up. She had half-finished the cup before the internet connection chimed, signaling it was okay to begin working.

She clicked on the link to open the payroll system; it also took a couple of minutes to completely load up. Her eyes roamed the room. She glanced at the cookie cutters and was again taken back to the smell of Grandmom's fresh-baked sugar cookies. She missed those days. As her eyes continued to pan, she saw the folder she had placed the applications in. Just from the look of it, she could tell that Pop had not touched it.

The computer gave out a *Ding*, and the program was requesting login information. Deborah obliged and grabbed the stack of papers in the wire basket that served as an inbox. There were a couple of bills that needed attention, a letter from the state about their annual review coming up in February, and two ink-punched timecards.

Deborah entered the information for the week, slowly sipping at her cup of coffee. She had this down to a science, not that there was much to it. Both had the same schedule every week, so it was rare that there would be any differences. She could do this in her sleep if needed. Simple, yes, but still at a level that both of her parents struggled. She had considered it was a ploy to keep her within the family business, but she never could bring herself to call them on it. That and part of her did want to be there—the memories at times wrapped her like a blanket.

She had completed both timesheets up until clock-in that morning, prioritized the bills, and written down the upcoming review dates. It was now 2:30. She looked over at the phone, wondering if she should call Aaron. While she was excited about their date, part of her was still nervous that he would cancel at the last moment. Silly, teenage knots in her stomach again played tricks with her mind.

She smiled and reached for the stack of applications. As her arm was extended the room went dim. She slowly lost her vision, the dizziness returned, and the ringing in her ears intensified. If she had not been sitting, she would have easily ended up on the floor. Instead, her hands went to her temple, and she put her head between her knees. She knew what came next, so she was already reaching for the wastebasket. To her benefit, she was not a loud vomiter, so no one heard.

After a couple of rounds, she was able to sit back up. The dizziness subsided, and she regained her composure. Luckily, there was a small fridge next to the desk with bottled water. She opened one and gently sipped until her knees would allow her to stand again. She looked out the office door—all clear. She was relieved that no one noticed.

Deborah took the can to the office restroom and cleaned it out, replaced the liner, and returned it to its place. Then she went back and washed her face. As she walked through the office, she looked at the phone again and thought about calling Aaron. She shook it off. She was already feeling better. No need to worry anyone. She would be fine.

TWELVE

Aaron, too, was watching the clock. It was almost the end of the day, and he had put the final touches on the La Cabaña piece. While Mexican food was not his particular favorite, he did enjoy what he ordered. The place had many of the nitpicky things that the elites up in Dallas have now been taught to watch out for. But these little things never bothered him, and he felt that they wouldn't bother his readers either. So, he rated the restaurant well, and while he wouldn't return there, he is sure that traditional South Texans would enjoy the place.

It was now 4:30, and he needed to occupy his time for another half hour. He thought about trying to begin the Davies Deli review, but every time he tried to open the file, his mind went blank. He just couldn't find the words to express what was needed about the old family establishment. Again, he laughed that a professional writer could come up blank, especially about something that meant so much to him.

He looked back up at the clock. 4:34. He had been staring at the screen for what seemed like hours, and his mind lived a lifetime within those four minutes with memories of conversations with Deborah and the anticipation of tonight's date. He wondered if she would be matching, or if that was just a work thing. He couldn't wait to find out. Maybe that's what made it challenging to write this particular review; it was personal. All of his other visits had a healthy level of detachment. He didn't know the owners, much less the staff. In the case of Davies Deli, he knew both. One had even threatened him. Aaron couldn't help but laugh.

At 4:36, Nate knocked at the door and made a crude remark about making the evening count and reminded him of his due date of the La Cabaña piece. He ignored the comment and told him the review was in his inbox.

At 4:40, Jessica came into his office and sat in a chair against the wall. She did not say a word but only smiled. Aaron waited for her to give him some print-worthy female advice. She sat there in silence for what seemed like forever, but she spoke at 4:41. "So, are you ready for tonight? You look nervous."

"I do?" Aaron responded, looking at his reflection on the now sleeping computer screen. "What makes you think I am nervous?"

"Because you are just sitting there doing nothing. That's not like you. You're usually active, always doing something."

It had not occurred to Aaron to be nervous. A little fidgety about the time, 4:44, but he wouldn't call it nervousness. He was excited to see her, not afraid. But it would be the first time they would be alone together; the first time that he would have to think about what to say, how to behave, and she had never really witnessed what he did for a living. It is one thing to stand on one side of the counter; it's quite another to sit on the other end. Okay, now he was nervous.

"Thanks a lot," he said, letting out a deep breath.

"Just calling it as I see it," she said. "You know me."

"Yeah, you're the one who put me up to this."

"Me? What did I do?"

"You told me that she was interested because of what she did with her eyes."

"Just calling it—" she began.

Aaron finished, "—like you see it. Yeah, you made that clear." He laughed.

4:46.

"Well, she came to you and agreed to go out with you, so I was right."

"Yeah, you were right about that. But I'm not nervous," Aaron paused. "Well, I wasn't until you got me thinking about it."

"Afraid you won't live up to the hype?"

"What hype? I am a newspaper writer, not Stephen King. There's nothing to live up to."

"Well, you've spent the better part of three weeks in that place, working up the courage to ask her out."

Is thirteen enough to ask you out? echoed in Aaron's mind.

"Now," Jessica continued, "you have the chance. What if the capture is not as entertaining as the chase? For her and for you?"

"I couldn't imagine her not being worth the pursuit. Not possible." Aaron defended.

"I would hope so. Let's just hope she feels the same way," Jessica said with a sly smile. She was baiting him. Her attempt to help him relax. But it wasn't working. If he wasn't nervous before she walked in, he was now.

"Don't you have a Lion's Club meeting to cover?" he returned the jest.

"Touché," she replied. Jessica smiled and said, "In all sincerity, I hope you two have a great time. Just trying to help you loosen up. You better get going, it'll be time to pick her up before you know it."

Aaron looked up at the clock, 4:55.

He sighed.

Deborah sighed as she closed the shop door after saying good-bye to Clarence. She looked up at the clock, 5:15. In a little less than two hours she would have to be ready for Aaron. She ran down a mental timeline. Forty-five minutes to finish books, 15 to drive home, which left less than an hour to get ready. Her earlier episode had passed. She felt fine and had no intention of canceling.

She was grateful for her head start, and she was done in no time, even with the lag of Pop's 1990s computer. She clicked 'finalized' as the second hand ticked 5:50; 10 minutes ahead of schedule. She shut down the computer, and it played the familiar Windows tone. Pop must've heard because he met her at the office door with a mop in his hand.

"The Aaron boy picking you up here?" he asked, trying not to pry.

"No. He's going to pick me up at my apartment. I just need to run home and grab a quick shower and to change. I printed up the checks for Erica and Miguel, they are on the desk, they just need your signature before you give them out, like usual."

Pop was looking at the ground now, fidgeting the broom from one hand to another. "You feeling okay, DeeDee?" He looked up at her with knowing eyes.

The trash can, he must have emptied it already.

"Pop, I am fine. Yes, I got sick. Must've been something I ate," she lied.

"And the ringing? You still get that?"

"Yes, Pop. The ringing is always there. But it's not what causes the dizziness or me getting sick. The doctor says it's not related, remember?"

"Oh, okay," Pop sighed. "Maybe you should go home and get some rest?"

"I am fine, Poppy. Really, I am." She called him Poppy to soften him up. He always relented when she called him by the name of her youth. It was endearing, just as DeeDee was for him.

But Pop did not smile or relent. "I am worried about you, Dee. That is twice this week that you have gotten sick."

Twice? Deborah thought. Her racing mind was evident in her face.

"Erica saw you the other morning," he admitted.

"Okay, yes, I got dizzy and sick in the parking lot, but that is nothing to be worried about," she said more trying to convince herself. "I feel perfectly fine right now. I always feel better after getting sick. I get dizzy and it makes me vomit. But just as quickly as it hits me, it goes away. Trust me, I am fine."

"Please, just get some rest this weekend," he said, setting the mop aside. "Rest tomorrow. Mom can go to the Flea Market another day. Erica and I can handle the lunch rush. I'm sure she would understand." He went in for a hug. She accepted. "I love you, DeeDee."

"I love you too, Poppy." She held him just like she knew he needed. "Now, if you'll let me go, I need to get home and clean up before Aaron comes to get me. I'm going out with him just like you said I should."

Deborah looked up, and she could see Mom with her head around the corner. She guessed that Pop could feel it too. She looked back to Pop as he studied her for a moment, then smiled, which made her smile.

"She's fine, Mom. She said so, and I believe her," he said into the hallway, never turning around.

"Oh good," Mom said. "I wouldn't want her to miss her big date with the Aaron boy. He is such a fine young man."

"I'll pick you up here at 9:00 in the morning, Mom," Deborah hugged her mom and left the deli. The sun was getting ready to set, casting an orange glow on the building. She walked to her spot, started her car, and was home in 10 minutes.

6:15, right on schedule.

Jessica's words did not end with her leaving his office. He carried them all the way home, through his shower, and into his closet. *What am I going to wear?* he anxiously thought. It was the 'living up to the hype' that got him worried. He did not want to be over-dressed; they were going to a carnival for crying out loud, but he also didn't want to dress down and have her dress up and feel uncomfortable. What was it his uncle used to say, a *schlemiel?*

6:35.

He went with middle-of-the-road jeans with a brown button-up long sleeve shirt. Jessica had once said that it brought out the color of his eyes. The night was warm, so he rolled up the sleeves. Comfortable, but still stylish. That, with his boots, completed the ensemble. He looked in the mirror, and the green eyes staring back at him were the eyes of a man nervous about his first date.

Dang-it.

6:50.

Deborah had adjusted her lipstick for the 12th time; *Would thirteen be enough?* she asked herself with a laugh that made it difficult to ensure she had it right.

She had also selected a pair of jeans, boots, but could not decide on which blouse went well with how she felt. She felt the excitement of a teenager, but bright colors were far too much for a first date, and she did not want to stand out in the crowd. And she was far too happy for a darker color, so what would be the middle of the road. Gray? Tan? White would be too much and could get dirty; this was a carnival after all. In the end, she went with gray, bright enough to reflect joy, but dark enough to blend in with the surroundings.

Deborah adjusted the shoulders on her top and tossed her hair a few times to bring out the subtle curls she had heated into her hair after drying. She felt warm and was not sure if it was nerves or the humidity of the bathroom. She grabbed a gray scrunchie and placed it around her wrist, just in case.

6: 55.

Aaron tapped his hands on the steering wheel as he waited for the light to change. Her building was around there some-where. To save him from having to find a parking spot she had asked him to pick her up in front of her complex. There would be a row of mailboxes under a streetlamp; she would be standing under it. The sun had set a half hour ago, the final glow of twilight was subsiding, and the streetlamp was beginning to take its intended effect.

He saw the row of mailboxes and the streetlamp, but he did not see her. He looked at his dash clock: 6:58. He passed by and made a right at the light so he could drive around the block and come back around. "Waiting on a Woman" played in his head as he made the final turn; there she was, looking at her watch; hair down and no scrunchie—she looked amazing.

He pulled up to her and rolled down the window. "Going my way?"

She smiled, and to her credit and Aaron's amazement, played along. "Only as far as Rainbowville."

He grinned, and she got in. The car immediately filled with her perfume. His grin only grew, and they were on their way.

"Not too many people like the classic cinema," Aaron said.

"Bing Crosby is one of my favorites. Although I prefer his Christmas movies."

"Yes, the Palladium is having a Christmas movie marathon day after Thanksgiving. I think both *White Christmas* and *Holiday Inn* are playing."

"Are you implying another date? What is that, our third, even before we have started this one?"

"Merely an observation," he laughed. "So, how was your day?"

"Busy," she said. She did not even consider telling him about her episode. "Seems like all the conventions in town seemed to find the deli. We were packed most of the day. Yours?"

"Slow. I finished up a review. But I was kind of preoccupied," he said, giving a side glance to see her reaction. Which of course, drew a grin.

"Nervous?"

"Me, no. Not at all," he said, remembering the set of eyes that stared him down at home. "Although that is not what my coworkers said."

"Well, you look fine to me. In fact, you look amazingly comfortable."

"Well, that is the outside. My insides are doing cartwheels, somersaults, and my mind won't focus."

"Want me to drive?" she jested.

That made him laugh. "No, I'm fine. You don't know how to get there, and besides, nobody drives my jeep, but me."

"Is that so?" she said.

"Yep, this is my baby."

"Will there ever be a time where you'll trust me enough to?" she asked.

"Not too sure about that."

"Will thirteen dates be enough?" She looked at him for a reaction.

Aaron looked back at her, and their eyes locked. She glowed under the light of a passing streetlamp.

They both laughed.

Aaron no longer felt nervous.

P arking was scarce, and Aaron could see the look on Deborah's face. It showed that she did not want to walk. Aaron had a secret, though. "Can you open up the glove box?"

Deborah did.

"That green hanging placard, please hand it to me." He took it and hung it on the rearview mirror. The sign read **Media Relations Pass**.

"One of the perks of the job, preferred parking."

"Very nice," Deborah said.

Aaron pulled up to a side entrance, away from the public craziness. "This is where the vendors park and have easier access to the facility. Not only is it closer, but my jeep will be safer with increased security." He nodded at one of the guards patrolling the area who saw the hanger and waved him on. Aaron slowly drove and found a spot near the entrance.

"Front door service. How about that," Deborah said.

"Only the best. Sometimes the job has its benefits."

"And other times?"

"Other times..." Aaron paused to gather his thoughts. "Other times, you are ducking potstickers that are being thrown at your head by an angry Asian woman."

"You're kidding me?"

"Nope. Last year I gave a less than popular review of a buffet over near Katy. Not only was I banned from the restaurant, she started throwing the daily special at me."

"Isn't that something."

"I can tell you, it's never boring." He got out and rushed over to open her door. She had a little more difficulty getting out than in; the jeep was slightly raised. "Sorry," Aaron apologized, taking her hand. She blushed.

The chill in the air that had been there the last few days was replaced by the regular gulf moisture, leaving a warm, almost damp feeling. Not uncomfortable—for a South Texan, that is. For them, it was a nice evening, nice enough to be out and about.

They made their way through a side gate and into a staging area. "This is where the action is. Vendors prepare some of their items back here when they do not have room inside their booths." He pointed to a couple of large industrial vats. Steam was rising from each of them and their senses were suddenly hit with the blended aromas of cooking meat. "The first one is chili. The other is most likely some type of pulled pork. You can tell by the utensils near the cookers."

"Do you wear a badge or a pin of some sort?" she asked.

"No. For the most part, other than the preferred parking, I try and blend in. I can give a better review when they don't know I am coming. I do get recognized from time to time, and while that can be exciting, because I get the best, but it is tainted. You do not get to see how the place really performs. It's why I try and show up an hour or two early to scope out a place. It helps when they have a bar or a form of entertainment. Easier to get lost in the crowd."

"So, are we late then?"

"Here? No, not at all. There is no ambiance to get used to. Here is straight food tasting. And the first batch is never the best. So somewhere around late evening is the best time. Gives the vats time to get seasoned and give a better flavor."

"You sure do know your food."

"Well, it's not that different than what your parents do at the deli. I am sure they can tell you a thing or two about seasoned pots and pans."

"True," she agreed.

"So, what do you want to try first, the Tilt-a-Whirl or the Ferris Wheel?" he said, pointing toward the carnival entrance.

"Uhhh," she said, looking a bit queasy at just the thought.

Aaron laughed. "I'm teasing." To which she looked relieved. "I wouldn't ride those things, even if the paper paid me to. Not my department. How about a lemonade? It's fresh."

"Sounds good to me," she said.

He led her away from the screams of riders twisting and looping and dropping several stories. The vendor they approached had a large container of yellow-tinted liquid with floating slices of lemon and limes. Aaron ordered two, and the girl behind the counter snapped her gum, pushed a lever, filled two cups with the concoction, and garnished the rim with a slice of lemon. He paid, and they were on their way further into the concession area.

Aaron attempted to look like he knew what he was doing, but really he was clueless. Not so much about the food court but being on a date. He did not want to be empty of words early into the date, but starting casual conversation was not his strong suit. Unless, of course, it was about food.

"How long have you done this," she asked. She was just as eager to fill the silence.

"Three years. Here and there. I started as a simple columnist writing about stuff that was happening around Houston. Things like this. But I once wrote a piece on a culinary class, and Nate noticed something about it. He asked me if I was interested in reviewing restaurants. I wasn't particularly keen on the idea, but after I did one, something clicked." Aaron paused in recollection.

"You found you had a knack for it."

"Pretty much. With food, words flow. I can't explain it. I couldn't write an editorial or sports piece to save my life, but food—"

"It's you," she finished.

"Yeah, I guess it is." He smiled, getting her recognition.

"So, what would you say about this lemonade."

Aaron laughed. "Well, it is a bit tart. But with fresh lemons, that is expected. Actually, lemonade is tough to judge. It all depends on the batch of lemons. How ripe they are will determine how sour your drink will be."

"And these?"

"Fresh off the vine. No doubt. No time to settle and age."

"Mmm-hmm," she said. "I like it."

"My conclusion, or the beverage?"

"Both," she laughed. "So, when do we eat."

"What would you like to start with?"

"Start?" she asked a little confused.

"I have to sample a little bit of everything. Well, not everything, but most of what they have to offer. Fair and balanced."

"Well, that chili smelled fabulous, let's begin there."

"Sounds good to me." He gestured the way.

For the next couple of hours, they made their way from booth to booth sampling the many offerings. At first, they ate from separate dishes, but as they grew comfortable, they began to share. They were sampling and not eating because of hunger. It took some getting used to for Deborah—she was used to eating until she was full—but Aaron had discipline. Eat enough to get a feel for the food, then move on.

After each booth, he paused to write in a small notebook he carried in his back pocket. He was thorough and would ask Deborah's opinion. "So, what do you think of this? How did you feel about the texture of that? Was this dish too spicy? Too salty? What was missing, what would make it better?"

Deborah felt a little overwhelmed, but she was learning to appreciate food better. Even if it was of the carnival variety, she could only imagine what a restaurant would be like.

Deborah suddenly noticed was how full she had gotten. Two hours of sampling chili, chowder, corn dogs, chili cheese fries, fried this and fried that, nachos, pulled pork, and everything barbecued. In addition to lemonade, they drank other fruity concoctions, tea, sparkling water, and a swig of a beer or two for comparison sake. She wasn't a drinker, but she could tell Aaron knew his way around a brew.

When she felt that her jeans were about to burst, she took hold of his arm and pointed to a set of benches. "Can we sit for a bit?"

"Yeah, sure," he said as they waddled to sit down. "You alright?"

"I will be after everything settles." As she sat and something caught her attention. A figure was walking away from them. There was something familiar about the tweed coat and hat.

"Oof," Aaron exhaled as he sat, followed by an, "Ouch! What the…?" He stood quickly and grabbed his shoulder. There was a screw sticking through the wood. It was part of the bench, but stuck out a bit too far. Aaron grimaced at the exposed screw and sat to the right of it, much closer to Deborah than what he had planned.

Their legs now touching, Deborah thought she should feel awkward, but for some reason, it felt right. His warmth transferred to her, and she could feel a tingle traveling up her spine. She was not sure if he was feeling the energy exchanging between them, but that question was quickly answered when his hand rested on her knee. She blushed.

"What a nice evening," he said.

"Yes, very," she concurred.

"Better than spending it alone or with a stranger."

The word *stranger* triggered Deborah's memory. "Did you see that guy walking away from us earlier?"

"What guy?"

"Tall. Tweed coat and hat. He was walking that way," she pointed in the direction he went.

"No, I don't believe so," he said.

"It is the strangest thing. I keep on seeing him."

"Who?"

"He is a homeless man, I think. He comes into the deli now and then. I saw him the other morning near my office. He was looking for the restroom. Then in the park across from my apartment complex. He was sitting on a bench in the rain. I gave him a ride to the library.

"The strangest thing happened after that encounter. I found a sand dollar on my back seat after I dropped him off."

"A sand dollar?"

Deborah realized Aaron wouldn't understand the significance. She told him the story of her and her father's close relationship and their walks on the beach. Then, about the day they found the intact sand dollar and how excited the seven-year-old was to find it. She gave details about how they both initialed the sand dollar and about the heartbreak when she thought she had lost it.

"It was the same one?" Aaron asked.

"As far as I could tell. If it was duplicated, it was an exceptional job. Even the aging was there." Deborah was again flooded with the confusion of it all.

"It was just odd that it was not there, then Carter was—"

"Who?"

"Oh, sorry, Carter is the man's name."

"Ok, gotcha, continue."

"Well, there was nothing in the backseat, then he was in my car, and after I dropped him off, it was there."

"How could he have put it there, much less have it. Or even know it belonged to you if he did have it?"

"I don't know. That is what is so confusing."

"And you just saw him?"

"I think so. He was walking away as you stuck your back with the screw."

"Well, I am glad I did. It gave me an excuse to get closer to you." He smiled.

She returned the gesture and looked up at him. Then it happened. That moment when the eyes of two people meet, and neither has much to say, nor remembers what they had to say if they had anything to say to begin with. The lengthy pause, the awkward smile. The heartbeat between the ears—all in anticipation of what was about to happen. Aaron leaned over and kissed her. The subtle connection of two unfamiliar pairs of lips, the warmth of shared nervousness, the electricity of the chemistry between them. It was a great first kiss.

Deborah was in her mid-twenties but felt like a teenager. Every touch, every word, every thought, all surrounded this moment. Nothing mattered; her job, the deli, her parents, her condition, nothing. She wanted to stay in this moment forever, but her adult instincts took over, and she knew life had to move on. She smiled as their lips parted. He put his arm around her, and time seemed to stop. Her fullness, forgotten. All that mattered was 'right now.'

Across the concourse, in the darkness of a shaded building, an older man in a tweed coat and matching hat put a screwdriver back into the shoebox he carried. He smiled. A hand touched his shoulder, the warm hand of one not of this world.

"Excellent job, Carter," Gabriel said. "Are we set up for tomorrow?"

"First thing," Carter assured his companion. "It will be in place. Are you sure he will find it?"

"Not a doubt, my friend." Gabriel patted him, and with another flash he was gone.

Carter watched them for another second, smiled, then disappeared into the night. Leaving the new lovers to revel in their newfound love.

FOURTEEN

They finally found the spot for dessert and had many booths from which to choose. Garish signs proclaimed, Fried Cheesecake, Homemade Fudge, and staple snacks like Pretzels and Cotton Candy. But the reason Aaron was drawn to this carnival was Francine's Fab'lous Funnel Cake.

"It won a Western County fried food contest last month," Aaron declared, and Deborah remembered from the peach cobbler that he had a soft spot for desserts.

"Are you sure you want to do this?" Aaron asked. "You don't have to. I am the one who needs to try it. It's the reason I am here."

"No, I want to," she said with a hint of reservation in her voice. "You need a female perspective, and I am giving you my full support."

Aaron turned to the clerk, "Two, please. One with powdered sugar, one with the strawberry topping." He rubbed his hands together with a Cheshire grin.

After the server handed them both desserts, they sat at a nearby table and took turns sampling each cake. Aaron looked like a wine connoisseur chewing on one side of his mouth, then the other. He pulled his notebook and placed it on the table. Then with his pen touching his lower lip, he furrowed his brows. When he seemed to find the right thought, he scratched a few words and took another bite. It made Deborah laugh.

"What?"

"Nothing, it's just you are so into what you are doing," she said as she mimicked his facial expressions.

"Is that what I look like?"

She laughed. "Yes." The truth was that she liked it. He had strong features, very masculine, sexy, something she had failed to notice at the deli. "You truly enjoy what you do."

"Yes, I do."

"It shows." She touched his arm, he placed his hand on top of hers. "But I am so full that I cannot eat another bite. I have already told myself I won't eat for a week."

He looked down at the half-eaten cake and nodded. He grinned and met her eyes. "Me too."

"So, what's next?"

"Definitely not the Tilt-a-Whirl." Aaron released her hand and leaned back a bit, then stood. "How about a walk?"

"If I can get up." She let out an *oof* as she stood. *Well, that was ladylike*, she thought. Aaron extended a hand, she took it, and they walked around as their metabolism kicked in and burned away that heavy, overindulgent feeling.

Deborah enjoyed every moment. It had been a long time since she felt this carefree. Through the years of schooling, she never had time for herself; her nose was always stuck in a book. From education to the business ledgers of Davies Deli, she was always busy, trying to please other people. And tonight, it had felt like she had stepped out of her life and for just a moment gave into the selfish desires of doing something for herself. It felt good.

As they walked the perimeter of the midway, she asked about what he was writing in his notebook. He went on to explain that for a carnival, it was a different experience. Since the aesthetics were a non-issue, he had to go by the trinity of food critiquing: scent, flavor, and content. This too she found fascinating. She had never really given thought to any of it, and she had spent her whole life living in a restaurant. Aaron's true passion was something she discovered that she took for granted every day. She could not wait to take this knowledge back to the deli and rediscover her family's deli in this new light.

They rounded a corner, and Aaron pointed to a gate. "This is where we came in. You ready?"

She wanted to say that she wasn't; that she wanted the night to last forever. But that was infantile, and she had to get up early to take Mom to the flea market.

"Yes, I need to get some rest for tomorrow," she said, following his lead through the backstage maze. The pots no longer steamed, and two workers were preparing to clean them out.

They reached his jeep, and he helped her inside. His hand on her side sent tingles up her spine; his touch was much more familiar now. He too struggled to get in. *Too much funnel cake,* he mused.

She giggled.

"What?"

"I think we both ate enough for an army."

He agreed with a grunt. "So, what's tomorrow?"

"I am taking Mom to the flea market in Edgewood. She is always looking for collectibles and memorabilia for the shop." She paused a moment and spoke before giving much thought. "Wanna tag along?"

Aaron laughed. "I would not want to impose on mother-daughter time."

"Oh, it's nothing like that. We always go once a month. Plus, I think she wants to meet you officially."

He nodded as he pulled into the traffic of other patrons waddling home. "What time?"

"I am picking Mom up at 8:00. I can swing by your place after I pick her up, say 8:30?"

"It's a date," he said, offering her his hand over the center console.

She accepted it. "Great." She hoped she did not seem too eager. Yes, she did not want the night to end. She wanted to spend more time with him, but to push him into a second date in less than 12 hours could be off-putting. And dealing with a family outing was something for more serious couples. She reasoned that with, he had been in the deli for the three weeks and already knew her parents, so it wouldn't be near as awkward as meeting them for the first time.

The drive home was, for the most part, spent in comfortable silence; soft jazz played on the radio. She had to agree with Louis, it was most certainly a wonderful world.

At 7:00 in the morning, Aaron was up and ready. He was relaxing on his recliner with a cup of coffee and an open Bible on his lap. He had been reading through the Psalms and had come across a stretch where the theme was remembering who God is. Psalm 77 spoke of remembering what God had done in the past; Psalm 78 admonished readers to not forget and to pass on traditions; Psalm 84 recalled the blessings of trusting God. Aaron felt encouraged.

He had been through quite a bit in his 26 years of life—the worst was when his parents divorced when he was 12 years old. While old enough to understand, he was left in the dark about what exactly happened. It had always been a blame game anytime he questioned someone about it. His mom blamed his dad's job. His dad blamed her lack of affection. Neither of them slept around —at least not that he knew of—they just did not get along. And they were not afraid to let it show.

He couldn't remember seeing them spend time together. Dad was always out of town, and mom was always working. They had little time for each other, much less him and his brothers and sisters. He was the youngest, so it was the hardest on him. Most of his siblings had already left the house by then, so on D-day, it was just him and his 16-year-old sister, Sally, in the house. Yet, they both toughened up and made the best of their years. He went to live with his dad, and she spent her remaining two years with mom until she left for college.

Even though Aaron had a poor experience when it came to adult relationships, he always had faith to turn to. His sister had an old beat-up Chevy she purchased from an ad in the paper. David, their oldest brother, helped her fix it up. She used it for school, her part-time job, and to take Aaron with her to Wednesday night service at the church they grew up in. It was something he always looked forward to, keeping him close to his sister and drawing him closer to the Lord.

After Sally moved to Atlanta, he was able to continue going through the friendships he had built. They continued to pick him up and take him to services and outings. He still kept in contact with some of them today.

He struggled in his faith when he moved to Houston. The college scene proved to be a tempting one. It was easy to get caught up in the party scene. While Aaron did not lose himself to it, he was knocked off track for a bit. It took a college professor who saw his potential to remind him of what he stood to lose by falling in with the wrong crowd. Aaron listened and quickly rebounded. By the next semester he was top of his class.

Aaron knew of the reminders God put in the path of a believer to keep them near. The Bible spoke of making paths straight, but Aaron always believed that straight was not necessarily the absence of curves and hills. His life experience taught him that God gave each person minor course corrections that kept the path aimed at Him. *A life path could be as crooked as Lombard Street in San Francisco*, he mused, *but if it led to Christ, then it was technically straight—straight to the Lord.*

Aaron prayed and thanked the Lord for all he had gone through; for the reminders that kept him close. He thanked God for his church, his pastor, his job, and for meeting Deborah. He asked God for another great day and for him to reflect Christ in a worthy manner toward Deborah and her mother. It suddenly occurred to him; he was not entirely sure what Deborah's stance on God was. He made a mental note that this was important to know and for her to understand his position.

"Mom, what are you up to now?" Deborah asked. "It smells like an Italian restaurant in here. Let me guess, Spaghetti Sandwich."

"Here, taste this," Mom said, sticking a steaming spoon full of sauce in her face.

"Mom, it's 8:00 in the morning. It's too early for spaghetti sauce."

"Just a taste—Pop's newest creation. He's been up since 4:00. He was tossing and turning all night. I finally told him to get up and get cookin'." Again she lifted the spoon.

Deborah relented and tasted the sauce. To her surprise, it was exceptional. "Pop, you made this?"

"From scratch," he proudly stated, stirring the pot slowly. "Tomatoes and all. No canned nothin'."

"This is amazing," she said, stroking his ego.

"I am glad you think so, DeeDee," he said. "It will be Saturday's special!" He paused and pointed to the dining area, "Mom, go get the window sign." He waved his hand in an arc. "All new flavor, Homemade Spaghetti Sub Sandwich."

"Pop, not now," Deborah said. "Mom and I need to get going. We are heading over to the Flea Market in Edgewood." She looked at the clock. "And we should get going."

"What's the hurry, Dee? We have all day," Mom said. "We don't need to rush off."

"Well, we kinda do," Deborah said.

Both Mom and Pop stopped and stared at her, "Why, what's going on?" Mom asked.

"Well, I sorta invited Aaron along," she admitted. She had planned on only telling Mom on the way. She knew Pop would make a big deal, which with his jaw-dropping, she saw he was about to just that.

"When did this happen?" he asked.

"Last night at the end of our date."

"Must have been some date," Pop said, raising his eyebrows.

Deborah smiled at the gesture. It must've pleased Pop because he smiled just as wide and made no further comment. She knew that seeing his daughter happy was all that mattered to him.

He began to whistle and headed back to his pot and stirred happily. He suddenly stopped. "Momma!" he said, and his voice elated, "We should toast the sub. Like garlic bread."

Mom was grabbing her purse from under the counter. "Yes, Poppa, you're a genius," she said, rolling her eyes. Deborah laughed.

"When will you be back?" Pop asked.

"I will be here for the lunch rush. Erica and Miguel will be here at 10:00 to help you open up," she explained like he was a child and didn't realize that it was the same time they always came in every day.

He danced around the island and kissed his wife on the cheek. "Love you, momma."

"Love you too, Poppa," she said, waving off his dancing ability.

"So, where does Loverboy live?" Mom asked with a sly grin as they walked to the car.

"Mom, really," Deborah said. "Just on the other side of the highway. Not too far."

Within 15 minutes, they were outside his building. It was different than she expected. Much older and taller. Deborah parked and texted him that they were outside. He replied, and moments later he appeared. She grinned, and her heart fluttered. Mom must've noticed because she gave a motherly, all-knowing giggle.

"Oh, stop it, Mom," Deborah pushed at her mother's side.

Aaron got in the back seat and greeted both of them. Mom still had a giddy look on her face, and Deborah was laughing silently.

"What did I miss?" Aaron asked.
Both women burst into laughter.

FIFTEEN

There was a doughnut shop across the street from the entrance to the flea market. Mom insisted it was a tradition to have coffee and a pastry before spending the morning shopping. She claimed that not only did it give you energy, but it was a foreshadow of the type of day you will have. Good coffee and you would find a diamond in the rough; weak coffee or a stale pastry would be indicative of going home empty-handed. They left the shop with high hopes and a big smile on Mom's face.

Aaron would have given the place four stars.

After a few minutes, they joined the stream of cars that filed into the market grounds. Aaron had been to flea markets many times in his younger days, only back then they were called swap meets. The name was spruced up after folks began to sell newer items, crafts, and food items. Before, it was simply a giant garage sale where people would buy clothes for pennies on the dollar, and a bargain shopper could haggle the price of mismatch tires, flatware, and unwanted appliances. Now bartering your way to a better deal was more difficult with the small businesses selling their crafted, canned, or specialty items. Another lost art that faded away into yesteryear.

Aaron reached into his jacket pocket, pulled out his press placard, and handed it to Deborah. "Here, use this. There should be a preferred parking area near the entrance. There always is."

Deborah hung the sign on the rearview mirror, and they found a spot three spaces from the entrance.

Mom smiled. "You feel pretty special with that thing, don't you son."

"The job does have its perks," he replied.

Aaron paid the admission fee, and they were on their way.

"So, where to first, Mom?" Deborah asked, looking at the three paths they could take.

Mom closed her eye and sniffed the air like a bloodhound tracking its prey. With a grin, she pointed to the left. "That way. I can feel it."

"Mom is trying to find old-fashioned coke glasses for the deli. She wants to extend the '60s feel. She has even considered bringing in a malt machine. But today's adventure is for those glasses. We have been to three markets and an antique fair so far with no luck."

"Let me guess, bad coffee," Aaron assumed.

"You catch on quickly," she said with a laugh, taking his arm.

As they made their way through the crowd of shoppers, peddlers, and looky-loo's Mom would pause for a moment at each station, give it a once over, shake her head, and move on to the next. She seemed to have a system, or a sixth sense, because at the third vendor her head popped up, and she said, "Here. This is the one."

They walked into the smaller stall, and Aaron saw why she had chosen it. The place was filled with antique signs advertising Mobil Oil, Texaco, and Pepsi. No Coke, but her target was not a sign. She filtered through the tables, moving stealthily as if she moved too quickly her quarry would escape her attack. Then, there they were. It even seemed to take Mom by surprise—two six-pack cartons with 12 identical coke glasses. The glass was even frosted—the perfect trophy.

Mom yelped with glee upon seeing them. "Look!" she said, then covered her mouth, perhaps afraid that they would scamper off into the field of other knickknacks on the table. "See, what did I tell you? Good coffee, good day!"

The shop owner noticed her excitement, and Aaron noticed the shop owner noticing her excitement. He knew that they both knew the game. The owner grinned ear to ear and walked over to them. "Can I help you?"

"Yes. How much for the coke glasses?" Mom asked.

"Just so you know, they come as a set. Can't break 'em apart. Buy one; buy them both."

"I do want them both. How much?"

"Well, these are antiques. Much of my shop is. Each six-pack is $90, so for the full set, $180."

Deborah's eyes went wide; Mom's grin fell from her face.

Aaron squinted his eyes, grinned, and took a deep breath. He stepped forward and extended his hand. "How are you doing? My name is Aaron."

Aaron let his hand float in the air until the man took it and shook it. The short, stocky man's grip was a little limp, and Aaron knew right away he had him. *You can tell how strong a man is by how firm his handshake is,* he thought. *This dead fish had no chance.*

"Chuck," the man said. It came out more like a question than a statement. He retrieved his hand and flexed the feeling back into it.

"Pleased to meet you, Chuck," Aaron began. "You do realize that you are charging $15 per glass?"

"That's the price," Chuck said shakily, then adjusted the ball cap on his head. It too had an antique motif—Pennzoil.

"Yes, of course, but prices are always negotiable," Aaron said.

Chuck looked at the two ladies, then back to Aaron, "What you got in mind?"

"How about $90? Buy one get one free?"

The man got some of his nerves back because he grinned, almost laughed, then shook his head. "I could get $150, easy, from anyone else."

"150?" Aaron questioned.

Chuck looked Aaron in the eyes, tried to remain firm, but failed. "$140."

"Okay, I can see you understand the situation. I am a reasonable man. $10 per glass, $60 per case, $120 for the set."

Chuck looked again at Deborah and Mom, then back to Aaron, who once again had his hand extended.

"Deal?"

The man nodded, smiled, and shook Aaron's hand. "Deal."

Aaron opened his billfold and handed the guy six $20s.

Chuck readily accepted them. "A guy's gotta try," he said.

"I completely understand. Hey, you got to make a living just as much as the next guy."

Mom grabbed the two packs—gently, but quickly—before Chuck could change his mind.

"You have a pleasant day, Chuck. Good doing business with you."

They left him there, but he was already moving on to the next patron who was eyeing a Gulf sign that was so rusted it was almost illegible.

"Well, that was impressive," Deborah said.

"Eh, you just got to know how to handle guys like that. He figured he had a group he could push over. He found out he was wrong."

"Boy did he," said Mom.

"There are two tricks to negotiating. First, you never let on how much you are interested in something. And two, you must always be willing to walk away, or at least convince them that you are willing to walk."

"Is that so?" Deborah asked.

"With him, it was easy. That is why I shook his hand before speaking about terms; sizing him up. With a weak handshake, I knew he would accept whatever I offered. So, I never had to go as far as walking away."

"But you said $90?"

"Yes, you always want to go lower than you are willing to pay. It gives the seller a reason to knock a bit off his original price, which is always higher than he would be willing to accept. After that, you find the middle ground. Most of the time it is a bit higher than you wanted to pay and a little lower than what they are wanting. Both parties feel like they won."

"As I said, very impressive."

"I don't care how you got them. I am just happy we found them," Mom said. She was looking at them like she held the World Cup. And relevant to the situation, they almost glowed in the sunlight. "God was shining his light on us today."

"Amen, sister," Aaron echoed.

"Oh, mom, do you have to?" Deborah said.

"Do what, sweetie?" Mom asked.

"Bring God into it." She paused, then continued, "Even if God did exist, He wouldn't care about Coke glasses."

"Oh, DeeDee, you know very well that He exists, even if you won't admit it. And He does care, even about the little things. All the small things we take for granted, all the little reminders He leaves behind for us to find. He's real, even when it comes to Coke glasses."

Aaron could see that Deborah was upset. He had not given a thought that she may not be a believer. He took it for granted that everyone thought like he thought. He had a sudden mini-epiphany. *There is a whole world filled with the lost, or those who have forgotten.*

"Where is the restroom?" Deborah asked.

Aaron saw a sign up ahead near a couple of food vendors. He pointed it out and offered to get a couple of lemonades and a pretzel. She accepted, gave a half-smile, and headed toward the sign. He and Mom found an empty table and sat.

"Please forgive Deborah. It has been a tough couple of years for her. College really did a number on her faith. She was not always that way."

Having dealt with the atheistic college scene, he understood. It almost enticed him to the mainstream way of thinking, which was all about self-promotion and not needing anything or anyone to be successful.

"I get it," he replied. "In college they teach you that if you rely on a higher power, it negates the hard work you experience climbing the ladder. In college, you're alone. No one is there to fight for you, much less join with you. So, it's easy to fall into the trap of self-glorification. You work on your own, at least that's the way it felt to me. It's easy to forget that God is there every step."

Aaron fell silent. He knew the struggle well. And when the voices crept up, then were confirmed through others, they became easier to follow. Even the strongest of people could fall victim to them.

Aaron could still see Deborah in the distance, and for the first time, he felt sorry for her; sad that she was missing out on one of the most essential things in life—knowing that there was a higher power at work.

"We don't need to understand it all," he added. We don't always have the answers. But isn't it cool that we get to rejoice in the little things, even if it is just a set of Coke glasses?"

Deborah could feel her cheeks burning. She was upset at Mom for making her look foolish in front of Aaron. She realized that they had not talked much about faith. Not that it was her favorite topic, but for the first time, she could see it would be something that they would need to address. He seemed to hang on Mom's words, and she now knew that he was a believer just as her parents were.

After making a wrong turn toward the men's room, she finally found her way but stopped for a moment to regain her composure. As she calmed down, she began to feel more embarrassed than angry. She had acted silly, like a child. She sighed as she stared at the ground where an empty popcorn bag rolled around in the breeze. Then a pair of shoes stopped in front of her. They were a worn but nicely kept pair of brown loafers.

"Do you like gelato, Deborah?" the voice asked.

Deborah looked up to see white hair under the staple tweet hat and piercing gray eyes. She smiled. It was Carter. He had a cup of what she assumed was the item he spoke of. He licked the spoon and went back for another scoop.

"I don't see the difference. Ice cream is ice cream," she said. "Are you stalking me, Carter?"

Carter laughed. "No, I wouldn't call it that. Stalking shows a deliberate act and in many cases infers ill intent. So, to answer your question, no ma'am, I am not stalking you."

"Well, I don't believe in coincidences," she said.

"Neither do I. But you didn't answer my question."

"I guess I do," she said as he took a seat next to her.

"Do you know what makes it smoother than ice cream?"

"Not really," she answered, not sure where this was going.

"Eggs," he said.

"Eggs?"

"Yes, eggs. Did you know that ice cream is part egg? Well, egg yolk, really. Other than the abundance of cream, it is one of the reasons it is so fatty. Gelato does not contain any egg. It also uses more whole milk than the heavy cream its partner uses. Thus, it is smoother and has half the fat that ice cream has."

"That is interesting," she said. Then, recalling the library, "Something you read, I suppose."

"Actually, no," he chuckled. "I was talking to the parlor owner just now."

Deborah laughed. "So what brings you to Edgewood? And don't say the gelato."

Carter nodded with his brows raised. "Fair enough. Let's just say I like rare items. I enjoy finding things—things people have once lost, sold without thinking, or have forgotten it is of worth."

She thought about the sand dollar. "Was that you?"

"Was what me?"

"The sand dollar. Did you put it on my backseat when I

was not looking?" she asked and watched his face for any form of deception.

"I do not know anything about your sand dollar," he said without a hint of lying.

"What was in that shoebox you were carrying that morning?" she pressed.

"That, my dear, is rather personal. Would I ask what you carry in your purse?"

Deborah felt guilty. She assumed again. Here she was accusing this poor homeless man of deceiving her and having less than honorable intentions. Maybe it *was* a coincidence.

"I'm sorry. I did not mean to offend you," she said, looking back at the ground. "I'm just not having the best of moments right now."

"Things are not going well with Aaron?" he asked.

She snapped again, "You *are* following me."

"Easy now. You wouldn't want to have to apologize again. I saw you two and your mom earlier, that's all. You seemed happy then. What happened to change your demeanor in such a short period of time?"

It was too much to explain. She was embarrassed by the whole discussion and answered simply, "I got upset at my mom about her talking about God. She got excited about finding some Coke glasses and was thanking God for it. I didn't understand. God wouldn't care anymore for Coke glasses than he would of the contents of gelato."

Carter laughed. "To you, maybe."

"What does that mean?"

"If she feels that small things are important to God, then they are, from her point of view. There is nothing wrong with that."

Deborah stayed silent.

"If you feel that God should only be concerned about the big things, then that is how you see things. And there is nothing wrong with that either."

"I don't know what I believe. I stopped caring a long time ago."

"Not so long," Carter interrupted. "College can do a number on one's faith. I have seen it a million times. A bright-eyed student is ready to accept the challenge. Bold in the faith and ready to change the world. But when they get there, the support they had at home is nothing but an echo. They realize how alone they really are and how much they depended on others—not only for life, but their faith. They see faith as work, and when they witness others around them who are just as busy and just as determined as they are, they begin to follow the crowd, neglecting their faith. And faith will slowly fade away when one does not work it out."

"How do you know that is what happened."

"Libraries are not the only places I like to spend my time. You would be amazed at the education one can receive by just walking the study halls of our university system," Carter explained.

"You surely do get around," she said.

"You would be surprised."

"I suppose I would. But what does that have to do with the big and the little things?"

"Let me ask you something. You went to college to get a degree, correct?"

"Yes."

"And you went there with a determination to do your best over the four years and to come out on the other end with a major accomplishment?"

"Yes."

"And on day one, your heart was sure that God had sent you there to achieve a dream?"

"Yes, I suppose."

"Okay, then consider this. If God cared about the end goal of you getting a degree, and He sent you to college to achieve a dream, then why would He not care about each course you took to get there? Why would He not care about each test that allowed you to pass each course? Why would He not care about each hour you studied that allowed you to pass each test, that enabled you to pass each course, that allowed you to get the degree, that helped you accomplish your dream?"

Deborah was once again silent. She had never thought about it like that and didn't have an answer.

Carter smiled. "You see, Deborah. God cares about the little things. Your mom's dream of building her deli into that malt shop in the sky is achieved through the little things. Today it was finding those glasses. It was one more piece to the puzzle. Was it God who placed those Coke glasses in that store for her to find? Maybe not. But it *was* God who directed her to the place where those Coke glasses would be.

"Either way, God is always sending us reminders of who He is. He loves each of us and wants the plans He has placed in us to succeed. He is more deliberate in some cases. Like those who once were so close to Him but have drifted away. Maybe like those who were drawn away through collegiate influence." He smiled at her, taking the last bite of gelato.

"So, God led me to find the sand dollar to remind me of what it meant in my relationship with Pop so that finding it would ultimately lead me back to God?"

"You catch on quickly." Carter smiled and stood. "I need to get going. And so do you. You don't want to keep them waiting too long. I will see you around." He gave her a slight bow and walked away.

Deborah watched Carter walk away, stunned for a moment, not sure what to do next. There were only two people who knew the full story behind her sand dollar—her and Pop. Of course, the legend of the sand dollar was widely known, but the fact that he told her the story that day no one knew but the two of them. But she would not let him break the sand dollar to release the five doves; it was far too pretty. He explained it would spread goodwill and peace. But when she started to cry, he relented. *It's funny how a little girl's tears can affect a father,* she mused. He also explained how the symbol of the sand dollar was there to help us share the Gospel.

Another fairytale, she thought.

But this time, she wasn't so sure.

Aaron and Deborah's mom chatted as they waited for her to return.

"Was she brought up believing in God?" Aaron asked.

"Oh, yes," Mom said. "She was always in church. If not with Pop and me, with my parents. Christ has always been a big part of our family. When Dee… Deborah… was little, she and my mom had a tradition of baking Christmas cookies, only instead of canes and trees, they would make crosses. As a little girl, it was her favorite part of Christmas. Almost as much as presents. And then…" her voice trailed off.

"She grew up," Aaron inserted.

Mom nodded. "My mom, her Grandmom, passed away suddenly. Grandpop followed not too long after. It always seems it's that way. One spouse passes on, the other almost gives up living, just wanting to be reunited with the one they spent so much time with."

"It happens. The good thing is that she knew them. And knew them well. You are a good mother for giving her the ability to know and to learn from family. I did not have that growing up. It is a blessing to hear it still happens."

"But Deborah…" again her voice failed her.

"Will come around." Aaron finished. "I came around. After my parents divorced, I was mad at God. While I never turned my back on Him, I did stray away from my faith. I bet Deborah is the same way. That is why she gets upset. She knows God is real, but for some reason, the connection has faded. She needs these reminders. So, don't get discouraged when she shuts you down. God sees you, and He sees her. I came back around. She'll come around too."

Mom smiled. "I knew I liked you from the moment you walked into the deli. You had that believer glow about you."

"Thank you," Aaron said. "The key for Deborah will be to find what is troubling her so much that she doubts her faith. That is where to begin."

"I think I know what that is," Mom said.

"Really?" Arron asked.

"Aaron," she began. Mom seemed reluctant to say what she was about to say. Aaron gave her his full attention. "There is something you should know, but I don't know if I am the one who should tell you."

"What is it?

"Deborah is—"

"Okay, I am ready." It was Deborah. She looked at both of them, a little puzzled. "What's wrong?"

"Nothing, dear," Mom said.

"Your mom was telling me about your Grandmom. She misses her, and I was just telling her how lucky both of you were to have the time with her that you did."

"Oh, okay," she said. "So, were we gonna get something?"

Aaron had almost forgotten. "Yes, sorry. I'll be right back." Aaron went for the pretzels and lemonade.

"I'm sorry, Deborah," Mom said. "I didn't mean to upset you."

"No, I am sorry. I shouldn't have behaved that way." Deborah sat and sighed, still a bit upset, but more embarrassed. "I'm such a fool. I can't believe I acted that way in front of Aaron. It did not occur to me that he was like you."

"Or like you."

"Mom, you know I don't believe in that anymore. How could a loving God allow me to go through this?"

"That same loving God has brought a loving man into your life. He has given you Aaron. Please consider that there are things we do not understand. Sometimes God works through the hard times we have. And sometimes He works through the little blessings. If you cannot accept your condition, at least thank God for Aaron."

Deborah was silent.

"Have you said anything to him?"

"Mom, we have been on one date, well two if you count this. The subject has not come up. Plus, I am fine. So I get sick from time to time, it really doesn't mean anything. And if I did tell him about it, I would risk losing him. I like him, Mom."

"I know, DeeDee. That is why you need to tell him."

Deborah knew she was right. It was not fair to keep him in the dark. Even though *the dark* was such a loose term. Even the doctors did not know what was wrong. They were just as uncertain as she was. So, she really had nothing to say. Maybe she would have more to tell after her appointment next week—no sense in rushing to reveal anything to him before then.

Aaron returned with the refreshments, and they snacked and talked about the deli—the plans Mom and Pop had for it. The Coke glasses were just the beginning. Aaron asked about the malt machine, and Mom gleefully went over the detail of reliving her younger years and having her first milkshake at a diner, much like the one she was trying to recreate.

Either he was genuinely interested, or he knew how to make people feel important, but Deborah was once again impressed with Aaron. She couldn't shake the words Mom used to describe him—*A blessing from God.*

She thought, *Maybe some fairy tales do come true.*

It was nearly 11:00 when they finally made their way toward the exit. They had made a full circle, not really doing any more serious shopping—that had already been done—and Aaron's wallet was a bit lighter. But Mom was still ecstatic from the experience, and Deborah knew that Mom's joy made the sacrifice worth it for him.

Even though she calmed down, their walk out of the market was not as close together as their walk in. Deborah did not have her hand in his; she was close but kept her distance, still embarrassed by her actions. She could tell Aaron wanted to say something but wasn't quite sure what to say.

"I know it's not the best time, and it's still a week away, but would you like to go back to Andretti's with me on Friday?" he asked.

Deborah went to answer but remembered she had a late doctor's appointment. "I can't."

"Oh, okay," he said, looking a bit confused.

"No, it's not what you think. I already have plans. Mom

and Pop are taking me somewhere," she explained without explaining.

"Oh, okay," he said again, relieved, but still a bit confused.

"Are you able to go on Saturday?" she asked, wanting to let him know it wasn't him, or what had happened earlier.

"I would have to check my schedule," he tried to jest. It was her turn to look confused. "You know, a big paper reporter like myself. You never know where I will be from day to day."

She caught on, but not as quickly as Carter had given her credit for. "Well, I know one thing for sure, you will be at my counter ordering a Spaghetti Sub on Monday for lunch."

"Pop really thinks that will sell?" he asked.

"Isn't that your job?" she asked. She could feel the tension easing.

"That's true. I still have yet to write my review of the place."

"Why is that, by the way?"

"I haven't a clue," he said. Which was partially the truth. But now that he had a clearer idea of where they stood, he thought it might make the process easier.

"DeeDee," Mom called from behind them. "Look at this."

Deborah excused herself and found her mother looking at a stack of placemats, all a bit faded, but bearing Coke, Pepsi, and 7UP logos.

"Nice find, Mom," she said. The stall owner came over to them. Deborah reached out her hand, the tall brunette accepted it. "Hi. My name's Deborah. How are you this afternoon."

The game had begun.

Aaron continued to walk slowly toward the exit. Not

wanting to get too far ahead, he began to window shop through the last few vendors. One of them was selling hand-crafted doilies, scarves, and blankets. Sitting on the edge of one of the tables was a solitary book. It was a worn pink color. It looked out of place among the knits and cotton. Aaron approached it and could just make out what was on the cover—a perfectly shaped sand dollar. He picked it up, thumbed through the pages, and quickly noticed that it was a Bible. "Excuse me," he asked the vendor. "How much for the Bible?"

"What Bible?" the clerk asked.

Aaron showed it to the lady behind the table. "It was at the end of the table."

"Strange, I don't know anything about it." She called over her husband, who was on the other side of the booth folding blankets.

"Oh yes," he said. "You remember that older gentleman who came by. He asked us to sell it for him. He said that he had sold everything else but the one item and wanted to make sure it got a good home."

"Did he give you a price?" she asked.

"No," he replied.

"Hmm," the wife responded. She turned to Aaron, "Make me an offer."

Aaron did not want to insult, and it being an item he wanted, he quoted a generous amount.

"Done." The husband responded without waiting for a communiqué from his wife. He took the money and went back to folding a stack of blankets.

"Do you have a bag I can place this in. It is a surprise, and I do not want the person I am with to see it just yet." The wife handed him a plastic bag with "Knits Around" nicely printed on it. Aaron took the Bible and placed it in the bag, but it looked odd. "Quick, how much for a scarf. That one, with the red and silver?"

They again conducted business, and soon Aaron had the Bible stowed away, just as Deborah and Mom walked up. Mom was flushed red with laughter. Deborah too was flushed red, but for different reasons. But she was carrying a box of mats she had just purchased.

"Uh-oh, what happened?" Aaron asked.

"Don't ask," said Deborah with a tone of frustration in her voice. "Let's go. It's nearly opening time at the deli."

"Need help?" Aaron asked.

"No, I got it," she said and walked past him.

Deborah outpaced both of them, and Mom waved him over. As they all walked to the car, Mom recounted the big deal that Deborah attempted to negotiate. Apparently, she misjudged her opponent and was shut down rather harshly. Mom told him about how she had gone wickedly too low on her counter. And while the vendor just laughed, another patron came along and wanted to purchase the same mats and was willing to pay the asking price.

Deborah, determined to win the battle, made her counter-offer. It went back and forth a few times, ending with Deborah winning —just under double what the vendor had initially asked. But that was just the beginning. After they packed up, they stopped to adjust the stack to make it easier to carry and saw that the person whom Deborah was at war with was one of the vendors. She had been hoodwinked.

Aaron laughed—apparently loud enough for Deborah to hear.

"Oh, shut up," she shouted back at them. Which only made him and Mom laugh harder.

They arrived at the car, and Aaron helped her load the box into the trunk. "So how many times did you go back and forth?"

"I think she raised the bid six times," she pouted, upset with herself.

"So, a dozen bids for placements?"

"No, thirteen. It was my final raise that got her to stop."

Aaron began to laugh again. "I guess thirteen was enough then."

Deborah's face turned red again. Then she began to laugh. "Yes, I guess it was. Our lucky number."

Aaron leaned over and kissed her on the cheek, "Good work, babe."

He could see her a bit taken back with the sudden nickname, but she did not say anything to correct him.

"So, what's in the bag?"

"Presents for my ladies," he said and then tucked them under his arm. "But they are surprises, so no peeking."

"Get in the car, Romeo. We need to get back to the Deli before Pop sends out the cavalry."

"Oh yes," Aaron said, slipping into the back seat. "Pulled pork today, right?"

"You got it. And it's on me this time. You have done enough."

"Fabulous," Aaron said. "Free lunch. Thank God for the little things."

Aaron saw Deborah look at him in the rearview mirror. He turned and glanced out the window. "You're all clear to back up."

She smiled and headed back to the deli.

Mom loved the red and silver scarf Aaron had given her. She rushed into the kitchen to show Pop. He had no intention of telling her it was an afterthought to conceal what he had purchased for Deborah. In reality, it was a split thinking decision. 'Concealment,' 'they sell scarfs,' 'mom likes coke products,' 'they came in red and silver cans,' *"that scarf right there!"*

Aaron was in his usual seat, the one that had contoured itself to his form. Deborah was hastily rushing around, helping Erica set up for an 12:00 sharp opening. "Sorry, Erica," Deborah said, as she came out of the kitchen with a bus tray full of rolled silverware. "I lost track of time."

"I heard. Trying to outbid a hustler." Erica said, hiding the desire to laugh.

"What? But how?" Deborah questioned, then, "Mom!"

"It's okay. I love it. Proves you are not Superwoman," said Erica.

"What do you mean by that?"

"You. You are doing everything for everyone, and you are good at it. You have an amazing heart and like things to be perfect."

Deborah looked as if she suddenly remembered something. "Did you set up the Decaf brewer? Because—" she began, but Erica finished her thought.

"—The Nixon's come in on Saturday for lunch, and they drink decaf. Yes, it is almost ready."

"Oh, and the cobbler—"

"—needs a couple of portioned bowls. Gus and Vernon don't like the idea of being served from the same tray as the other customers. Yes, I remembered that as well." She smiled.

"Great. Okay, I think we are ready."

"See, perfection," Erica said to Aaron. Then she walked to the counter to start up the electronic register. It was one of the only things modern about the deli.

Deborah excused herself to go open the doors. Aaron had wanted to give her the gift he had for her, but there wasn't enough time. And a gift of this magnitude, especially after the train wreck at the market, would require some finesse.

Erica brought him a tea, already in a to-go cup.

"Trying to get rid of me?" Aaron said.

"Of course not, but what are you going to do when you do leave?" she asked, but answered for him, like she had done with Deborah, "Ask for a to-go cup. Saves me time and Miguel from having to wash another glass."

He smiled and sipped at his tea, as was his normal routine. Although this time, it seemed much different. He didn't feel like a customer anymore, more like an insider. It gave him a thought, and he pulled out his notebook form his inner jacket pocket and began to scribble.

Erica passed by to place a couple of tickets in the window. "Uh oh, paper boy is writing," she observed. "Just remember, my name is with a 'c' and not a 'k'."

Aaron smiled and continued to write. Once through, he read it over. Satisfied, he closed the notebook and tucked it back into his coat.

Pop came out of the kitchen, "Mr. Aaron," he said, but Aaron corrected him.

"Please, Mr. Davies, just Aaron," he said with a chuckle.

"Ok, Aaron. Then you can just call me Pop," he said with a welcoming so-now-that-you're-dating-my-daughter tone. "Aaron. I want to thank you for what you did for Mom. She tells me you helped her get a good deal on her find." He reached for his back pocket; Aaron stopped him.

"Mr.—sorry, Pop, no need to thank or pay me back. It is my investment into what you and your family are doing here. I feel honored to contribute."

Pop froze a second, ready to insist, but he shrugged with raised lips, then a smile. He patted Aaron on the shoulder. "Thank you. You have made both of my girls happy. And that makes me happy." With that, he headed back to the kitchen as tickets were filling the wheel, and he could hear Mom calling for him.

The lunch rush settled down around 2:30. Deborah's red scrunchie had fallen to the side of her head, and she sat next to Aaron as she adjusted it. "So, what are your plans for the rest of the day?"

"I am meeting up with some of the guys from my church. We're going to play basketball at the gym."

"Sounds interesting," she said plainly. The last thing she wanted to do is get into another discussion about religion. So, she left it at that. But she felt she knew what was coming next.

"So, what are your plans?" he asked. She was relieved it was not the *church* question.

"Not much. Finishing up here, then I need to work on some paperwork to extend my leave of absence at work. Pop still has not found a replacement. He seems to be dragging his feet."

"How, so?" he asked.

"Pop has always wanted me in the family business. He was disappointed when I went off to college. And even more when I accepted the job with the insurance company."

"What makes you think that? Did he tell you that?"

"No, he didn't have to. This is what he and Mom have always spent their life doing. They were unable to have any other children. I am the only one to continue their legacy. Me saying no to it must be very discouraging to him."

"I don't mean to sound rude, Deborah, but what has he *said* to you to make you think he feels that way?"

Deborah thought about it. She could not remember Pop ever expressing his displeasure with her career path. Yes, he wanted her to spend more time at the deli, but he had never shown any animosity toward her. She must have been giving a blank look because Aaron spoke.

"See," he said. "Your dad is proud of you, that much is evident. So, do not even think for a moment that he is disappointed in you. You continue do what your heart tells you that you should do. And Pop will support you because it is your dream."

Aaron was right, and she knew it. She had been so busy feeling guilty, not because she felt she was leaving him hanging, but because she was happy where she was. She never considered that he was actually happy with her. "You really think so?"

"Yes," he said.

"It still doesn't explain why he hasn't hired a replacement for Josh," she reminded him.

"Just ask him," Aaron said. "I am sure he has his reasons. It's the only way you will know for sure. And I am confident you will be surprised at what he really feels about you and your chosen path."

She looked up at the pass-through window. She could see Pop's white chef cap bobbing back and forth; he looked like a duck in one of those shooting games. She laughed as she fixed her ponytail. She kissed Aaron on the cheek. "Thank you. I needed to hear that. I better get back to work."

Deborah felt a bit lighter as she finished out her day. The job, while she enjoyed interacting with the customers, was draining. She was not sure if it was a natural thing or the result of her condition, but she felt more spent at the end of six hours than she did working 10 at the agency. She wasn't sure she could live the life of a server. Maybe that was why it appealed to the college student; it was temporary.

Aaron had left an hour earlier with a good-bye kiss telling her he was off to shower and would see her on Monday. Again, to her surprise, he said nothing about church on Sunday. In fact, she felt a little left out. She shook it off because she would have obviously told him no and would have had to come up with a reason why she couldn't, or give him the same speech she'd given Pop for the last year and a half.

She wiped down a few tables, showed Clarence out, and locked the doors. Erica was helping Miguel buss the last couple tables, everyone working on getting home for what was left of the weekend.

Erica saw Deborah and called her over. "Aaron left something for you. It's behind the counter."

My gift! Deborah was excited to see what Aaron had gotten her. It was rare for her to receive a gift other than on birthdays and holidays. And she had never received a 'just because' present from a man she was not related to. She walked over to Aaron's seat, on the counter side, and saw the bag the scarf had come out of. She picked it up and quickly could tell it was a book.

Hmm. I don't ever remember discussing my taste in reading with him. That was with Carter.

She walked around and sat in his seat, feeling almost comfortable in it. She slowly pulled the book out of the bag. The first thing she saw was the pink leather of the back cover. She may not have been a regular at Sunday services, but she knew right away; it was a Bible. Not sure what to feel, she turned it over and noticed what had drawn his attention to it. With a tear in her eye, she caressed the sand dollar on the front cover. It had a glassy texture, almost as if a real shell had been woven into the fabric.

She opened it to the first page. On the right were the words Holy Bible, NIV version 1984. On the left, in a freshly written script,

"I can understand how you feel about the big picture. God does care about the great adventure of life, but He cares more about you and the little things that make you who you are. He knows every star in the sky. He knows every strand of hair on your head. (If you need proof, read Luke 12:7.) I have heard you once knew Him so well, dancing and singing as stories of His love comforted you. I just ask that you remember who you once were and consider giving Him another chance. Because He has not forgotten you. Our Father always sees us for the child that is in each of us. Through that view, we have eternal youth.

And it is a little thing of a childlike faith that will remind us of who He is."

It was signed, *"Love, Aaron."*

With tears now streaming down her face, she made her way to the office before anyone could see her. She shut the door and set the Bible on the desk. Deborah cried harder than she could remember. It was one thing to have a parent try and reach you on that deep of a level; it was their job, and always had little to no effect. It was quite another for a suitor to make the same attempt and break through that barrier to open your eyes.

She knew she was pushing God away, but she did not know why. She could not place a finger on where things went off track. But she did know that she was far gone now. *How far?* She had no clue. She was still fearful of taking the step of finding out. But Aaron had done one thing for sure, two if you considered the entire picture. For one, she once again believed God existed. And two, she knew that there indeed was another man on the planet that she could love as much as she loved her father.

EIGHTEEN

The next week flew by faster than anticipated. Deborah contemplated going to church with Mom and Pop on Sunday, but for the first time in a long time, they didn't ask. And she felt odd about asking to go, so she slept in, but did manage to read a couple of familiar passages from her Bible that she remembered from her youth. One of them was Psalm 23, the other was I Corinthians 13. Both spoke of God's love and guidance. She was encouraged, and it brought many memories to her weary mind.

She did not tell her parents about the Bible. Nor did she mention anything about church. All things aside, the week went as usual. The only real difference was Pop's Spaghetti Sub on Monday. It went over relatively well, better than Deborah anticipated. The only reason people turned it down was the carbs, mainly the health nuts. But Houston was not like Austin. People loved their carbs here. Aaron had been especially fond of the it. Deborah felt that it was more of a show to score extra points with the dad of his girlfriend.

That weekend she decided to try to make things work at the deli and attempt to maintain a relationship with the agency. The adjustment had her feeling overly busy. She and

Aaron still saw each other every day when Aaron came in for lunch, and they also spoke on the phone every night. This had her feeling like a teenager with the sleepless pillow talk, *no-you-hang-up-first* type of conversation.

They did have one engaging discussion. He talked shop about the work he was doing for the week. With the Thanksgiving holiday approaching he had to visit locations each day that would be offering meals on Thanksgiving Day. The piece would be highlighting only locations that provided meals to the less fortunate. She told him of Mom and Pop's dream the last couple of years of doing just that. But when they began to look at the possibility, there was no way they could afford it. She had run the numbers last year, and even with donations it was well beyond the means of a small business like Davies Deli. They were disappointed that it would have to remain a dream. Aaron expressed his empathy and said that that if God wanted to happen, then one day He would provide the means.

This made her think of the Bible, but neither he nor she spoke of it. She figured he did not want to push her too quickly, and she still carried the embarrassment of her behavior. But she was growing eager to discuss it with him. With each read, she was feeling stronger, but still could not understand why she was going through what she was facing. Why would a loving God allow someone to go through an illness? Why would he let the doctors remain clueless?

She was hoping for some good news when she saw the doctor on Friday, or at least for them to finally discover a reason why she was feeling the way she was. Deborah had experienced two more episodes, and they were both identical to the first two. Once she was reaching up to a shelf in her closet when the feeling hit her, and the other was when she was trying to adjust the showerhead. In that case, she was lucky that she didn't slip and fall. As with the first two instances, she kept it to herself.

It was Thursday, and she once again escorted Clarence out and locked up. She already decided that tonight she wouldn't go to the insurance office. She had done plenty of work on Wednesday night, so there would be little to do. It would be a wasted trip. There was a Rockets game, and she was not in the mood to battle traffic. Instead, she wanted to surprise Aaron and drop in to see him. He had told her during the previous night's conversation that he had planned on relaxing and watching the game.

She and Erica cleaned up, she said her good-byes to Mom and Pop, and headed to her car. She felt that she needed to bring something, but what? She figured he would have his meal and beverages figured out, so that left snacks or a dessert. She swung by a supermarket and picked up some fresh pastries from the bakery.

It was shortly after 7:30 when she arrived at Aaron's building. She had spent the last couple of miles trying to remember if his apartment was 502 or 205. She hoped there would be mailboxes to point her in the right direction as she parked her car and entered the lobby. It was brighter than she assumed and much nicer than the outside led her to believe. Black and white tile lined the floor, and larger subway tile wainscoting rose to just below the gold-plated mailboxes. She got halfway lucky. Apartment 205 belonged to someone named Murray; 502 must be his.

The elevators were just as impressive; paneled, gold trim, and all the lights worked. It was a smooth, quiet ride to the fifth floor. The car reached the floor, *binged*, and the doors opened to a receiving area, much like in a hotel. To the left was a large window that overlooked the city; the other buildings in the area were single story. She hoped his apartment was facing east. If it did, what a view he must have.

With her purse around her shoulder and the pastries in hand, she walked down the hall reading off plate numbers. Just like in a hotel, the wall guided her. A plate showed 500–510 to the right and 511–520 to the left. She found 502 and stood in front of the door for a moment.

What am I doing? she asked herself. *A surprise visit? What if he isn't alone?* She had not considered that. She deliberated for a second forgetting about it and heading home, when the door latch clicked and the door opened.

Aaron was in red sweatpants and a white t-shirt with the iconic Houston Rocket "R" on the front. His face lit up, "Deborah? I thought you were the pizza guy. He's 10 minutes late."

"Guess the pizza is free," she joked.

"They stopped doing that years ago. Too many free pizzas and too little care for the customer."

"Figures you would know that. I was in the area and remembered that you said you were going to be home watching the game. Could you use some company?" she said in a pleasant, but nonsuggestive manner.

"Yes, of course," he said, standing aside. "Please forgive the size of the place. It's always been just me, so I have the smallest apartment they have."

Deborah walked into the studio apartment. It was definitely small, but very much spoke of who Aaron was. He had a recliner set up in front of the 32" television that was currently on mute and commercial break. There was a breakfast area just behind the chair with a table and two chairs. One was stacked with books, the other set up for working with an open laptop, a pad of paper and pencil, and his cell phone.

"Were you working?" she asked.

"No, not really. Doing an online search for other eateries in the area that I could review."

"Isn't that work?"

"Not to me. Eating and writing are working. I really don't consider the research part of the job work."

She stood in place, taking it all in, not sure what to do next, or where to sit.

He must have noticed her discomfort and quickly went over to the unoccupied chair and pulled it up next to the recliner. "Please sit," he said. Then he sat—on the chair he just moved. He gestured to his recliner. She blushed.

"I can't take your recliner. I'll be fine in the chair." She remembered the pastries in her hand. "Oh, I brought dessert. I figured you'd have dinner."

"Are those raspberry Danishes?" he said, standing with eyes opened wide.

"Yes, got them over at the market. Where can I put them?"

"In my stomach," he said, taking the bag.

Deborah laughed. "That's dessert. You eat it after supper."

"What, are you my mother?" he laughed. "Life is short. Eat dessert first!" He removed the tray from the bag, opened it, and handed one to her. She accepted it, took one for himself, and they took a bite together. "Please sit," he said again.

She sat in the chair. "I will be fine here. Can't rob a man of his throne."

"Hey, I have learned that it's best not to argue with you," he said, sitting and then reclining the chair. "But you don't know what you are missing. This chair costs more than the TV."

The game had come back on. Houston was losing, but the game had just started. He did not touch the remote.

"You can turn the volume up," she suggested as they finished their danishes.

"In a minute," he said. "How was your day? How are Mom and Pop?"

"You know, same ole same ole. Pretty routine. Mom and Pop send their love," she said, blushing once again. They were talking like a couple; she liked it.

"How were the numbers for the Spaghetti Sub?"

"You know, it did much better than I thought it would. Yeah, we got some turned noses, but for the most part, we had a positive response. Of course, Dad was tickled pink. He was dancing around in celebration."

Aaron laughed. She loved to hear him laugh. It had a soothing tone, not hacking like so many. Who knows, maybe it was, and she could not hear it; maybe love was truly blind.

"So, of course, now it will be a staple on the Monday menu."

"Good for him," he said, glancing at the TV every so often, but still giving her his attention.

"Please, turn on the game. Do not let me keep you from enjoying your evening." He tried to protest, but she stopped him. "No, really. Can I stay and watch the game with you?"

"Did not realize you liked basketball," he said.

"Honestly, I know nothing about the game. But I am more interested in the company, than the game," she said. Juvenile, she knew, but truthful.

He smiled and clicked on the volume button, and the squeak of shoes on the court, the play by play of the announcers, and she was sure the beating of her heart filled the room.

By halftime, the pizza and Danishes were gone, and it was evident the Rockets were not playing their best game. She had to hide her amusement with each call that went against Houston; Aaron was a bit animated. She had not seen him behave this way, and she found it adorable. She could not understand how people could get worked up about a game. She had heard her share of sports enthusiasts use words like *our team*, or *we won*, to describe *their* team. Yet those fans had never played a down, quarter, or inning of a game. She smiled. He noticed.

"What?"

"You," she said with a chuckle. "You are so worked up over a game."

"I have to root for my team," he said. To which she burst out in laughter.

"What?"

"Nothing. I just think it's cute that you throw yourself so deeply into it."

"Cute?" he said.

"Too feminine? Okay, it's attractive."

"Well, I could throw in a couple of f-bombs if that turns you on," he said just as Harden threw up a three-pointer and was fouled. "Yes!" he hollered, "And one!"

"May I use your restroom?" Deborah asked.

"Certainly. It's up the stairs, the second door on the left," he said, not missing a beat, and not looking away from the TV. Harden made the free throw. "Alright!" he said.

Deborah had a grin ear to ear, happy that she stopped by. Taking chances was not her style. She had a meticulous, organized way of doing things. Flying by the seat of her pants would usually frighten her. But with Aaron, it didn't feel risky. She felt a comfort level with him that she had never experienced before. And she was enjoying every minute of it.

It was the end of the third quarter, and Harden had hit two more threes, and the Rockets had outscored the Clippers 14–6 and were only down by four points. "We can do this boys," said Aaron to the TV. At the commercial break, he looked over at the restroom door, which of course, was actually just 10 feet from where they were sitting. He smiled. What had been meant to be an evening of alone time, *decompression mode* he liked to call it, turned into an even better stay-at-home date night. He hoped she was enjoying herself as much as he was.

He was not used to having visitors, so the place was not as tidy as he would like it to be. But at the same time, he was rarely home. Always out on the town, trying new things out, experimenting, and being the food aficionado his column made him out to be. So, there was not too much of a mess.

Aaron had a rare evening where nothing was planned but his recliner and the ball game. He did not think it could have gotten better, until the knock on his door two hours earlier. Now he could not imagine it any other way; could not have written a better scenario. He was happy—grateful for walking into that out-of-the-way sandwich shop.

A sudden ruckus came from behind the bathroom door. Then silence.

"Deborah?" Aaron called, his head whipping around.

Nothing.

"Deb? Are you okay?" Aaron said, pushing the mute button on the remote.

No response.

Maybe she slipped and is embarrassed to reply. He already learned she embarrasses easily.

Aaron got up, went to the door, and knocked. "Deb?"

Still nothing.

"If you don't respond, I am going to come in there," he warned.

Silence. He thought he could hear a faint sound of labored breath.

"Okay, Deborah. I'm coming in." He turned the knob, but it was locked. "Deborah, I need you to unlock the door. Can you do that?"

No movement, just the silent breath of someone who was not okay.

Aaron planted his feet and threw his shoulder into the door. It budged a bit, but not enough. He was afraid of busting through and hurting her more than she already may be or frightening her if she were okay. He centered himself with the sweet spot and drove his shoulder into the door; the frame gave way. But he was more frightened by what he found.

Deborah was lying on the floor; she appeared to be unconscious. He quickly checked for a pulse. Her heart was racing, and she had a sharp breathing rhythm. Aaron called out to her, hoping she would snap out of it, but she didn't respond. He tapped her on the face, but it had no effect. He was beginning to panic. But he knew better. He took a deep breath and ran through his mind what he needed to do next.

Aaron ran to the table and grabbed his phone. He dialed 911 and gave them as much info as he could. Then he found Deborah's purse and felt a little guilty, but opened it to find her cell phone. It was in a pouch on the side. Luckily, she did not have a screen lock. He quickly found the phone number he needed. He clicked on the number labeled "POP" and let it ring.

"DeeDee, was just about to go to bed, what's up?" said the cheerful voice answering the line.

"Mr. Davies, it's Aaron," he said, trying to remain calm.

"Aaron, how do you—" Pop asked but was quickly cut off.

"Listen Pop, Deborah is at my apartment. We were watching the game, and she went into the restroom. I heard a loud crash and found her passed out on the floor. I have 911 on the other line, and an ambulance is on the way. Do you know why she would just pass out like that?"

"Oh my," Pop said, and he shouted away from the phone for Mom. "Deborah passed out at Aarons place. What? No, I'll ask."

"Do you know what hospital they are taking her to?" he could hear Mom asking questions faster than he or Pop could exchange information.

Aaron asked the other phone, "Ma'am, you wouldn't happen to know where the paramedics will be taking her, would you?"

"No, sir. I am just the operator who dispatches them. It would be determined by where you are located and the seriousness of her injuries. Paramedics will determine that when they get there."

"No, not yet. The paramedics have not arrived. I am afraid to move her. I don't see a bump on her head, so I don't think she hit any porcelain, but better safe than sorry."

"Sir, just tell the paramedics everything you told me, plus if she were to have been drinking or taken any medication let them see the bottles," the operator informed.

"Pop, is there anything I need to know to tell the paramedics? Is she taking any medications I need to tell them about?"

"Oh, umm," Aaron heard him say. Either he didn't know, or he felt that he was overstepping his bounds, either way it was something that needed to be said. "She takes medication for her dizzy spells, Aaron. I don't know the name of it. Check her purse. She carries her pills with her."

Aaron found the bottle. Antivert. *Take twice daily for dizziness and nausea as related to vertigo.* "Vertigo?" Aaron asked himself. He knew nothing about what was going on. He remembered he still had Pop on the line. "I found it. She has vertigo?"

"Well, the doctor doesn't know what she has; she takes those to treat her symptoms. She is supposed to see the doctor tomorrow afternoon," Pop said.

Well, that explains why she couldn't go out tomorrow.

"Operator, she is taking medication for Vertigo."

"Did she take any pills before she passed out?"

Aaron had to rethink the evening for a moment. The door knock; a surprise visit. The excited thrill of having her over, the easy conversation over a rudimentary meal, the comfort of her laugh, but nowhere was he led to believe there was an underlying issue. Swallowing hard he said, "No, I did't know she even had the pills until just now. I've never even seen her with them."

"Okay. Just let the paramedics know when they arrive, Aaron."

"Okay, Thank you," Aaron said taking a deep breath.

Aaron could hear the siren in the distance. "They're almost here," he spoke to both phones. "They may need to use the service elevator to get the gurney up here, though." He looked out the window, and sure enough, the ambulance pulled up to the rear of the building where the service elevator was. "Pop, they're here. I promise to keep you posted. Please, pray as you've never prayed before. I will stay with her, and when I find out where we are going, I'll call you." He said his goodbyes and hung up the phone. Two minutes later, after speaking to Aaron, the two EMS members were securing Deborah in a neck brace. Then carefully placing her on the gurney, her body still limp. "Should I bring her pills with us?"

"Sorry, buddy, only family can ride with the patient."

"Well, I am her fiancé," he lied and sounded very much like he was doing so.

The two looked at each other. The female said, "Works for me." She was the senior member of their team. The other nodded and said, "Let's go. And yes, bring her pills, and her purse, just in case the doc needs to look through it for anything else she may have taken. Has she been drinking at all this evening?"

"No, we drank soda. No alcohol," he said.

"Okay, good. Alcohol does not mix well with this medication. You sure she didn't take or drink anything today?" the female asked.

"She got here a couple of hours ago, probably straight from work, don't see how she could have," Aaron explained.

"Okay, Melissa, she's secure," said the male technician.

"Let's go," Melissa said.

Aaron locked up his place, still in his sweats and Rockets shirt. With the addition of a hoodie, he followed the two techs to their rig, and they headed to the hospital.

"Which hospital are we going to, I need to call her parents," he asked as Melissa shut the doors and yelled to the driver to get going.

"10-39," she shouted to the driver who flipped on the siren and accelerated onto the street. Then she turned to Aaron. "Mercy Regional. It is a little further, but with the game letting out, we will get there quicker. No traffic to deal with."

"Can I make a call?" Aaron asked, making sure he was able to use a cell around their equipment.

"Sure," Melissa said. The male was the driver.

Aaron looked at Deborah; she was unusually still. He was scared for her. He dialed the number and gave Pop the information, telling him he would see him there.

Just under 15 minutes and they were pulling up to the ER entrance of Mercy Regional. The tech delivered the specifics to the orderly receiving the incoming for the night. Aaron was as close as a shadow the whole way. The attending doctor grabbed the notes the tech had, and he looked up at Aaron. "You will have to wait in the waiting area until we get her prepped. Nurse, can you take this man to the admitted waiting area?"

An older lady in her 60s with a blonde-dyed bob directed him to a sitting area near the nurse's station around the corner. From there, he could hear the hustle of the crew, but could not see anything.

The nurse called to him. "Sir? Can I have your name and relation to the patient?"

He remembered that they were engaged and gave his personal info to the attendant.

"Does she have any kin that we need to notify?" she asked.

"No, I have already done that. They are on their way." Aaron could only imagine how they were feeling, but maybe they expected this; maybe even have gone through it before. "Has she been here before?" He asked out of curiosity.

"What's her full name?" she asked.

He thought about it and realized he did not know a middle name. *Some fiancé I turned out to be,* he thought. He gave her first and last name only.

"Does she have an alias?" the nurse asked.

He thought about giving Pop's nickname, but thought the better, "No, not that I am aware of."

"No, no Deborah Davies. She has not been in here before."

Well, that is a good sign, he thought. He wished he knew what to do. He was at a complete loss; confused why she had not said anything to prepare him for something like this. He knew they just started dating, but something like this could be life-threatening.

"Was she taking any medication?" the nurse asked.

"Yes," Aaron said. He forgot he was holding her purse. He reached into it; he was over the violation part of it and handed the bottle to the nurse. "Antivert. It is for vertigo, but her Pop said that her doctor was still exploring the cause and was not sure why she was having dizzy spells. That's all I know. He should be here shortly."

"Had she been drinking this evening?" she asked after typing all he had just recounted.

He knew these were routine questions, but explaining it again only frustrated him. "No, all we had was Dr. Pepper."

"Is she pregnant?" she looked a bit uneasy, "Sorry, I have to ask."

"No, she isn't," he said.

"What was she doing when she lost consciousness? Was she doing anything strenuous?"

"No, she had gone to the restroom. She gave no sign of anything being wrong. I was watching the game, and the next thing I know, she is passed out on the floor."

"Does she have a family—" she began, but Aaron cut her off.

"I am sorry, I know you are doing your job, but her parents will be here shortly. Can you ask them these questions? I don't know of any family history anyhow. When can I see her?"

"Soon," she said. But that was it.

Aaron could hear a firm, panicked voice on the other side of the wall. "I think that is Deborah's father. If you can let him back here, I would appreciate it. He can answer any other questions you may have."

The burly voice grew louder and eventually made its way to where Aaron was sitting. "Aaron," Pop said, "where is she? How is she?"

"The doctors have her right now. They are stabilizing her, I think. She remained unconscious the entire ride here. No movement at all. They took her into the other room, led me here, and I have been answering questions since."

"When can we see her?" Mom asked.

"Soon," both the blonde-bobbed nurse and Aaron said in unison.

Mom looked at Aaron. He could feel her stare. "Are you okay?"

"Yes, I am fine. Just shocked and confused. I had no idea anything was wrong with her."

The nurse chimed in, "You're her fiancé. How could you not know?"

"Fiancé? You proposed to my DeeDee?" Pop said as confused as he felt. "Why am I the last one to know about these things?"

"Relax, Poppa," said mom. "I am sure there is an explanation."

"Mmhmm," said the nurse taking the chart around the corner.

"I am sorry," said Aaron. "I told them I was her fiancé so they would allow me to stay with her. I apologize if I offended you."

"Oh," Pop said.

"No, you did the right thing, Aaron," Mom said, placing her hand on Aaron's arm. "Thank you for taking care of Deborah."

"Not sure how much I did for her," he said, peering around the corner. There was a curtain where he could see several pairs of shoes underneath. "All I did was stand there. Actually, I felt pretty useless."

"I am sure you did fine. You were there for her and got the help she needed." Mom reassured him. "Now, we just wait."

"I should have done more," Pop said. "She got sick the other day, and Erica saw her get sick earlier last week. But we said nothing. She assured us she was feeling fine."

"Poppa, you can't blame yourself. DeeDee is a grown woman. If she said she was fine, either she was, or she thought she could handle what was going on."

"Yes, but now we know she can't. So, I am guilty of not doing anything earlier."

Pop asked Aaron to recount his evening with her. He repeated it like he had told the paramedics and the nurse. He was a bit calmer this time and did not have to pause to keep his composure. Pop nodded as he listened, satisfied that he now knew all there was to know.

"So now we wait," Aaron said. "Please sit down. No need for all of us to be standing." Both Mom and Pop sat. Aaron stood, as close to the corner as he could, occasionally sneaking a peak for any activity exiting the curtained area where Deborah lay.

"You tried to tell me, didn't you Mrs. Davies," Aaron said finally. He remembered their discussion was cut off by Deborah's return from the restroom.

She nodded with tears in her eyes. "Yes. I felt you should know. She is very protective of her privacy. But for honesty's sake, and for situations like this, I told her she should tell you."

"Well, her visit to me tonight was unexpected. Maybe that is why she stopped by. But we never really got the chance to speak. We—well I was busy watching the game." Aaron hung his head. Did he allow the game to get in the way of her saying something?

"Don't go blaming yourself, sweetie." Mom was patting his arm again. "You had no way of knowing something was on her mind.

Now tears were filling his eyes. He should have seen it. His job was to be observant—to notice the things that most neglect to see. He had learned to trust his senses when he entered an establishment, to pick up on the little things, it was those that mattered most. Not nit-picking like Ethan had grown so accustomed to but discovering that there is good in every nuance. But this he completely missed. Were there signs? If there were, he failed to notice. And now he hoped his short-sightedness would not cost Deborah her life.

Still in these thoughts, he missed the nurse's return. She clicked on her keyboard and typed for a minute or two. She then turned to them and said, "The doctor says you can see her now. She is still unconscious, but they have stabilized her heart rate and breathing."

Aaron looked at Mom and Pop. "You go. I will wait here."

They did not protest, but both rose and followed the nurse. Mom turned, smiled, and said, "Thank you, Aaron, for being with our baby. We are grateful for you. Please don't beat up yourself. There is no way you could have known. That is the way she wanted it, and she would have told you when she was ready too. I am sorry you have to find out this way. But know this is not your fault. Sit, relax, and when we find out more, I will let you know. But please don't leave. I am sure she will want to see you when she wakes up."

"I am not going anywhere," said Aaron. "They couldn't drag me away."

She smiled and left to catch up with Pop and the nurse.

Aaron sat in silence. Then he looked up to the ceiling, closed his eyes, and began to pray.

Chapter
TWENTY

After a couple of hours of sitting with no new information, Aaron was eager for a walk. He asked the duty nurse where the cafeteria was. She gave him directions and the assurance he would be easily readmitted if she left duty. He did not see Mom or Pop but left a brief message for them at where he would be.

He walked the halls following his directions and the well placed signs that appeared at every turn. It was a typical hospital—off-white walls that shone brightly under the buzzing of fluorescent lights overhead. He passed orderlies in scrubs, other medical professionals, a maintenance crew member pushing a wastebasket on wheels, and other visitors trying to make their way around the endless maze. He could smell coffee, and other stale cafeteria smells as he made the final turn. A sign hanging from the ceiling pointed to the left. The clanging of dishes and a hushed murmur of tired, stressed, and burdened staff and visitors hit him as he entered.

Coffee decanters, creamers, and sweeteners were set up to the right of the entrance. A wooden sign above the row of lids, spoons, and stirrers informed him the coffee was complimentary, but it was to stay within the cafeteria area. He poured a cup and sat at a table where someone had abandoned a newspaper. The sports section was on top with the headline, "Rockets to Face-off Against Clippers Tonight." He had to laugh a little to himself. *Too early for today's paper.*

It was coming upon 3:00 in the morning, and he felt he should eat something because after going back to the ER, he was not sure when he would get another chance. He wondered the same about the Davieses. He figured he could smuggle something into them if needed. He hoped they were okay. He could not imagine experiencing having to go through an emergency room visit with a child, no matter what age.

Aaron drained his cup and found the line for breakfast. It was a simplified buffet table, with a couple of hair-capped ladies dishing out scrambled eggs, meats, and oatmeal. There was even the ability to make breakfast tacos to an extent. He decided on eggs, bacon, and potatoes. There was a counter at the end of the line with an assortment of bread, bagels, and muffins. He toasted an English muffin and grabbed another cup of coffee. He sat down, and as he was about to eat, Mom and Pop walked in.

He immediately stood and met them halfway to him. "What's wrong? Why aren't you with her?"

"They are admitting her. She is stable but still unconscious. They are going to do an MRI then take her to an assigned room. The doctor said they would call us when she was in her room, or if…" Mom could not finish.

"Oh, Mom," Aaron said, realizing what she was about to say. "I am sure she will be fine. Please, sit and eat with me. We can wait together."

The couple looked at each other. Somehow, they looked older this morning.

Worry and lack of sleep will do that to a person. Aaron thought. *I can only imagine how I look to them.*

Still, Aaron wanted to do his best to help them feel comforted. "Please, sit." He had Mom sit where he was. "Here, eat this. I'll go get another plate. Do you want anything, Pop?"

He shook his head and sat next to his wife.

"Are you sure? We may not get another opportunity for a while once we get up to her room. I know once you are back with her, you won't want to leave."

Pop looked down at the table, lost in his thoughts. Aaron thought he hadn't heard him, but he replied, "Just like Mom, but sausage, not bacon. And wheat bread if they have it."

"No problem." Aaron went on the food run and returned shortly with two plates. Mom was slowly playing with the food on her plate, taking a bite every so often.

"Thank you, sweetie, you are a good boy," Mom said softly.

Aaron sat and offered to say a prayer. They agreed.

"Thank you, Lord, for this family. I thank you that they share a love so strong that nothing can shake it. I pray that you carry Mom and Pop through this time of uncertainty. I pray for Deborah, who is somewhere above us. I pray for the doctors to discover what is happening and that they know how to treat her. Help her to recover. Help her to see who you truly are. Use us to influence her life and bring her back to your loving side. Bless this meal to our bodies, and give us the strength to get through this day. Amen."

"Amen," they both echoed. Mom smiled and patted him on the arm. "Thank you, Aaron."

They all ate in silence. Aaron realized that Mom's delay

was more about waiting until they all were eating than not being hungry. Both seemed eager to eat. Maybe it was more than just hunger, though. Maybe then needed something to occupy their thoughts. Eating was better than doing nothing at all. Aaron went back for coffee refills a couple of times; it was actually pretty good coffee. Aaron chuckled as he found his mind slipping into work mode, evaluating each aspect of the cafeteria. *Better than doing nothing at all,* he told himself.

When all plates were clear, and enough curious contemplation took place, Aaron broke the silence. "So, how long has she had this condition?" he asked, figuring all secrecy and waiting for her to tell him were out the window.

"Three or four months," Pop said.

"Closer to six," Mom corrected. She obviously knew before he did. "She had her first dizzy spell back in April. It was shortly after the insurance agency she works for got a new contract. She was really busy at the time, having to make sure all the paperwork was filed correctly and that the employees were taken care of."

"I did not know this," Pop said.

"She, I mean we, did not think much of it. She was exhausted and figured that it was just fatigue. And her allergies had been bothering her that week. She mentioned it to me, but we reasoned it away."

"You should have told her to go see a doctor," Pop scolded.

"Relax Poppa. You would have done the same. Have you gone to the doctor for every little symptom you've had?"

Pop just grunted.

"Then in May she had another episode, but this one is where the," she paused and looked around, then mouthed the word 'vomiting,' then continued, "began. This time I urged her to see a doctor. She did. He said it was overexertion, and that she should take it easy. With her workload decreasing, she pretty much did. But shortly after the Fourth of July, she had another. We went back to the doctor, and he did not feel running expensive tests were the answer. Since it looked like an imbalance, he sent her to an ear specialist who said it was probably an inner ear issue and prescribed her medication for vertigo."

"But has she ever ended up in the hospital, like this?" Aaron asked.

"No," said Mom.

"I wonder what made this time different?" Aaron asked, more to himself. "When was her last episode?"

"That is hard to tell," Mom said. "Deborah is so headstrong. She is not one to admit she needs help. So she could have had one and not said anything."

Pop spoke up. "Last Friday afternoon, before your date," he said, eyes never leaving the table.

Mom looked up in surprise. "Now who's the one keeping secrets?"

He shrugged. "She said she was fine. She looked fine. I wouldn't have known she had one if she had cleaned the trash can better." He paused. "And Erica saw her in the parking lot a couple of days before. That is the last I know of."

Aaron could not understand why they did not get her to see a doctor sooner or be more adamant about finding out what was wrong. But he knew hindsight was 20/20 and that focusing on the past only hurt the here and now. Plus, she was above them getting the tests done that could help determine if it was, in fact, vertigo, or heaven forbid, something worse.

"We are grateful she was with you this time," Mom said,

again with her hand on Aaron's arm. "If she had gone home, none of us would have known. It could have been…" she started to cry. He placed his hand on top of hers.

"But she didn't, and she will be fine," he tried to sound reassuring. "So, she was supposed to see a doctor tomorrow, well, today?"

"Yes," Pop said for Mom, who was wiping her eyes with her napkin. "Her appointment was for 4:00 PM. She wanted it late, so she could spend as much time at the deli as she could. By then, Erica could handle things until closing." He, too looked disappointed in himself. "I let her work too hard. This is my fault. The doctor told her to take it easy, and all I did was keep her working. I should have found the replacement for Josh she asked me too. I did this to her." This time he lost it.

"Poppa, this is not your fault. Remember, she is like you, strong-willed. She could have said 'no' at any time and would have."

"She loved working with you, Pop," Aaron said, remembering his conversation with Deborah. "Yes, she wished you would have found the replacement, but that was only because she felt she needed to get back to her job, not because she was weary or did not want to be around the deli. She loved it there and has many fond memories there. She mentioned a few of them to me. So, like Mom says, don't blame yourself. She was happy there."

Pop nodded in acceptance. "Thank you, Aaron. Momma's right. You're a good boy."

Aaron had to laugh; it was not often that he was referred to as a boy. He saw that one of the workers was bringing out trays of pastries, it reminded him of Deborah, handing him the bag of Danishes, and their evening together, just hours ago. "Would either of you care for a Danish?"

Both Mom and Pop looked over. He could see tiny smiles come across their faces. Maybe in remembrance of an encounter they had with their daughter. Another thing he learned about her; she has a sweet tooth.

"Raspberry," Pop said.

"The cream-filled ones," Mom said with a bright grin, "if they have it."

They spent the moment in silence. Each enjoying the sweetness, not only of the baked good, but of the memory each was experiencing of the one they loved. Aaron was topping off everyone's coffee when his phone rang.

Unknown number.

"Hello," Aaron answered. "Yes, doctor. 503, you say? Okay, we are on our way up. Thank you." He hung up and apologized. "Sorry, they must still be under the impression that we are engaged. They should have called you."

Mom smiled. "That is quite alright, dear. Nothing you have to apologize for. For as much as I am concerned, you are part of the family now."

Aaron still felt bad. He couldn't understand their acceptance so quickly. After all, he had only known them for a month. But it was good to see a healthy family, something he didn't grow up with. Here before him were two people who loved each other, who had experienced so much, and yet held it together. He admired them and was more than happy to be accepted into their family.

All three ignored the sign that still hung above the coffee decanters. They found their way to the elevator that led to the patient rooms. A few minutes later, they were all in a reception area near a line of rooms; Deborah was back there somewhere. Aaron knew Mom and Pop were even more anxious to get back to their little girl than he was, but first things first.

A doctor was heading down the hall with a clipboard in his hand. He had that look all doctors have. The straight poker face. Inside he knew what had to be said to the patient's family. Good news, bad news, it was all the same; it had to be. Aaron did not know the feeling of experiencing life and death each day but understood it must be difficult. Now the one that hopefully had the answers was walking toward them. He felt the tension build-up, preparing for the worst, but still praying for the best.

The doctor stopped in front of them, stone faced. J. Mattheson was embroidered on his coat.

"Why don't we sit down," Dr. Mattheson said.

TWENTY-ONE

Dr. Mattheson led them through the hall to a waiting area for admitted patients. He was tall and well dressed. Most of all, he was young, probably post-grad, excited about his new position and spending every dollar the second he made it just to prove his success. Aaron could tell his shoes cost more than he could ever afford.

His youth was a little unsettling. Aaron would have preferred to receive medical advice from someone older, more experienced; someone who looked like they knew what they are talking about. Mattheson's smooth face and blonde locks did not exuding a level of experience needed for this type of work. But Aaron decided to to give him the benefit of the doubt. What choice did he have?

Preparing for the worst, Pop took Mom's hand. Due to the hour, the sitting area was empty. Mattheson opened the chart and put on the pair of glasses. They did make him look a bit older, but didn't take any uneasiness off the situation. Then, surprisingly, he gave them a slight grin.

"First of all," the doctor began, "Deborah is in stable condition. Her heart and breathing rates are normal. Right now, she is pretty much sleeping." Then his face became a bit somber. "However, when she will wake up, we still cannot tell."

"So, what's wrong with my daughter?" Mom asked.

"That we are not sure of right now, Mrs. Davies. I am waiting for the results of the MRI. Those will take another hour or so. I can tell you that if it were anything serious, her heart rate would be elevated, her breathing could be labored, and her blood pressure would be much higher. Again, right now, she is sleeping."

"Like a coma?" asked Pop.

"You could call it that," said the doctor. "We can try different stimuli to wake her, but I want to wait for the MRI results before we try anything. There could be cranial swelling that is healing, and the rest she is getting right now is the best thing for her if that be the case. So, we will know more in about an hour."

"When can we see her?" Aaron asked.

Dr. Mattheson looked at Aaron like he had just arrived. "Are you the fiancé?"

"Yes, Aaron Stephenson," Aaron stuck out his hand. The doctor accepted it.

"Let me speak with the nurses and see if I can arrange for Deborah to have visitors," he said. "Do you have any questions for me? I am about to head up to Radiology to see if the doctor is there."

"No, just please, find out when I can go see my little girl," said Pop.

"Give me just a moment," the doctor said and walked away.

Mom and Pop did not look any more relieved. They didn't know any more than they did when they left Deborah two hours ago. Waiting was the hardest part. Luckily, there was a TV on the wall in the back corner of the room which helped pass the time. The volume was extremely low, barely a whisper. Right now, a weatherperson was talking in front of a map of Texas as a long blue line moved through the state. Another cold front was on its way. The caption read, "Coldest Temps of the Season So Far."

With it being the second week in November, it was about time for a strong cold front. It had been a pretty warm summer, and fall was not much better. The blast they got a couple of weeks ago was a big relief from the humidity. Aaron remembered the day. It was the day he decided to ask Deborah out. He smiled. Pop noticed.

"Thinking about my DeeDee?" he asked.

"Actually, yes," Aaron said. He nodded up to the TV. "The news was just saying that a big cold front is on the way. It reminded me of the last one that blew through." He told them his story of talking with his boss, asking Deborah out, and how he felt like an utter failure after she shot him down. He left out the *is thirteen enough* line. Some things he wanted to keep to himself.

Pop acknowledged that he had heard and confronted her about her reluctance. Mom added that she, Pop, and Erica convinced Deborah to accept his invitation.

They all shared a laugh and continued telling stories to occupy the time and to distract their minds from thoughts that led to the worst-case scenario. *The mind has a strange way of doing that,* Aaron mused. *It far more often considers the dangers involved than the possibility of a victorious conclusion. Having positive influences to help you talk through it, or take your mind off of it, is such a blessing.* Aaron appreciated the Davies more and more each moment.

Dr. Mattheson returned and informed them that they

could sit with Deborah under two conditions. First, they could not disturb her—sleeping right now was the best medicine. Second, only two of them could be in the room at a time. He said this while looking at Aaron.

"If she is unconscious, what matter does it make how many of us are in there?" Pop defended.

"Pop, it's okay, I'll wait here. Go be with your daughter," Aaron said, not wanting an argument.

Pop looked at Aaron with an apology in his eyes. Then he nodded and stood. He took Mom's hand. "Let's go," he said to her. Then to the doctor, "Show the way."

After they left, Aaron moved closer to the TV. They were playing highlights of the Rockets game. The sports anchor could hardly be heard, but Aaron could make out some of what he was saying. "If you turned off your TV early during last night's game, you missed one heck of a finish." He felt guilty for his thought on that comment. He sat back in the chair, and somewhere between the repeat of the weather forecast and a special interest story of a laughing dolphin, he fell asleep.

Aaron was awakened by the volume increase on the TV. An older gentleman in a tweed cap was fiddling with the volume button. He made it loud enough to hear, but not too loud to draw the scolding of an attending nurse. The news was over, and the local morning talk show was on. Aaron wondered how long he had been out.

"Good morning," the man said. "Sorry if I woke you, I couldn't take the silence. And you snore a bit loud."

"Sorry, it's been a long night," Aaron said.

"Yes, I figured. That is why I let you sleep. I also took the liberty of grabbing you a cup of coffee," he said, pointing to the table next to Aaron.

"How long was I out?"

"You were sleeping when I came in. I sat for about an hour and then went down for a Danish and coffee. They have a great sweet roll down there."

"Yes," Aaron agreed. "So, I drove you away?"

The older man laughed. "It served dual purposes."

"Well, thank you for the coffee," Aaron stuck out his hand. "I'm Aaron."

The older gentleman reached out his tweed coated arm. "The name is Carter."

"What time is it?" Aaron asked, not recognizing the name. With no windows or clock, time was evasive.

"Almost 8:00," Carter said. He sat back like he was relaxing in the park.

"You have someone in here too?" Aaron asked, not sure what else to say. Why would someone be in a hospital waiting area if they didn't?

"You can say that," he answered. "You said a long night. When did you arrive?"

Aaron yawned, "Been here since 10:00 last night. My girlfr—fiancée," he corrected—He wasn't sure why, but figured it was better to stick with the story that allowed him to stay—"passed out last night and would not wake up. I called 911, and they brought her here."

"Sorry to hear," Carter said. "Have they told you anything yet?"

"Just that she is comfortable and sleeping. And that she will wake up when she is ready. Something about part of the healing process." Aaron shook his head. "I just wish there was something that I can do."

"Ahh, there is always something you can do, Aaron," he said. He sat up and leaned toward him with a smile. "You can pray."

Aaron returned the gesture. "Yes, I know. And I have. But do you ever get the feeling that it isn't enough?"

"Yes, I find that it is normal for people. Many feel they have to be in control of their life and must have it all figured out. When they are faced with the unknown, they feel lost. Or if they are told to sit and wait, they get nervous because they feel they must be taking action. For some, to put control in the hands of the unknown is a frightening thought."

"Yeah, I guess," Aaron admitted. He sipped his coffee; sure it was going to be sweetened and creamed. To his surprise, it was black, just the way he took it.

"But you see, God is bigger than all of that. Just because a situation is not working does not mean that He is not at work. People just need to have the patience to let Him do His job."

"You're right," Aaron said. *This man knows his stuff,* he thought. He had to admit that he was feeling the helpless anxiety that was paired with the waiting. Time was the real enemy. The longer the wait, the greater the sense of helplessness. *Maybe that is why people occupy themselves with the mundane. It helps time loosen its grasp.*

"Trust me, Aaron, you are not helpless when He is in control. Yes, patience is the most difficult discipline to learn. But it is during this time that we grow closer to Him. We never know how much we have in Him until He is all that we have. Right now, you need to keep focused on the things you can do and not be so concerned with the things that are beyond your control.

"God will always do His part. Let the doctors do their job. And you do yours. First, pray. Second, be there for that adorable couple who are suffering over their daughter."

Aaron sipped at his coffee. He was at a loss as to why God placed him in this position. He had no family experience. His own family dissolved before his eyes. To him, both his parents were failures. His mom disappeared when it got too tough, and his dad was present but never there. How was he to guide Mr. and Mrs. Davies through this, and now to quite possibly be the glue that would hold this family together through this crisis? But like Carter just pointed out—God is bigger. Aaron knew God had a plan for all things, and that He used people for specific purposes. He prayed that he had the strength to be that shoulder, that listening ear, the one who remained strong through it all.

They both sat in silence for a while. The TV had some show on, interviewing some actor, who was in some movie, that was about to be released somewhere. Carter seemed to watch it with interest. To Aaron, it was just background noise. While his eyes were on the screen, his mind was somewhere between them and the room down the hall.

Carter laughed at something the host said, bringing Aaron back to reality. He drained his cup and stood with a labored grunt. "Well, I need a top off. You need anything?"

Aaron shook his head; his cup still half full. "I'm good, thank you for bringing it up. It's good to know I'm not the only rule bender."

"Well, Aaron, it was a pleasure to meet you. If I don't see you again, I wish you the best. I will be praying for Deborah." Carter made his way out of the waiting area just as Mom and Pop came back in, both looking dead on their feet.

"How is she?" Aaron asked.

"She wants to see you," Mom said warily.

"She's awake?" Aaron asked.

"Yes, she woke up not too long ago. Then she kicked us out," said Pop.

Mom slapped him on the arm, "She did no such thing, Poppa. She told us to go home and get some rest, that she would be fine. We tried to fight it, but you know Deborah—"

"Yeah, she's headstrong and usually gets her way," Aaron said with a chuckle.

"She's a little embarrassed, but she wants to see you. She feels bad for giving you such a scare," Mom said.

"What did the doctor say?" Aaron inquired.

Mom and Pop look at each other. "We will let her tell you, but all in all, the doctor says she is going to be fine."

Aaron breathed a sigh of relief. "Praise God."

"Yes, God has had His hand on our little angel. And He has given us you. Thank you for all you have done, Aaron," Mom said.

"I don't know that I have done that much, but you're welcome nonetheless."

They said their goodbyes, and the Davies headed out the way Carter had left. Aaron walked around the corner to the nurse's station. The shift had changed, and there were two men in blue scrubs behind the counter. One was typing on a computer, the other was writing updates on the board behind him. He saw Deborah's name as D. Davies next to 502.

"Good morning," Aaron said, "Room 502?"

The nurse on the computer pointed him in the right direction, and he followed the signs that led him to Deborah's room. He stood out front the door for a moment. "What am

I doing?" he asked himself. He took a deep breath, knocked on the door politely, then pushed it open.

TWENTY-TWO

Deborah was nervous to see Aaron again. She knew she had given him quite a scare. While she didn't remember exactly what happened to get her here, she did remember being at Aaron's apartment and having a pretty good time. She remembered the pizza and Danishes, the game, and then going to the restroom. But she did not remember anything after getting up from the chair.

She wanted to freshen up before he came in, but being tethered to machines and monitors made that difficult. Mom had brought her a warm washcloth and helped her clean up the smeared makeup, but that only made her more apprehensive, Aaron had never seen her without makeup. What would he think? She still felt a bit unkempt, but there wasn't much she could do about it. He was on his way, and she was as pretty as she was going to get.

The soft hospital room type knock on the door, though quiet, startled her. "Come on in," she said. It wasn't Aaron; it was her doctor. She let out the breath she held.

"So, how are you feeling, Miss Davies?" Dr. Mattheson said, reviewing her charts updated numbers. "Have you eaten anything yet?"

"No, I'm not hungry," Deborah said.

"You need to eat soon, we've already stopped feeding you intravenously," he explained.

"I will. So, what's the latest?" Deborah asked, wondering if anything had changed over the last hour she had been awake.

"Well, right now, it simply looks like you got a pretty good sleep out of it," he began. "The MRI is inconclusive. In their haste, they did not run it with the contrast, so I would like to repeat the MRI, this time with a contrasting agent. Until then, it is too early to say."

"Doc, please, put it to me straight. What do you think?" Deborah said a tone that was sweet but demanded an answer.

"Let me ask you a few questions first. Are you up to that?"

Deborah nodded.

"Your chart says you are taking a medication for vertigo. What exactly are your symptoms during your episodes?"

"Sudden dizziness. My vision goes black. Pain in my temple, just behind my left eye. Then I get sick."

"How long does it last?"

"No longer than a few minutes. Just as suddenly as it has comes on, it's gone. After I get sick, my vision comes back, and the pain goes away, then I feel fine. Well, other than the sour taste of getting sick."

"How often does this happen?"

Deborah thought for a moment. She knew she had to be honest here. No more lying; no more hiding it. This was serious now. "It started off every so often, but it happens more frequently now. Even when I take the medication. I don't understand, isn't the medication supposed to help me?"

"Well, it would help you if you had vertigo."

"So, I don't have vertigo?" Deborah asked.

"How often," he asked again.

"Twice last week. Three times this week, that includes last night."

"Any other symptoms? Anything at all, no matter how inconsequential."

Deborah thought for a moment.

"Any tingling or numbness? Ringing in your ears?"

Deborah was so focused on the dizziness and pain that she couldn't recall. "Well, I have always had tinnitus. The doctors said that it was normal and not part of the vertigo. Other than that, I have been feeling a little weak, but I also have been working pretty hard lately."

The doctor wrote on her chart. And looked lost in thought.

"Doctor, what do you think?"

"Acoustic neuroma," he said.

"And what exactly is that?" She asked.

"It is a tumor that grows on the primary nerve that leads from your ear to your brain."

"A tumor? Cancer?" she asked.

He raised his hands defensively. "Relax. Nearly all acoustic neuromas are noncancerous. So that is not necessarily a concern. The concern is its location."

"You said the inner ear?"

"Not exactly. The location is on the nerve between the ear and the brain, but it is on the inside of the skull. They are generally slow-growing, so they can often go undetected unless a doctor runs the right test. But occasionally, one can grow rapidly and cause unexpected issues."

"Issues? Like vertigo?"

"Something like that. The slow-growing ones can affect equilibrium problems and make you dizzy and cause you to blackout, but it is not vertigo per se. The symptoms are similar, and I can see why they diagnosed you the way they did. It is just that they did not run the right test. So, there is nothing to compare its current size to."

"How big is it right now?"

"A small neuroma would be around 1.5 centimeters. It would cause simple ringing in the ears, a little bit of dizziness, maybe come coordination issues. The larger it is, the more severe symptoms surface. Like blackouts, vomiting, and loss of consciousness."

"So, mine is not small?"

"Let's not get ahead of ourselves. I cannot speculate that is what you have. You said to let you know what I *think*. We will know more after we run the second MRI. I have it scheduled for 7:00 PM. That is as soon as I could get one in, and that was on an emergency basis. But with the total loss of consciousness and the length you were out, I am leaning in that direction."

"What are my options?" Deborah asked.

The doctor sighed. "Are you sure you don't want your parents here to discuss this? Maybe you're fiancé?"

"My what?" Deborah asked, taken back by the sudden title change.

"The man that brought you in. Your fiancé."

"Oh," she said, recalling the patient privacy rules. She had faced those many times during her tenure at the insurance company. "Yes, Aaron. And no, I am a grown woman. I would like to know my options."

"It is too early to tell. We will know more—" Dr. Mattheson said but was interrupted.

"—after the second MRI," Deborah answered.

"Right. And we would need to consult a neurologist to confirm the diagnosis and proceed with treatment."

"Which is?"

"Most likely, surgery."

"Wow," said Deborah realizing the severity of the situation. "All of this from a little dizziness?"

"Now, please, don't get worked up yet. We still have to run more tests to be sure. Remember, you asked me what I thought. I am not a neurologist; I could be completely off base, and I have probably said more than I should have."

"Yes, I know," said Deborah. "I thank you for your candor, doctor."

He looked over at her monitors and took more notes. The blood pressure cuff inflated again and gave him a reading that he recorded. He nodded in approval, "Well, I have to say, your numbers look good. You seem perfectly healthy."

"I just have a rock in my head," she said with a grin.

"We'll know more this evening. I put a rush in on the results. We should have something by 9:00." Dr. Mattheson returned her smile and replaced the chart on the hook across from her bed.

There was another polite knock at her door. This time it was Aaron. He looked beaten up and exhausted but attempted a smile. He looked at the doctor. "I'm sorry, should I come back?"

"No," both Deborah and the doctor said at the same time. The doctor continued, "I was on my way out. I will let you have some time with your fiancée," he said to Aaron. Then to Deborah he said, "I will check in on you before we take you back, around 6:00, 6:30, okay?"

"Thank you again, doctor," she said. With a nod, he left the room. "Fiancé? I wasn't out that long. What did I miss?"

Aaron laughed. "I'm sorry. It was the only way they would let me stay with you."

Deborah smiled. It didn't occur to her to care. She was even a bit uncomfortable with the idea.

"So how long have you been awake?" Aaron asked.

"What time is it?" she asked.

"Just about noon on Friday," he said.

"A couple of hours. But I am still sleepy."

Aaron smiled again. She was reminded of how much she loved his smile. It helped comfort her, giving her the feeling that everything was going to be alright. It made her forget for a moment where she was and what she had gone through the previous night.

"What are you grinning at?"

"You do the math," he said. "You have been out since around 9:00 last night."

She was too clouded to think straight. She gave Aaron a *can you give me a clue* look.

"I guess thirteen hours of sleep was enough." He smiled again, a bit softer, but still adorable.

Deborah smiled, then laughed. "Yeah, I guess it was. Our lucky number."

"So, how are you feeling?" he asked.

"That's the weird thing. I feel fine," she said, holding up her arm. "If I weren't hooked up to all of this, I wouldn't even know anything happened."

He was quiet for a moment. He looked to the ground; the smile gone from his face. He looked at her then to the equipment that was beeping and hissing, "You scared me, Deb."

"I know," she said. "All I can say is that I am sorry."

"Why didn't you tell me?" he asked.

She had been wondering the same thing. But she knew. Her parents called it headstrong, but it was stubbornness that kept her quiet about what she was battling. She now knew it was more serious than she could ever expect. And she was ashamed for not opening up to someone before.

"For what it's worth, not even my parents really knew what was going on," she said, trying to justify herself.

"But they knew. You got lucky last night."

"Yes, lucky that I have you. If I had not met you, then I would have been alone last night," she said in an attempt to lighten the mood. It didn't help how she felt or Aaron's mood.

"That's not what I mean, Deborah, and you know it. I appreciate the sentiment, and I am blessed to have you in my life, but you should have told me."

The last thing she wanted to do was hurt anyone. Her stomach tightened up, making her want to cry. She knew he was right, but they couldn't change things now. "I know," she said in a whisper. Then she let her tears flow.

Aaron sat on the bed beside her. He took her hand in his and kissed it. "I apologize. I didn't mean to upset you. I was just so scared. I thought I was going to lose you."

"I know. I'm sorry," she said again through her tears.

Aaron sighed and looked up at the monitor, which was beeping a little faster. "The good thing is that you are awake and getting better now. I am sorry I upset you. Try and calm down, or they are going to come in here and kick me out," he said with a hint of a smile.

She smiled. After a sniff, she asked for the tissue box that was sitting on a side table. He handed it to her. "Have you been here the whole time?"

"Of course," he said. "I couldn't just leave my *fiancée* now, could I?"

They both laughed.

"Mom and Pop said that you called them."

"Yeah. Another lucky thing, you didn't have your phone locked."

"I wouldn't know how to set it," she said, laughing again. She wiped her eyes, now feeling more unattractive than ever. "I must look hideous. No makeup and now puffy eyes from crying."

"You're beautiful," he said, brushing a strand of hair from her face. He looked her in the eyes and leaned over to kiss her cheek. She turned her head and met his lips with hers.

"Thank you," she said.

"For what?"

"Saving my life. If I hadn't been with you last night, I could not imagine what could have happened," she said again, but this time she meant it.

He leaned over and put his arms around her the best that he could among the wires and tubes. She felt good in his arms.

Deborah could not remember feeling safer or more comfortable. Being near him felt as natural as breathing. She did not want to be in any other place than right here, right now. Not wanting it ever to end and maybe letting the moment get the best of her, she uttered the three words that best described how she was feeling.

"I love you, Aaron."

TWENTY-THREE

Before Aaron could respond his phone chirped out its ringtone. He fumbled with his pocket and silenced the ringer; it was Nate. In all the confusion he had forgotten about work, he had forgotten about everything. He answered the phone. "Hey Nate, sorry. I meant to call you," he said in a half-whisper.

He stood and walked to the window, which had the drape shut and created a reasonably good wall; no light from the outside escaped into the room.

"Where are you? You do know it is a workday? Where is the La Cabana piece?"

"Boss, calm down. I am at the hospital," he said. That obviously got Nate's attention because he went silent, processing what he just heard.

"What? Are you okay? Were you in an accident?"

"Nate, no. I am fine. It's Deborah," he said, but not wanting to violate her privacy again. He thought of her purse and that he still had to explain that to her. "I am at the hospital with her. I can't go into specifics right now. But I won't be in today, and if you checked your email, you would see that I sent the La Cabana piece to you last night."

"I did check my email. I learned from the last time, but it wasn't there."

It hit Aaron that he was working on the piece when Deborah showed up before the game. He had just finished the final edit but had not sent it yet. *Dang it,* he thought. "Yes, it is on the screen on my computer. Sorry, everything happened so quickly. I will get it to you soon."

"Not too late, remember we need to get it to formatting by 8:00," Nate reminded him.

"Yes, I know. You'll have it. Look, I gotta go. I'll call you later," Aaron said and hung up. He looked at Deborah, who had an *oh, you're in trouble* look on her face. He smiled. Even without makeup, she looked like an angel. "That was Nate. He was looking for my article. Guess I forgot to send it in all the confusion."

"Oh sure, blame me," Deborah said with a laugh. "At least it is a better excuse than your dog ate your homework."

Aaron laughed, then remembered where they were before the interruption. He looked at his phone and made sure it was on silent mode and set it on the food tray. He again sat next to her and took her hand. He was just as sure as she was. Somehow, from the moment that he walked into the deli— from the moment he set his eyes on that bouncing ponytail, he knew. "I love you too, Deborah." Then he kissed her again.

"I think we are the first couple who got engaged before telling each other how they felt," she said as he rested his head on her shoulder.

"So, what did the doctor have to say?"

Aaron listened to Deborah recount all the doctor had told her. He heard her say it was mere conjecture, but he knew a doctor would not be so loosely lipped if he wasn't confident in what he was saying. It worried him, but he did his best not to show it. He nodded in all the right places and gave an occasional, "I see." He was praying in his heart as she spoke, and when she finished, he acknowledged that he had heard everything.

"We will know more after my MRI at 7:00," she said. "Until then, we wait."

He took a breath, soaking it all in. "So, Pop says you kicked him out."

Deborah smiled. "They needed their sleep. Pop gets grumpy when he is sleepy, and he was growling at the nurses and barking at the doctors. So yes, I told him to go home and get some sleep. I assured them I was in good hands and reminded them you were here. You were the one who saved me in the first place, so they didn't have to worry."

"And you can be headstrong," he laughed.

"Yes," she said, "I am stubborn. Go ahead and say it. I know I am, but it's just who I am. Take it or leave it."

"Yes, ma'am," Aaron said defensively. He had hit a nerve. But her agitation only made her more attractive. "I'll take it. Any day of the week, and twice on Sundays."

Sundays made him think of church; church made him think of the Bible he had given her. He wanted to say something but held back. It didn't seem like the right time. He just watched her as she laid her head back. Her brown hair was not in a scrunchie, nor did she have one around her wrist. But he could see it in a memory. "I love you," he said again.

"I love you too," her eyes remained closed, but a smile came across her face. "Let's just remember who said it first."

Aaron chuckled. There was a knock on the door—a little louder than polite—and a nurse came in. She was not in blue scrubs like the desk clerks. She was in teal green. "Hello, Miss Davies. My name is Carolyn, and I will be taking you for your bath."

"What about all of this?" Deborah said, raising her arms, displaying all of her connections.

"The nurse will be in shortly to remove the IV. Your test came back normal so we can remove the fluids, you'll just have to drink more water for a while, or else we will have to put it back in. The rest of it we can simply take off and put back on when we return." She looked at Aaron, "You will have to wait in the waiting area, sir."

"How long will she be?" Aaron asked.

"An hour or so," Carolyn said.

"That's fine," Aaron said. "I have errands to run anyhow." He turned to Deborah. "I gotta get that piece turned into Nate, grab a shower, and change. I'll be back later."

"Okay," Deborah said.

He kissed her on the cheek and turned to leave.

"Wait," she said. "Can you do me a huge favor?"

"Anything," he said.

"Can you go by my place and pick up a couple of things?"

He had never been inside her apartment. The feeling of violation once again hit him. His face must've shown his discomfort.

"Please," she said with that endearing smile of hers.

"What do you need?" He said, wondering what it could possibly be.

"Two things. In my bathroom, there is a pegboard on the wall with my scrunchies. Can you bring me a few?"

"Sure, and the second?"

She looked to the bed, almost shy about asking. "The Bible

you gave me. Please bring it to me." She looked up at him and her look said everything; she had been reading it. That pleased him.

Again, his facial expressions gave his feelings away. She blushed.

"Most definitely," he said. "Where is it?"

"On the nightstand next to my bed."

"I will have it here this evening." He kissed her again, this time on the forehead, and left her to the nurses.

Aaron's place was just as he left it. Pizza box and empty pastry container on the table, TV and lights on, and the scattered mess from the paramedics rushing Deborah out of the small space. He found himself getting emotional for a moment, remembering her lying on the floor, helpless. He had to remind himself that she was okay now. Last night was in the rearview mirror. Just a bad memory that they would recount to their children one day.

He turned off the TV and sat at the table in front of his computer. He woke it up and went to dial Nate to tell him the piece was on its way, but his phone had died at some point. His charging cord was next to the computer, and he plugged it in. After the system loaded up, the article appeared before him. He gave it a quick once-through and saved it, then sent it to Nate and headed for the bathroom.

Other than the bath rug being askew, there was little sign that anything had happened. It did not occur to him to see if she had any bruising from hitting her head, but he was sure he would have noticed. He recalled her facial features from the hospital. Her smile, her bright but tired eyes, her mussed up hair—but no bandages, or swelling. Thinking of her smile made him relax. He smiled himself remembering her telling him that she loved him.

He was in and out of the shower in 15 minutes, changed in another 10, and out the door again, having spent less than an hour at his apartment. He almost forgot her keys and had to go back upstairs to retrieve them, but now that he was home, he was able to drive; he had to take a cab from the hospital. He had forgotten that too when he left the hospital. He had ridden with Deborah in the ambulance, never considering how he would get home.

Mid-afternoon traffic was already piling up, and it took Aaron almost a half hour to get to Deborah's place. He found a parking space quickly and wondered if it was her spot. He had assigned parking at his building, and it would make sense for her to have such amenities as well. Either way, he took the spot; he wouldn't be here long anyway.

The building itself was fancier than he remembered, but the last time he was here, it was already dark. His main concern was a doorman, but he was relieved to find a standard lobby. Once inside he saw a door with a key card bypass, but he found that attached to her key ring. *Fancy*, he thought. The keycard read 411, so he got onto the elevator and hit the four on the keypad, and a smooth ride later he exited on her floor.

He had yet to see anyone; another concern he had. He knew that the tenants easily recognized a stranger. If it was anything like his complex, people looked out for each other. He knew his neighbors, and more importantly, they knew him. Any stranger who approached his door would immediately be written down, or if needed, a friendly call to local law enforcement would be placed.

He quickly found 411, and he entered her apartment. After he closed the door, the unfamiliarity overcame him. He felt the guilt of crossing lines and shame as if he were violating her privacy. But he took a couple of steps through the entryway and into the living area. It was considerably larger than his all-in-one. There was a partition that separated the living area from the dining area, and the kitchen was a separate room altogether.

The first thing he noticed was the smell of her perfume hanging in the air. He closed his eyes and accepted the greeting. It set him at ease and began to melt the initial weight of remorse. He looked over the room. It had the feeling of being lived in, and a bit messier than he anticipated. He knew she had not expected company. He imagined her doing a quick clean up in preparation for a visitor. He was seeing behind the curtain at how Deborah lived in real life. She may have exuded organization and discipline on the outside, but he had to laugh; her place was a mess.

Not wanting to pry any more than he had to, and wanting to get back to the hospital, he found the bathroom. It was cleaner than the living space, but there were piles of dirty clothes, and a towel hung from the shower curtain. Here, there was a damp smell mixed with lavender he assumed was shampoo. He quickly found the pegboard she spoke of. Sure enough, and just as he suspected, there were colors of every shade hanging neatly in color-coordinated rows. *Impressive*, the thought. He knew where her priorities lay. He thought about it for a moment and grabbed a half dozen, then froze. He smiled, then grabbed another handful—All the different shades of the hospital gown she had worn: maroon, blue, and yellow stripes.

He was most nervous about entering her bedroom. This was the sacred space of the single adult. Not many people get to see this room. If he had known the layout, he may very well have closed his eyes and felt his way to where the Bible was. Not having this knowledge, he slowly opened the door and turned on the light.

The perfume smell was stronger here. The room was sparsely furnished, but every piece had a purpose. She had a queen-sized bed covered by a cream colored comforter with a red and green floral pattern. The bed was a bit messy, but he was confident she was a left side sleeper. He would have been able to tell even if the Bible was not on a nightstand on that side of the bed. There was an armchair in the corner, and it strongly resembled the pattern of the comforter, a couple of garments and an overcoat were tossed across it. Against the opposite wall was a long dresser with a mirror. It reflected the theme in the room—comfortable and functional.

Before he could feel the violation of her inner sanctum again, he grabbed the Bible and exited the room, closing the door behind him. He looked over the apartment one last time, anticipating the next time he would be in here. He could see them sitting on the sofa, enjoying a drink together, discussing their future. *Soon*, he told himself. He smiled as he pulled the keys back out of his pocket. He locked up behind him and headed back to the hospital; a little wiser regarding the life of Deborah Davies.

TWENTY-FOUR

Aaron returned to the hospital around 5:00 and found Mom and Pop in the waiting area watching the evening news. The TV was back to its original hushed volume and quietly announcing the Sunday cold front was on its way. Aaron could not imagine working in television media. His job was stressful enough. While not a major paper, a periodical was just as much a platform, but your face was not front and center. To have such a spotlight on you, Aaron couldn't bear the thought. He hardly liked to be recognized now, even though it did happen on occasion.

Mom met him halfway and hugged him. "I'm glad you came back," she said.

"Why wouldn't I?"

"Well, now that you know, we weren't sure you would want to stay."

"Mom, I'm not going anywhere," Aaron said, taking her by the shoulders and looking into her eyes. They were gray, much like Deborah's, but with more life experience behind them. "I only left because they were going to remove the IV, and she was going to take a shower. So, I went home to freshen up, and she asked me to pick up a few things from her place." He lifted up his arm to show thirteen scrunchies around his wrist. Mom laughed.

"Well, I'm glad you're here," she said. "The doctor took her back early for the second MRI. You just missed them. So, come, come sit with us."

Aaron sat. Pop had a blank look on his face. Part sleepy, part unsettled. "You okay, Pop?"

He looked up, surprised. "Aaron, my boy. When did you get here?"

"Just now," he explained.

"You just missed Deborah, they—"

"Yes, Mom told me. They took her in for her MRI. How are you doing? I thought you would be gone a bit longer."

"Couldn't sleep. Figured I could just as well not sleep here and be closer to DeeDee than be not asleep at home and be miles away. What if she needed me?" Pop said. "Where did you go?"

"I went home to freshen up and then…" he was almost afraid to admit he had been in her place. "Deborah asked me to grab a couple of things from her place." Again he displayed the train of hair ties on his arm.

Pop gave a hearty laugh. "That's my, Dee," he said. "Would not feel like herself without one of those things up in her hair. She has her priorities."

Aaron looked up at the TV. "Anything good on?"

"Is there ever?" he retorted.

Mom sat next to Pop, and he took her hand and kissed it. She blushed at the display of public affection, even though the room was relatively empty. A couple was sitting in the far corner, both reading from the stack of magazines on the table. Not surprisingly, one of them was the Houston Gazette.

"How long will she be back there?" Aaron asked.

"The doc says an hour, hour and a half. They want to be thorough." Pop saw the pink book on Aaron's lap, "What is that? Looks like a Bible."

Aaron smiled. "It is."

"You have a pink Bible?" Pop questioned, furrowing his brows.

He held it up to show the sand dollar. It took him a moment, but the insignia brought a light of recognition to his eyes. He just wished he had gotten to see her reaction to seeing it. "This is Deborah's."

"She has a…. When did she get a Bible?"

"I knew you were up to something. Nobody buys a scarf for a someone on their first outing. You were hiding that from Deborah," Mom said.

Aaron blushed. "Well, yes and no. Yes, I needed to hide the Bible, but choosing the scarf's colors was truly from the heart."

"I don't understand," said Pop.

"Poppa, he found it at the Flea Market last week. He had to hide that he bought it because Deborah may have gotten more upset than she already was that day. So, he bought the scarf I showed you to hide it."

"And you gave her a Bible?" Pop asked.

"Yes, and I think she is reading it," Aaron said with a smile. He handed Pop the Bible. He thumbed through it and came across several dogears. Aaron pointed out, "Those were not there when I gave it to her. She's reading it, Pop. It was one of the things she asked me to bring her."

Pop smiled the fatherly smile of a proud man.

"And you just told me that she has her priorities. I would say this is a good sign."

"But how did you know about the sand dollar?" Pop asked.

"She told me about the day the two of you found the sand dollar on the beach when she was seven. That you both initialed it with the date. She also said that she thought she had lost it, and that it mysteriously appeared a couple of weeks ago."

"Yes, she asked me about it. Said she found it in her car."

"She told me that, as well. She said she was confused at finding it because she keeps her car pretty clean." Aaron chuckled. "She even thought that the homeless man whom she had…" It hit him like a ton of bricks. He could feel his face go pale and his heart skipped a beat.

Both Mom and Pop noticed too. "What's wrong," Mom asked.

"I don't know," he said, gathering his thoughts. *What an odd coincidence.* "Has Deborah ever mentioned a man named Carter? A homeless man that lives in the neighborhood?"

"No, not that I can remember," Mom said.

"She said he wears an old tweed coat and hat and has white hair and beard. He may have visited the deli."

"Hmm. No, doesn't sound familiar. But we get a lot of customers. It's difficult to keep track of them all."

"Deborah told me that she had given a ride to a homeless man named Carter the morning that she found your sand dollar. Since it was not in the car before she gave him a ride, she thought he might have put it there."

"How would a homeless man have my and DeeDee's sand dollar?"

"I don't know. I am just saying that is what she told me," Aaron said.

"Then she saw him at the carnival last week."

"Did you get a look at him?"

"No, not then. I was busy being stuck by a screw that was sticking out of the bench. I had to—" Aaron blushed, "—had to move closer to Deborah to get away from it." He didn't mention their first kiss.

"So, what is important about him?"

"I don't know. But I think I saw him here this morning," Aaron said, recalling his conversation with the old man. "I had fallen asleep, and when I woke up, he was turning up the television volume. He brought me a cup of coffee. He introduced himself, but I did not make the connection until just now. We talked for about an hour, about prayer, and allowing God to work."

"Why would he be here?" Mom asked.

"He never said, and it never occurred to me to ask. He asked about Deborah, though. Well, not about her directly, just the reason I was here. Then he left to get a refill. In fact, that was right before you came to get me. Do you remember seeing a man in a tweed coat and hat after you left Deborah this morning?"

"Son, I can't remember coming to see *you* this morning. I was so tired. I wasn't noticing much of anything." Pop said.

"You don't think—" Mom said.

Aaron answered, "No, couldn't be. Just coincidence. He's older, could be visiting a friend, or a loved one. Well, there's one way to find out." Aaron stood. "I'm going to ask the nursing staff."

"Carter," Gabriel said, obviously a bit unnerved. "You know you're only supposed to make contact with your assignment. Getting involved beyond that can be dangerous. And you, above anyone, should be able to understand that."

Carter met his eyes. "I know the risks. But it was harmless. A small conversation was all it was."

"But that small conversation could turn into a big fiasco if your playing around leads to the wrong impressions. What if they see you as a threat and keep you from her? How will you be able to help her then?"

"Relax, Gabriel. The final drop is not even for her. I may not even need to see her again, but if and when I do, it will be safe enough. He is not the only one who knows things. This is my job, and I do it well. I know what I am doing. He gave me this assignment because He trusts me. All I ask is for you to give me the courtesy of trust as well."

"Just be careful," Gabriel said. "You are not the only one who has something at stake here."

"You? In hot water with the Almighty?" Carter said with raised brows.

"Who do you think vouched for you on this assignment?"

"Gabe, I'm touched," Carter said, placing his hand on Gabriel's shimmering robe. "I apologize for doubting you. Alright, then. I'm sorry. I will tone it down. You have my word."

"Good," Gabriel said. "Have you placed the final reminder?"

"Soon," Carter said.

Gabriel laughed. "That is your answer to everything."

"Perhaps. But as you have said, I am performing admirably," he said, handing Gabriel's words back to him.

"Yes, but this one is the most important one."

"He will find it by the end of the week."

"She may not…" Gabe said, then stopped.

Carter was taken back, "May not what?"

"Nothing," he said. "Just get it placed and ensure he finds it."

"What are you insinuating?"

"Carter... nothing. The longer people have to think about things, the longer the enemy has to mess with their heads. Delays cause doubts, and doubts cause hardened hearts. And hardened hearts are difficult to convince. Just don't wait too long. Her heart is softened now. It's time to act."

Carter accepted Gabriel's perspective but had already planned out how Aaron would find the final piece. He could not see any other way to make it seem natural. He would stick to his plan for the time being, and prayed it would work out in the end.

TWENTY-FIVE

N one of the nurses remember an older gentleman in a tweed coat and cap," Aaron said as he sat back down. "But that doesn't mean he wasn't here. We'll have to wait until the night shift comes on at 9:00."

"I don't like it," Pop said, shaking his head.

"He seems harmless, Pop," said Aaron. "He seemed to know his scripture and a lot about God and how He works. I don't think a stalker would be as spiritually minded as Carter was." But he wasn't so sure. *You never know nowadays.* He was close enough to the news media to know that many tragic incidents were conducted by those who claim that spiritual forces caused them to do what they did. He only wished he had made the connection, then he could have handled the situation then and there.

Aaron looked up at the TV again, the news was recycling itself for those who just got home from work. It occurred to him that it was still Friday. "What happened with the deli today?"

"I called Erica and told her to take the day off. By the time I called Miguel, he was already there. I asked him to put a sign in the window letting people know we would be closed for the remainder of the week," Mom said.

"Oh, I'm sorry," he said, not really sure how to reply.

"Being here is more important," Pop said. "What about you? Did you call your boss?"

"Yes, he knows and understands."

"Good," Pop said. They were silent for a moment, then Pop broke the stillness. "So, why haven't I seen a review of my shop in your paper yet?"

Aaron laughed. "A small sandwich shop is below the standards of Aaron Stephenson."

"You sound like that bigwig, Ethan what's-his-name," Pop chuckled.

"You know who Ethan Chadwick is?" Aaron was astounded Pop would know who he is.

"Of course. I read things. He is the putz who said that small mom and pop establishments are on their way to extinction," Pop said, then made a *pfft* sound. "What does he know. We have been going strong for three generations. Long before his father was playing tiddlywinks on his grandfather's front porch."

"You never cease to amaze me, Mr. Davies," Aaron said. "First, the spaghetti sub, now I learn you are an Ethan Chadwick fan."

"I wouldn't go that far," he admitted. "I heard a customer talking about it and wanted to see it for myself. DeeDee found the article for me. Before that, this Chadwick fellow could have been a lawyer or stockbroker for all I knew."

"You are right about one thing," Aaron jested.

"What's that?"

"He is a putz." They both laughed. Aaron continued, "The conference I went to last week, he was the primary speaker. I was about to pull my hair out. He is oblivious to what a genuine culinary experience is. He is so blinded by the sizzle of $75 steak that he fails to see the subtle excellence of a meatloaf sandwich."

"Yes, but that sizzle grabs the attention of everyone in the restaurant," Pop said.

"True, but it's all fake. The sizzle doesn't come from the steak. It's a kitchen trick to drive sales for those who want the attention of that sizzle coming to their table. It's all a façade. The plates that they place the steaks on are heated in an oven. And while the steak will sizzle on the skillet, it is far from the spectacular show the waitstaff puts on. You see, right before they take the food out, they place cold water onto that 400-degree plate. The sound you hear is the water dancing around and evaporating. And that is who Ethan Chadwick is. He is the water on the skillet. Loud for everyone to see, but just as fake as they come."

Pop was quiet for a moment, then he chuckled. "You still didn't answer my question."

"To be honest, I don't know why I can't seem to get it written. Every time I try, I draw a blank. I can't place my finger on what is keeping me from just doing it. Everything about Davies Deli is five-star. I just—"

Pop elbowed him in the side, "You have it big for my DeeDee. You are blinded by her."

Aaron nodded; he couldn't deny that she may well have everything to do with it. "Perhaps," he agreed. "But that isn't professional. In my business one needs to remain impartial. Any personal connection and the review is tainted. So if people knew I was involved with the daughter of the owner, it could hurt business instead of drawing attention to it."

Pop gave another *Pfft*. "You write what you feel. It's what you do. Don't worry about what some reader thinks of your connection to our shop. If they feel your view is tainted and not worth listening to, then Mom and I don't want them in our place to begin with. Right, Momma?"

Mom nodded in agreement, "You do your job, Aaron, we'll do ours. Your relationship with DeeDee is irrelevant. It's none of their business. You go ahead and court our little girl, you marry her, and give us little grandbabies. And let people think what they're gonna think. God is in control of it anyhow. If He wants us to have business, He will bring it, regardless of a little article in a little paper."

"Let's not get too far," Aaron raised his hands. "We've been on two and a half dates. It's a bit early and a little uncomfortable to talk about marriage and babies."

"How so?" Mom said, "You obviously love her. I knew there was something about you the day you walked into the deli. God pointed you out to me. He knew you were the one for my Deborah."

"Why would you say that I love her?"

"Because you're here. A steady would have taken off already. He wouldn't keep an old man and woman company while their daughter was off having magnets taking pictures of her head. A steady would have handed her off the moment we got here and moved on with his life. And if you don't see that you love her, you're in denial."

Aaron looked everywhere but into Mom's eyes. He even looked over at Pop, a desperate attempt at some masculine connection. But his eyes were as fixed on him as hers. "Okay, you got me. And I think she feels the same way. She told me so," he admitted, now looking at the ground.

"Well, she better. You're here." Mom repeated. "God has you right where you are, for this very moment. For us, for her, and for yourself. Sometimes we don't like the way things happen, and sometimes we can't explain them. But we fail to see because we are so focused on ourselves that we don't pick up on the little things God leaves in our path that lead us to where His hand is guiding."

Aaron was astounded at the depth of this couple sitting before him. All he ever heard from them was coded messages that produced fries instead of potato chips and provolone instead of cheddar. To hear such guided and educated words from them was refreshing. He wondered how Deborah could have gotten lost in such a Christ-centered atmosphere. He was grateful for the Bible he held. He was convinced that God had placed that Bible at that Flea Market for him to find, for him to give to Deborah, for her to discover what He had once been to her. Aaron was eager for what would come next.

And what came next was Dr. Mattheson entering the waiting area.

Does he ever sleep? Aaron wondered.

"Well, the exam is complete. Sorry it took so long; we wanted to be sure not to miss an inch. The contrast made her a bit queasy, but that will wear off. I should have the results by 8:00. Do you have any questions for me?"

"When can we see her?" Pop asked.

"She will be back in her room shortly, and I will tell the nurse to let you know when she is available." He turned to leave and remembered something. "Oh, and I personally signed off on extra visitors, you all can go in together. If they say anything to you, tell them to page me."

"Thank you, doctor," Mom said, patting Aaron on the hand.

The doctor left them, and Aaron could feel the tension

in the room was much lighter. He could also see it in Mom and Pop's eyes. He was relieved. With them at ease, he felt less obligation to perform. Now he could relax.

Deborah's queasiness was a little more pronounced than originally explained, so they were kept out of her room for longer than they expected. They passed the time discussing Aaron's parents, or lack thereof would be a better description. He explained about them not being around and how disconnected they were from his life. He spoke of their divorce, and them leaving him and his sister to basically raise themselves. He encouraged Mom and Pop by praising their relationship. However, they felt their life was normal. *It is how families are,* Mom said, but realizing her mistake, she quickly apologized.

Aaron continued on about his sister being there for him after the split, taking him to church. But after she left for college, that all changed. If it hadn't been for the group he'd grown to know through church, he would have wandered away from the Lord. He spoke heavily of Nate's influence in his sophomore year, how they both enjoyed journalism and worked together on the school paper. He skipped ahead and told them how Nate was now his boss but still treated him like a high school buddy.

"It is hard to find good friends like that," Pop said. "Right, momma?"

She smiled like they had a secret. "Yes, Poppa. Few and far between." She took his hand and kissed it.

Aaron loved to watch the interaction between couples. It was another reason why he would show up early to restaurants. He was able to witness how people reacted to each other. He could easily tell how far along a couple was simply by how they entered the door, interacted with the hostess, and their mannerisms as they sat before receiving their food. He saw himself as much of a relationship critic as a food critic. And Mom and Pop—they were lifers.

It was 7:30 when a nurse who introduced herself as Sarah came out and said they could go back to be with Deborah. She did give a warning that she was weak and needed her rest, so they would not be able to stay very long. She said nothing about exceeding the visitor maximum. Dr. Mattheson must have informed them.

"Thank you, Sarah," Aaron said as she led them down the hall to her room. It was quieter than the previous evening; he could hear the tapping of each of their shoes on the linoleum—one of them squeaked, the other had an airy squishing sound. Sarah politely knocked on the door and called to Deborah, "Miss Davies, your family is here to see you."

"Come in," a weak voice answered. Aaron wasn't sure if it was sickness or fatigue.

Aaron noticed that extra chairs had been brought in and thanked Sarah again.

"If you should need anything, I will be making my rounds, but Alec at the counter can help you. I will check on you before I go off shift in half an hour." She left them and the room was silent except for the occasional beep from the monitor.

Aaron and Pop sat. Mom approached the bed. "How are you feeling, Dee?"

"They gave me some medicine for nausea. The contrast they used really did a number on me. I am feeling fine though. Just tired." She looked over at Aaron, let out a hoarse laugh, and reached out her hand. "I can take those from you."

Aaron had almost forgotten about his nylon bracelets. "There were so many I did not know what colors to bring. But I know you color coordinate, so I brought you the colors in your gown."

She looked down, then up at the scrunchies. "I'm impressed, paperboy. But you brought too many."

"Don't be too sure about that," he said with a wink and a smile, "Count them."

She did.

"Is thirteen enough?" he asked.

Now it was their turn to share a secret knowing glance. They both laughed just as there was another polite knock on the door, but not feminine like Sarah's would have been. It was Dr. Mattheson.

He had a chart in his hand. "The results are in. Why don't we all sit down." He was looking at Aaron as if to excuse him.

Pop picked up on it, and before the doctor could make any request, said, "He stays doc. He's family. He saved my DeeDee's life. He hears this too."

The doc nodded in acceptance. He sat, opened the chart, put his glasses on, and took a deep breath.

Despite having gone over this, Deborah was stabbed with every word. The seriousness of her condition was now confirmed. What was normally slow-growing and relatively treatable had moved over into words like *rare* and *grave*. She had what the doctor had assumed, acoustic neuroma. The usually small tumor was growing just inside her skull between her ear and her brain. The pressure on the nerve is what had been causing the dizzy spells. The last onset of symptoms was severe enough to place her in a mild coma.

The doctor went on for nearly an hour. She remained silent and let the doctor speak to her family, answering the same questions Deborah had asked when she was first told: Size, placement, symptoms, how long she has had it, and options.

"Right now, I am waiting to hear back from the neurologist. Only she can confirm what we have found, and then she will consult with a neurosurgeon that will give you details about what your options are. I am no expert, so I can't give you any more information than what I already have."

"When do we get to see her?" Pop asked.

"I will be meeting with Dr. Krauss in the morning and will fill her in on my notes. She will be taking everything over from here. I will remain around of course, until the introductions are made. If you need anything until then, the nurses can page me. Do you have any more questions?"

Mom looked at Pop. Pop looked at Mom. They both look at Aaron. Dr. Mattheson had covered pretty much it all. There was one question on Deborah's mind.

"Do you have any idea when I can go home?" she asked.

"That would be up to Dr. Krauss. I can't release you because I've already submitted for the transfer of care. While technically I am still your doctor until she signs your chart, I don't think it's wise for you to be discharged just yet."

Deborah nodded, accepting his answer.

"If you need anything, just ring the nurse. They can reach me anytime. We'll talk again in the morning." Dr. Matheson closed the chart and left the room.

The room was silent for a long moment, but Deborah broke it with a sigh. "Okay. Let's not give in to speculation. Dr. Matheson said they were still unsure of what happens next. So, let's wait until we talk to Dr. Krauss. No talking about any of this until then, okay?"

She looked at Mom and Pop with raised eyebrows. They exchanged concerned glances but agreed. Aaron's eyes locked on hers. He nodded.

Deborah looked down at her hospital gown, pulled her hair back, and stuck out her arm to Aaron. "Orange, please."

Aaron smiled slightly and pulled the baker's dozen off his arm and gave them to her.

"Thank you again," she said. Then asked in a much softer voice, "and my Bible too?"

Aaron placed it next to her.

The three of them sat there unsure of what to say. It was

Pop who broke the silence this time. "It makes my heart happy to see you with a Bible, Dee. You've been reading it?"

"Yes, Pop. I've been reading. I was a little unnerved at first, Aaron, that you would give me such a gift. But when I saw the sand dollar on the front, I understood why you did it. All three of you have been very patient with me, and I am grateful that I have such loving people surrounding me. I know I have been stubborn and selfish."

She paused to swallow back tears, then continued. "For that, I am sorry. Seeing this Bible reminded me of so many things—" Fighting it was no use, so she let the emotions flow. "I once understood how much God meant. I let the world take that from me. I allowed my friends, well, so-called friends, to dictate what I believed in. I lost my way. But I just want you three to know I am trying."

She wanted to say *four* because Carter had as much to do with her transformation as they had, but she did not think they would understand the ramblings of a vagabond they have never met, much less seen. She would keep their conversations to herself, at least for now.

Pop came and sat next to her on the bed, while Mom stood beside him, taking her hand. Aaron stood at the end of the bed with a studious look on his face. She wished she knew what he was thinking. It was more than a curious contemplation. *He's researching us like he does the restaurants he writes about. Is he evaluating our family dynamic? Judging our interactions? How do we rate on his expert scale?*

"Penny for your thoughts?" she finally asked.

"The three of you," he said, swinging his arm around. "I have never seen such a close family. I mean, neither of you are too busy for Deborah. And Deborah, you pretty much gave up your career to help them in a pinch. I never knew something like that existed."

"Son, forgive my boldness, but just because you had a less than perfect childhood, does not mean that all families are that way," Pop said. "While I cannot make up for what your parents put you through, you are welcome to be part of ours." Pop smiled. Mom smiled. Deborah smiled. He smiled.

Listening to Pop, Deborah realized that there were things she still did not know about the man that stood before her. She had proclaimed her love for him but was still far short of really knowing him. She was eager to know more about this dark-haired stranger. As she looked into his eyes, she could see her future, and everything in her tingled with the anticipation of discovering everything there was to know about Aaron Stephenson.

For the remainder of the evening, they did not discuss test results, treatments, or her being released from the hospital. They enjoyed the moment. She knew her parents were trying to be comforting to her as well as Aaron. She had not heard it from his mouth, but she assumed he had a rough childhood, maybe his parents were no longer together. She was grateful that her parents were that loving. She knew that type of love came from their relationship with God. She only wished God was that real to her. Maybe He was, way back when, but her current journey was still on shaky ground, and she knew it, more than she was willing to admit.

After another hour, Deborah was ready to get some rest. More than that, she wanted Mom and Pop to get some rest. She encouraged them to get back to work and open up the deli on Saturday, but they were not having it. And she had learned not to try and convince them against something that they had set their minds on. She accepted that they would see her in the morning. They agreed to gather again at 8:00 when Dr. Krauss was to meet with them.

Mom and Pop shared goodbyes and hugs, and they were on their way, leaving Aaron and Deborah alone.

"So, how are you, really?" Aaron asked her.

She looked away for a moment. "As I said before, I feel fine. I can't explain it. I wish I could explain what I feel when I feel it, but I can't. One minute I feel fine and will feel fine for quite some time, then all of a sudden, I am not fine. But it only lasts for a moment. What you experienced the other night was the first time I had an episode that severe. If I had known, I would have said something. Aaron, I am sorry for what I put you through. I never meant to freak you out. I thought I had it under control. Boy, was I mistaken."

"I am just glad you are okay," he said.

"Well, we will see when Dr. Krauss reviews my chart. Dr. Mattheson thinks I'll most likely need surgery. He said not to quote him on it, but in most cases, it's what is needed, especially if the tumor is rapidly growing."

The color drained from Aaron's face. He stared at the floor.

"Hey," she said. He looked up and gave a half-hearted smile. "It's going to be okay."

He laughed. "I'm supposed to be the one telling *you* that."

"Yeah, I know. Then you need to be doing your job, fiancé." They both laughed.

"Deb, it's going to be alright." He took the spot Pop had been sitting in. He took her hand as Mom had. But he kissed her gently on the forehead, then with a bit more passion on the lips. It was a wonder her monitor did not sound, but he knew the art of being gentle as well. Their lips parted, and he laid his head on her shoulder, "I missed you. I am glad you are feeling better."

"Me too. Thank you for the scrunchies, and for the Bible. Ya know, I was upset at first, but I can't begin to thank you. I don't know why your gesture was the one to get through. Maybe it was the culmination of everything that has happened over the past six months, you were just the tipping point. Not to discount what you have done, but God has used you to give me the final push I needed."

"When I saw it, I remembered what you had said about you and Pop finding that sand dollar. And I understood how disconnected you were. I had to take a chance."

"I'm glad you did," she said, choking back more tears. "I love you. And I mean it. It is not just emotions or the medication. I know we have only really known each other for a few weeks, but I have never known anything so deeply in my entire life. I love you, Aaron."

He smiled. "I love you too, babe. I understand what you mean. It just seems natural. I cannot explain it. I would really love to think that it is God shining His light on us, saying that this is meant to be. Right now, I couldn't picture moving from this moment on apart. When I am here with you, I feel calm. When I am away from you, I feel like something is missing."

She loved him talking like that about her. It was just how she pictured it. It was like the love Pop had for Mom. They were inseparable. Like salt and pepper, tea and lemon, George and Gracie, meant to be. *Are things moving a bit too quickly?* she pondered. *Perhaps, but love makes you do crazy things.* She thought again about the teenage emotions of falling in love. She was a bit embarrassed; her cheeks flushed giving her a giddy smile.

Aaron must've felt it. He leaned up.

"Did I say something wrong?"

"No, you said something right," she said, kissing him on the forehead.

He leaned back against her shoulder and back into a comfortable silence. They remained there for quite a while and must have gotten too relaxed because she found herself dozing off. She jerked awake. "Sorry," she said.

"You fell asleep," he said.

"Yeah."

"You were snoring," he said, a bit reluctantly.

She laughed softly.

"I better be going. You need your rest."

"So do you," she said honestly concerned by how much sleep he has really gotten the last couple of days. "Please, go home and get some rest. Don't worry about me. I'll be fine. I love you and will see you in the morning."

He didn't argue. Through a yawn, he held onto her for a long moment, kissed her on the cheek, and they said their good-byes.

Deborah laid there a moment, alone in the stillness, and dozed off. Tomorrow would be another day. Whatever lay ahead, she felt she was prepared for it. She had wanted to read a bit but couldn't keep her eyes open. The last thing she remembered was her pressure cuff taking another reading, showing she was in perfect health externally when she knew there was something much more serious going on underneath it all.

Chapter

TWENTY-SEVEN

Aaron had never fallen asleep so quickly. He figured he must have only had six or seven hours of sleep in the last 48 hours. He was gone even before his head hit the pillow and did not stir again until the grind of his alarm told him it was time to get up. Aaron never believed in snooze buttons. They were a foreign concept to him. He could never understand how someone could hit a delay button two or three times, or worse, have two or three alarms set up 10 minutes apart. For him, when the alarm goes off, it was time to get up.

This morning, however, he woke up but stayed in bed for a moment staring at the ceiling. He was grateful it was the weekend; he didn't have to be concerned about work. Although he did have to revisit Andretti's, it was definitely not top of his list and not an immediate concern. The plan had been to go back with Deborah.

After a shower and a quick breakfast of buttered toast and coffee, he was out the door. The mugginess that only came before an imminent front hung in the air. *Tomorrow it will rain for sure*, he thought as he pulled his car out of the lot and headed to the hospital. Still a week from Thanksgiving, everything was business as usual. Congested highways, classes in session, and work to do. Arron knew sometime this week he would have to finish his Thanksgiving article for next week's holiday issue. He still had two restaurants to visit before he would feel it was well rounded.

For Aaron, it was easy to understand why some would choose a restaurant and forego the traditional homemade Thanksgiving meal. The big day actually involved days of preparation. People bought ingredients that they would use once, then store in a cupboard until they threw them out the following year because they had expired a month earlier. What followed was hours of tedious baking that only made a gigantic mess. And to top it off, they would get up at the crack of dawn to get a stuffed bird into the oven so they could eat at a decent hour. *Who needs all of that when you can simply go to a restaurant where everything is already cooked?*

For Aaron, it was an easy choice. He didn't have a place to go to for Thanksgiving. His mom had remarried and moved to Seattle after Sally left for college. She rarely kept in contact, not even a Christmas card. His dad was far from affectionate. He was just as alone. Both of his parents had passed. He spent his holidays with a hungry man and the remote and was none the wiser that there were better things.

That's not to say that Aaron didn't try. But after one rather heated rejected invite, he never brought it up again; never even attempted to drop in. Was that resentment part of his dad surfacing? Perhaps, and he knew he would eventually have to deal with it. But not this year. He had heard through the grapevine that his dad had flown up to a buddy's place in Chicago to see the Bear's game. With no real family to spend Thanksgiving with since childhood, Aaron had become an expert on what restaurants had to offer.

Last year he had reviewed a place down in Stafford. He learned later his review brought the place double the revenue they usually pulled in on the holiday. He went there because he had heard they also fed the less fortunate by setting up a special area for those families to come in and receive a free meal. This was done through donations from the patrons of the restaurant itself. That is what stood out to Aaron. It was not a company wanting to get its name out there. It was the local community understanding that sometimes folks go through hard times, and wanting to provide for them during the time when it was needed the most.

Not only did they serve more within their regular restaurant, but their makeshift setting also welcomed families from all around. Times like those proved to Aaron the power of words. It was a mixture of what Paul told the Romans, "How will they know if they are not told," and a play on the *Field of Dreams* quote, "if you write it, they will come."

He was reminded of what Deborah had said about Mom and Pop wanting to turn their deli into one of these places that offered a Thanksgiving meal to the needy. He felt for them not being able to make their dream a reality. He understood about restaurant costs, but he could only guess what it would amount to to be able to feed a multitude. And to not have funds coming back in to compensate? It would take an act of God to make it all possible. But he also knew that God was the God of impossibilities. God could bring about the means through the most unlikely of circumstances. He sent up a quick prayer. *Lord, if it be Your will, provide a way for Davies Deli to one day be on my list of restaurants that meet the needs of the hungry through a Thanksgiving meal.*

This year he had eight places on his list—two that stood

out: a diner on the outskirts of Katy, which he had visited last week, and a buffet-style kitchen near the colleges. Both had Thanksgiving menus and were open, at least part of Thursday, but only the Katy diner was offering support to less fortunate. But with the proximity to the colleges, the buffet did offer a discount to college students. Having recently been one, he knew that even $5 off something could be a big deal. He would have to find the time this next week to visit both locations.

In all fairness he would visit all eight on the list. He knew better than just to visit the ones that struck him. There could always be a diamond in the rough. Davies Deli had been one of them—an unassuming sandwich shop on the outskirts of town. He had almost skipped it over. *Who wants a cold sandwich when you can get a hot meal elsewhere?* he had initially told himself. *Boy, was I wrong*, he mused. So, one of those six could be the next Davies Deli—not likely, but he would never know unless he went, so he would go.

But this morning, he was focused on Deborah. Today they would know how serious her condition was and what needed to be done from here. While he knew God was in control, it did not keep him from worrying about her. The was the complex dilemma of trusting in the unseen.

Aaron pulled up to the hospital, wondering if the Davies were already there. He spent a moment in prayer and contemplation of Deborah's situation. He thought about how quickly things had escalated. Several weeks ago, he was pining over a cute girl in a ponytail. Today he was sitting by her bedside in a hospital room, professing a love they both held for each other. *Did we allow circumstances to push us into a forced emotional state, saying things neither of us really mean?* He shook his head to clear the unnerving thought.

He took another breath and gave it all to God and once again chose trust over worry. He knew it was never a once and done event. It was day by day, hour by hour, minute by minute process. He fully understood because from the walk from his car to the elevator, he had regiven it another two or three times.

Deborah had expected Mom and Pop to be up before the sunrise and at the foot of her bed before she woke up, but when the day nurse came in at the change of shift to check on her, she was alone. In a way, she was relieved because she did not want them to worry about her more than they should. But with the impending discussion with Dr. Krauss, she wanted some company. She wondered what Aaron was doing.

"How are you feeling this morning, Miss Davies?" the nurse asked.

"A little nervous, to be honest," Deborah said.

"Yes, your blood pressure is a bit up," she said, writing in the chart, which in the 21st century meant using a stylus to selected fields and tapping in information on an electronic tablet that uploaded to a virtual chart.

Deborah knew the benefits of electronics just as well as anyone. She could have a new hire sign employment paperwork and have the documents to the corporate office in a matter of seconds rather than the snail mail version or inter-office mail. She pictured other hospital staff or maybe Dr. Krauss herself getting instant notification that her pressure was up and shaking her head. Deborah took a breath and exhaled. *Relax Deb,* she told herself.

"Do you know when Dr. Krauss will be in?"

The nurse looked at her wrist. "Well, it's 8:30 now. I would expect to see most doctors anytime now. No later than 9:00, but I am not sure of her schedule once she gets here. You may be number one on her list or number 10. But if I see her, I will make sure she at least pops in."

"Thank you," she said. A little relieved. That should appease the updated numbers in the sky.

"Need anything?"

"Can I disconnect and wash up?"

The nurse came over and removed her blood pressure cup and the pulse monitor. "Let me know when you are through, and I will hook you back up. Anything else?"

"Just a refill on water, if you could."

"Not a problem," the nurse said and left.

Deborah washed her face, brushed her teeth, and put her hair up in another scrunchie—blue today. When she returned, another orderly was changing the sheets on the bed, and there was a fresh pitcher of water on the night-stand. She poured a cup and sat on the bed. "Thank you both for everything."

The orderly smiled and left the room without a word. The nurse reconnected both monitors, then turned to leave. "If you need anything just buzz."

The room went quiet again. Being still was one thing Deborah couldn't stand. Being active was something she had grown accustomed to; there was always something to do. From the time she woke up until the time she laid her head down, she was in motion. All of this sitting around made her feel uneasy. She was comfortable but had the feeling that she should be doing something.

In the kitchen, there was creation, prep, cooking, serving, clean up, put away, wipe down, and prepare for the next shift. In the office, there was an endless cycle of paperwork. No matter where you were, something needed to be written up, collated, filed, copied, or expedited. There was always something to do to keep busy. But right now, there was nothing to do but hurry up and wait.

She heard a familiar rumbling in the hall along with cheerful banter and a hearty laugh—Aaron's laugh. She smiled. Now the flutters in her tummy were no longer the anxious nerves of boredom.

There was another hospital room polite knock on the door, followed by a "Good morning, beautiful." He looked her over and grinned. "Blue today. I like it."

She laughed. "Yes, I gotta change it up. Keep 'em guessing. I am sure it kept you coming back. If not to see what concoction Pop was going to come up with next, to see what color I was going to be wearing."

"Ah," he said, waving a finger at her, "so you do it on purpose?"

"Not deliberately. But yes, I am intentional with being coordinated."

"Even in a hospital gown?"

"Even in a hospital gown. But you had a hand this go around."

They shared a laugh.

Aaron looked behind the curtain, "Mom and Pop?"

She shrugged. "Guess they slept in."

"Good for them," he said. "They needed their rest. They can do you better by getting rest at home than sitting around here waiting for nothing to happen."

She agreed.

"Have you heard anything yet?" he asked.

"No. Dr. Krauss should be in shortly. That's what the nurse said."

There was an odd silence between them. She could tell something was on his mind. It was not like her to jump to conclusions, but now having the time to really think about things, she was wondering where he stood on things. So much had happened in the past couple of days. The past two weeks had been filled with first dates, long phone conversations, and some unpleasant revelations. Then a tragic event, some uncertainty, followed by hurried expressions of emotions. *Could we have allowed this whole thing to get ahead of us? No. No jumping to conclusions.*

Aaron looked at the door as if waiting for someone to walk through it, when no one did, he took a breath, then looked at her, "We need to talk."

"Yes, I know," she said, not sure if this is where it all ended.

"First, I ask you to please let me finish what I am about to say before you reply to any of it. While it may seem like I can easily communicate, understand that only applies to paper. With writing it is easy to edit a document before it goes to print. With the spoken word, I tend to be all thumbs, and there is no delete key on the human mouth, so please bear with me."

"Okay," Deborah said, gripping the bed sheet in her hands.

"It has been a crazy couple of weeks, right?" Aaron asked.

She remained silent. He looked a bit nervous. "You said to let you finish," she reminded.

He laughed, which eased the tension a bit. Just a bit. "Okay, you can answer that one. Sorry. I just want to be able to get this off my chest. And I do not want to be sidetracked and forget something by having to answer questions in the middle."

"Yes, it has," she answered, although *crazy* may not necessarily be the word she would have chosen.

"And while I can't speak from your end, I know from my end, I was attracted to you from the moment I walked into the diner. I don't know, must have been the scrunchie. It was—"

"Purple," they both said in unison. And laughed together.

He continued. "I was so mesmerized by you that I don't even know what I ordered that day."

She smiled. She knew it was chicken salad but was told not to answer. She recalled noticing the tall, dark-haired stranger walking into the deli. He seemed a little lost and out of place. Maybe that was why he sat tucked away against the display case—on the edge of the counter, out of the way and secluded. She did not know he was actually casing out the place, planning to put Mom and Pop across the headlines for the city to see.

"I think I had two things going for me that kept me from crossing the line of being a stalker. One was the regulars who were in there just as frequently as I was, and two, that Mom and Pop always had something new on the menu; I had to show up to see what was next.

"I know we rarely spoke at the beginning other than shop talk, but I loved to hear you talk. Your voice was soothing. I could just sit at the counter and listen to you bark code back to Pop and relay orders to Erica all day. It was the best hour of my day.

"I often thought of what it would be like to sit and have a long conversation with you, just talking about the weather or your feelings on the man bun, whatever, just to hear you speak. I wanted to have the opportunity to ask you out. But either ran out of time, or plain ole chickened out.

"Then that Friday, I took my chance. Well, I did have some support. Nate had known of my visits to Davies Deli. He has known me since high school, so he knew something was up and called me on it. I told him about you, and as expected, he rode me about asking you out that entire week. Finally, he told me as a friend, not as a prankster, to just do it. And I did. Very poorly, I might add," he laughed.

She remembered the day vividly. Her blushed and rushed reaction and hiding in the office, Mom and Pop's inquisition, and her regret over her behavior. She recalled what Mom said to her that afternoon. *He may be your knight in shining armor.*

"Ever since you said yes, I have been in a state of elation that is only equivalent to a teenage infatuation. I felt the nervousness of calling you on the phone partnered with the fear of your father if I screwed things up. I had the sweaty palms when I went to pick you up, the jitters of striking up our first date conversation, and the butterflies of sitting near you; then felt the passion as our lips met for the first time. I've had the next day withdrawals, the anxiety that comes with the anticipation of the next moment alone together.

"Then you surprised me with your unexpected visit. That showed me that you may very well be having those same feelings too. Then, you relaxed around me. It was not about how we could impress each other or being on our game. But then… then you scared me to death, Deborah." Aaron paused.

Deborah wanted to say something, but she remembered her promise and let him think. She knew she earned what he was about to say. She had kept him in the dark, and that could have cost her her life. She knew that it was his quick thinking that saved her. So, whatever he had to say was well deserved, and she was ready for it. She gripped her bedsheet again.

"I thought I was going to lose you. I had known you a little over a month, and I was scared to lose it all. Every second we've shared flashed before my eyes when I saw you lying there," he swallowed back the memory, "brief as it was, I saw it all—every smile, every laugh, every kiss.

"Most of all, I was scared and confused. I had no clue what was going on. I did all I could, and it still did not feel like enough. When your parents told me of your condition, for a moment, I was angry with you for not telling me. But the more I thought about it, you barely know me and as your parents said, no one really knew how serious all of this was until that night. I was still upset, but I understood your secrecy. But not knowing what to do last night was excruciating. I am just glad it wasn't anything lethally serious. Because I don't know what I would do if it became a 'well if you only had…' I just thank God that the paramedics got you here on time, that I was able to get hold of your parents, and that you are going to be okay.

"Speaking of your parents, I got to spend time with them. They opened up my eyes to a new world I did not know existed. My parents divorced when I was 12. To make a long story short, my mom moved away and forgot about me, and my less than attentive father attempted to raise me. My sister helped as best as she could, then I hopped between high school buddies's homes, then on to college as soon as I could. I never knew what a normal family looked like, much less a Christian home. And to see the love that Mom and Pop have for God and each other is inspiring. It gives me hope.

"They really think a lot of you. More than you realize. I don't think it's about the deli as much as it is about your happiness. Don't ever take them for granted. You never realize what you're missing until it's not there. For me, I never got to take anything for granted because I never had it in the first place. But your parents showed me that love is real, that families are real, and that it is all out there for us to find.

"But as I laid in bed this morning thinking about you and I rushing into this thing too quickly, about us allowing what happened to overwhelm us with emotions causing us to react without thinking, I considered that we may have said a thing or two in haste, and now that things have calmed down a bit, we may regret them."

He looked to the floor and remained quiet for a moment. She was not sure if he was going to continue or was looking for some sort of response. The truth was she had been feeling the same way. But she had come to a conclusion about all of that, and she was hoping he had done the same. It would save both of them much heartache.

He opened his mouth to speak again, but there was a polite hospital knock on the door.

"Miss Davies?" A woman in her 50s with shoulder-length black hair came in with a tablet in her hand. "I am Dr. Krauss, chief neurologist. Sorry it took me so long to come up to see you. I have been making myself familiar with your chart."

Deborah looked over to Aaron. Their conversation would have to continue later. He smiled at her and got up to leave.

"Do you have to go?" Deborah asked.

"I can stay if you'd like," he said.

"Yes, I'd like you to stay," she said with a smile.

Aaron sat, and the doctor began with the series of routine

questions that every doctor since the beginning of all of this asked. She gave all the same answers she had given them. It seemed she was more confirming than learning as she did not take any notes. She asked Aaron what he had witnessed, and again he gave his answers, and again she nodded in approval of the one who had taken the original notes.

She walked over to the door and called out to the nurse. "Tell Mr. and Mrs. Davies they can come in now."

"My parents are here?" Deborah asked.

"Yes," Dr. Krauss said. "The nurses said that they were letting you have some time together, and that when I was ready to talk with you that I could call them back."

"So, you know what's wrong with me?" Deborah asked half-filled with skepticism.

"That I will discuss when we are seated together," she said. "I need to go up to my office and finalize a couple of things. I will be back down in half an hour."

She left. Mom and Pop came in, and they exchanged greetings, then sat and waited for the doctor to return. Deborah and Aaron exchanged glances. Deborah couldn't read him, not sure if he was ready to say goodbye, and only stayed out of courtesy, or wanted to stay, but was willing to leave for the same reason.

Those answers would have to wait as the doctor made her return. She sat on the circular swivel chair, sweeping her coat behind her like a grand pianist. She cleared her throat and gave her diagnosis.

Chapter
TWENTY-EIGHT

All eyes were fixed on Dr. Krauss as she gave her opinion of what was ailing Deborah. Just as Dr. Mattheson had suggested, it was acoustic neuroma. And just as Dr. Mattheson had assumed, what had once been slow growing, was now most likely in a rapid growth stage and had caused the most recent episode. What she explained that Dr. Mattheson did not, or rather could not, was about its exact location and how it was spreading.

"There are irregularly shaped tumors," the doctor explained. "Picture an ice cream cone with a large scoop of vanilla on top. That is how these tumors look. The more massive they are, the more pronounced that picture is."

"How big is the one inside my head, doctor?" Deborah asked.

"A small size is a half-centimeter to a full centimeter. A large can be up to two and a half centimeters. Your cone is just over 2 centimeters. It is close enough to be classified as a large VS tumor."

"VS?"

"Vestibular schwannoma is the technical term."

"But it is not cancer," Pop asked.

"The tumor, as with most VS tumors, is non-cancerous.

However, with the possibility of it being a rapidly growing VS tumor, there are still serious concerns. Since we do not have any earlier neurological exam to reference, we have nothing to compare the size to. At this point, we are going by the onset of symptoms. And that's why you have had to answer the same questions over and over. We need to confirm before we give a full diagnosis.

"With how rapidly these symptoms came upon you and how quickly they escalated, especially with the consciousness loss, I am concerned. Loss of consciousness is rare for a VS tumor that is slow growing. Such pressure is indicative of something going on. The tinnitus is typical and even expected, even with smaller sized tumors. The fact that you still have most of your hearing is a good sign.

"I don't like to be the type of doctor to say, 'wait and see,' but we need another MRI to confirm growth so we can determine how much time we have."

"How much time we have?" Deborah echoed the doctor's words.

"Brain tumors are unpredictable without having comparable scans. Usually, you would need two or three to judge a growth pattern accurately. We do not have this in your case. If we go simply by symptom onset, then we could be seeing a rapidly growing tumor. But at the same time, if symptoms are just manifesting now, and the tumor has just shifted slightly, then we risk forcing surgery too quickly and may do more damage than good. A second scan will tell us if we need immediate surgery or if we could wait a couple of weeks."

"So, I will need surgery."

"Yes, that is a given. Whether it is next week or six months from now, you will need to have the tumor removed, cancerous or not. Right now, we are simply determining how long we can wait."

"What about chemo," Mom asked.

"Unfortunately, with these types of tumors, since they are not cancerous, they are not responsive to chemotherapy treatments. There are certain radiotherapies available that inhibit growth, but if it's as rapid as it seems, then we would only be wasting time. Thus, you see the importance of a second scan. This is the only reason why I would say 'wait and see.'"

"How would that work?" Pop asked.

"In-patient, of course. We would move you up to the neurological wing so we could better monitor you, and it's close to the surgical room should things turn for the worse."

She is surely blunt, Deborah thought. *But I suppose that is what I need. This is life and death. And even though I feel fine, to be given a warning that things could change quickly is better than being told things are fine or downplayed just to make me feel better.*

"How long?" Mom and Pop asked together. Then touched hands as they always did when they spoke in unison. It was their 'pinch, poke, coke.'

"I'd like to do the next MRI in the middle of next week. I would prefer a month, but I do not believe we have that luxury."

"But it's Thanksgiving," Mom said.

"Yes, I realize that. Unfortunate, but necessary. I will most likely schedule the scan for Friday morning, and I will have the reading by Friday evening. We will know more by then. After we see that scan, we can make plans for the surgery."

"Why wait a week, then?" Aaron asked.

"Honestly, because of the lack of symptoms. If she were experiencing paralysis or deafness, then I would be more concerned. Like I mentioned, your fiancée still having her hearing, vision, and full function is a good sign. Immediate surgery is not warranted.

"Of course, if that should change, my prognosis would change. Another reason is the location. Another scan would give us a better idea of how to better proceed with surgery. I would like to get her up to the neurology wing. That will happen by the end of the day."

The doctor stood and tapped on the screen a few times, made a few notes, and said her goodbyes. She softly closed the door behind her.

No one said a word for a moment, unsure of what to feel. Deborah was numb inside. Was she to supposed to be relieved that they finally knew what the issue was? Or should she be concerned that she needed brain surgery? The doctor didn't give them a real seriousness level—just that it was necessary. Perhaps that was a question that could have been asked. Concerned eyes met her gaze. Her parents were wondering how this could have gotten this far.

And Aaron... she still could not read Aaron. She wished she knew what he was thinking. It brought to mind their unfinished business. *Well, this complicates things*, she thought. If he were about to walk out, then what is his feeling now? And if his plans were to stay, would he be concerned that this diagnosis would appear to be the reason he stayed?

She felt she needed to be the one to say something. She mustered a smile and said, "So, how about those Rockets? I hear Harden can't miss."

Deborah spent the next hour and a half convincing Mom

and Pop that they needed to go back to the deli and conduct business as usual, that she would be fine. She told them that there would be nothing they could do anyway but sit and wait until the MRI was done next week. She tried to get Pop to begin making phone calls on the stack of applications sitting on the desk to hire help for Erica.

"Call Michael. He seemed the most promising. He has two years of expediting and waiting tables. He attends one of the colleges and will most likely be off for the holiday. And he lives locally, so you won't have to worry about him traveling. Please, Pop, go. I know the business will survive, but all the food in storage will not. And that will hurt your bottom line. So, if not for me, do it for Davies Deli. Go now, both of you. Please. You can see me at the end of the day, just bring me some of the daily special. The stuff in this place would make anyone go insane."

Pop nodded and grabbed his coat. *The front must have blown in,* Deborah thought. "Let's go Momma. We got work to do."

Mom silently got up, came over to Deborah, and kissed her on the cheek. "Love you, DeeDee."

She could tell Pop was a bit upset to be spoken to in such a manner, but it needed to be done. She couldn't just lie there with them staring at her for six days with pity on their faces. At least with the hustle and bustle of the restaurant to keep them busy, their minds would be occupied, and the time would fly by. Aaron on the other hand, she wasn't sure where he stood either way, and she knew she was about to find out.

The nurse came in and took her lunch request. Even though she knew it would be awful, she asked for the tuna salad. *It will most likely be dry, but at least I can enjoy the carrot and celery sticks that accompanied it, and who doesn't like apple sauce,* she reasoned to herself. *And anything is a welcome change to water.*

The nurse left them alone, and she gave Aaron an 'alright everyone is gone, let's get this done' look. "You were in bed thinking, you were considering that we may have said some things in haste, and now maybe reconsidering some of the things we said," she reminded him where he left off.

She could tell he wanted to laugh, but to his credit, he held back. She must have had that serious look on her face; that *human resource, don't mess with us* stare. She softened it up a bit, "Sorry. Please continue."

"You amaze me Deborah. Through all of this, you are remaining strong. I have been praying for you and that God would keep you strong through this time in your life. You are an inspiration to me. I don't know if I could handle what the doctor just told you. You have a solid foundation that your parents have laid. I am glad to see your roots are holding firm."

"I appreciate the sentiment, but you are not answering the question."

"Oh, but I am. Please let me finish."

"Okay," she said with a little caution.

"I am glad to see your roots are holding firm. I am proud to see the family that you are part of. And I am grateful to have found the woman who is strong enough to say what she means when she sees it and is not afraid to take a chance. Sometimes haste is a good thing. Sometimes passing up an opportunity causes more regrets than saying or doing anything in haste would.

"All I know is I do not regret anything for a moment. I love you, Deborah Davies. I would not change a single moment, well other than the obvious, of course."

Deborah laughed through her tears. It was exactly what she needed to hear, exactly what she felt, exactly the conclusion she had come to. "I love you too, Aaron."

He sat by her side and gently took her in his arms. She fell in close to him, allowing him to be closer than they had ever been. "I am so sorry to have put you through all of this. I am sorry I scared you. Thank you for staying with me. Thank you for not leaving."

He whispered, "Where else would I be. My world is right here, right now." He kissed her in a way that she knew he recognized the closeness she had opened the door to. Before he could trigger any alarms, he broke off the kiss and sat back.

"I also see that God has put us together. Everything that has lined up. I know he had placed you in my life for me to see that truly loving families exist. I grew up not knowing what that was like. I was turned off to the whole idea of family. Now, seeing you, Mom, and Pop, I have renewed hope. And forgive me for being so bold, but I think He has placed me in your life to show you how real God is. Not that I am life-changing, but I think that the Bible you have begun to read has a lot to do with where your heart is today. It is a blessing to see you growing stronger every day."

She had to admit, there was truth in what he was saying. She had a good idea where her strength was coming from. The Bible had a lot to do with it. She had rediscovered the faith she once knew. She thought of Carter. He had much to do with her transformation. He had her thinking again. Something she hadn't done since college. She had given up on God, and he had challenged her to look at the little things. Those little things that had always been there. She had just been too blind to them. Aaron was just the one that pulled the string. He had shown her that those stories she had grown up with were not fairy tales, as she had convinced herself they were in college. Every one of them was true. Maybe even the one about the knight in shining armor.

Chapter

TWENTY-NINE

Come Monday morning several things had been agreed upon. Number one was that neither Aaron nor Deborah's parents were to spend another moment away from their responsibilities. The only real reason Deborah was staying in the hospital was for rest and monitoring. Having someone continually feeling like they had to attend to her would make her uncomfortable.

Aaron agreed to go back to the paper first thing on Monday. He had to ensure formatting was correct for the Thanksgiving piece to be released on Tuesday anyhow. He arrived at the paper early. He beat even Jessica, who usually opened up the office. He had the main coffee pot brewing and his computer booted before the first car pulled up. Jessica always brought breakfast on formatting day. It was always a long and tedious operation because everything had to be perfect. All print had to be error-free, fitted into the allotted space, photos had to be matched to stories, and captions and pull quotes had to match the photos; everything had its place. One mistake could mean disaster.

Everyone had to work together to put the pieces of the puzzle together. This expended energy, and Jessica knew that giving the team a morning boost would give them a good start. Jessica also took it upon herself to learn everyone's favorites. She was not only well-liked because she was the boss's daughter, but because she took an interest in those little things that many tended to overlook.

"Good morning, Aaron. Didn't expect to see you here," she said, setting down the bag with the assorted goodies. "How's Deborah?"

Aaron explained the situation, recounting the high points of what needed to take place this week and his reluctance to have to be at work versus by her side. He then found the bear claws and snagged both of them before Nate came in.

"I understand you want to be with her, and if she understands that too, then that is great. But if she expressed that she wants you here, then working is the best way to help her feel better. Being there, you may think you are helping her, but in reality, you are making her feel worse because she probably feels like she is holding you back. So, miss her and wish you could be there, yes, but work your butt off while you are here. That will make her happy; and Nate too."

"I guess that makes sense," Aaron agreed with a chuckle. He smiled. "Thanks, that helps."

"Not a problem. Is there anything you need before I get started on my work?"

"Did you or Nate do anything with my piece after I sent it?"

"Just the final edit. Oh, and we pulled three photos from the Facebook pages of the restaurants. Those should be attached to the bottom of the existing piece. Nate said you could finish embedding them into the piece where they are to go. They will also need captions."

"Got it. Thanks." Aaron headed to his office. Settling in

front of his computer, he found his file and began to scroll through it. It always interested him to read a final edit—to see what an editor did to his work. He would not always agree with the changes, but most of the time they were necessary. This piece seemed rather untouched. He liked that. It meant that he was getting better at doing his job.

He found the three photos and got to work placing them where they belonged in the article while enjoying his morning jolt of energy. There was a knock at his door; it was Nate.

"Hey buddy, how's it going?"

He went through the same speech he gave Jessica, only he added about the connection they had made. He did leave out the mushy parts.

"Wow, that's crazy?" Nate said. "So, what are you going to do?"

"What do you mean?" Aaron asked.

"I don't mean to seem harsh, but are you planning on seeing this through?"

"Why wouldn't I?"

"You barely know her."

"What does that have to do with anything?"

"A little over a month ago, you barely had the courage to speak to her, and now you want to stand beside her through a critical illness?"

Aaron thought about it. What Nate said didn't make sense at all. It was true, he just met Deborah, and put in his shoes he would have the same doubts and reservations. But to Aaron, what made the most sense, was that it made no sense at all. "Yes, I guess I am."

Nate shook his head.

"Look, I can't explain it. I just know that I am right where

I am supposed to be. I have no doubt. It's not logical, and it goes beyond description. It's not a 'me' thing, it's—"

"—a God thing," Nate finished. A saying he was well familiar with. A common theme from their Youth for Christ days; the catchphrase of their generation. It was always about fulfilling the call God has on your life, not what you had planned for yourself. It was the one statement Aaron could use to help Nate understand—the one phrase that would allow him to see he was doing this because he felt he needed to.

"Exactly. Many things have pointed to this moment. I don't know why or where they are going, but God is using this for His ultimate purpose. And I have to see it through, wherever it may lead."

"Okay," said Nate. He nodded at the half-eaten bear claw. "I see where the other one up and went off to."

Aaron laughed. He knew the subject was dropped.

"So how are we looking at the Thanksgiving piece?"

"Finalizing now. I will have it prepped for formatting within the hour."

"What about the Andretti rewrite?"

"That'll have to wait another week. I'm prepping the La Cabaña piece. I'm about to head out for my drive by. I don't know though; the directions were a bit vague. This one is not starting off very well. Don't worry, I'll be sure to get the Thanksgiving piece over before I head out."

After assisting another columnist to sift through photos for her art column and Jessica with a final edit, Aaron headed out early to lunch. This was only going to be a drive by of the establishment to see it in daylight and to get familiar, more reliable directions for his readers. With the fear of getting lost with the left-left-left directions he had found, he decided to eat first. Even though it was in the opposite direction, his jeep just drove itself toward Davies Deli.

Part of him was torn because he already knew he would not see the colored-scrunchie-tailed waitress that made his heart swoon, but he knew there would be a meatloaf sandwich with his name on it. As he pulled up the lot was already filling up. He smiled, knowing that they were taking the advice of their strong-willed daughter, just as he had.

He found his seat empty, as it usually was, and took his place. Erica was buzzing around and gave him a wave from the other end of the diner. There was a new face in the mix. A tall young stocky boy that looked like the center of a football team, but he was moving about just as gracefully as a color guard. He was barking back orders to Mom and Pop just as if he had done it all his life. "Be right with you, sir," he said, zipping a tray of sandwiches and salads to a nearby table.

"How ya doin', Aaron?" Erica said, setting down a to-go tea in front of him. Her eyebrows narrowed filled with concern and empathy.

Aaron smiled to ease her worry. "Things are fine. Just trying to keep busy. I see you got some help."

"Yes, his name is Michael. Pop hired him on Saturday. He was excited about it too. He is on holiday this week and did not know what to do with himself."

"He seems to know what he is doing."

"Yeah, he has two years of experience working at a steakhouse uptown. But they let him go when he started taking a night course and couldn't work evenings."

"He looks like a center," Aaron chuckled.

"Actually, he's a wrestler."

"Is that right?"

"Made state his senior year in high school, been battling up the ranks ever since. But he expected that for a couple of years. Much more competition at the college level, or so he says."

Michael passed by, and Erica introduced them. Aaron was a bit nervous taking his hand but shook it nonetheless and still could feel his fingers afterward. Erica said her farewell and tended to the busy deli, and Michael took his order.

After lunch, he knew that this sandwich would be the centerpiece of the article he would write on Davies Deli; it was even better than the last one. He hadn't seen Mom or Pop the entire time he was there other than Pop's chef hat drifting back and forth across the window. He could still hear the *ping* of the pellet hitting the ducks. He laughed.

He looked at the time and grimaced; he needed to get going. He paid his bill, swung around the display case, stuck his head through the swinging door, and shouted a greeting to Mom and Pop.

"Is that you, Aaron?" Mom replied.

"Wait a second," Pop called to him. He came around the corner, spatula in hand.

"The meatloaf is spectacular, Pop," Aaron said.

The older man's eyes glowed with pride. "Say, can you swing by here before you head over to the hospital?"

"Sure," Aaron agreed. "Everything okay?"

"Yeah, but have you seen what she gets in that place? She needs some meat. Can you smuggle something in for her?"

Aaron laughed. "Yes, sir. It would be my pleasure. I'll be by around 5:30. Will that work?"

"Yes," he said with a wink. He gave Aaron a fatherly slap to the shoulder. "I will have it ready."

Aaron had to ask for forgiveness twice trying to find this place. He hit a dead end once, and now he was stuck in a construction zone. He could see why the directions were so vague; the city was changing the roads around. The traffic lane merged into a left-hand turn lane only, but he needed to go right. Not wanting to make another circle he pulled into a shopping center hoping to cut through to get to the right he wanted to make. But the constable two cars behind him also noticed his attempted short cut and followed.

Aaron asked for forgiveness again. He saw a pawn shop that had a couple of parking spots open and pulled into one to avoid getting a ticket for an illegal right turn. The constable parked in the space behind him and sat in his vehicle, calling his bluff. Aaron decided to commit to his hand and got out and entered the pawnshop.

A bell sounded as he entered. A middle-aged couple sat at opposite ends of the counter. The woman was Windexing the glass display, and the man was watching a ballgame on one of the many televisions they had for sale. A half dozen bargain shoppers were milling around through someone else's hocked belongings. Still feeling like he had to play the part, he melted into the pot and began his window shopping.

He saw power tools, fishing poles, old stereos—something grabbed his attention. It was an old-fashioned booth jukebox selector. He had only seen them in movies. In one, two teens were on a date in a soda shop, and they pushed a button on the device and their song came over the speakers.

"This is a must for Mom," he said aloud. He anticipated it being more than the tag showed. *May not need to do much haggling on this one.* He tucked it under one arm and headed for the counter when he noticed the constable was gone.

The female clerk was now arranging jewelry in the display case. There were various pieces like rings, bracelets, and necklaces. Knowing the primary purpose of a pawn shop, he wondered about the story behind each piece. A broken engagement here, a bill payment there, perhaps maybe even a revenge story somewhere—each one held its secret that would forever be untold.

There was one item that immediately caught his eye.

The clerk noticed his interest. "You like the pendant? It's new. We just got it this morning. The seller said that he felt that someone in the world could use it more than he could. I don't know what that means. I don't even know what that symbol is."

Having learned the Greek alphabet in college, he knew the pendant to be two letters intertwined: Alpha and Omega.

Those two letters, when combined, had special meaning. Aaron recalled one of Deborah's Bible dogeared passages. Revelation 1:8, *"I am the Alpha and the Omega, who was and who is and who is to come."* He did not know why she had highlighted the verse, but it obviously meant something to her, it carried deep meaning.

Without any attempt at haggling, he paid the price for both items and left the store.

Aaron completed his delayed illegal right turn, and he found La Cabaña not 10 minutes later. It wasn't impressive, but he never let outward appearance affect his judgment. Some of the most unassuming places had the best tasting food. The parking lot was half full; decent traffic for the tail end of a lunch crowd. It had ample space and was easy to get around. He could see into a lobby area and part of dining area that looked rather spacious. *So far so good.* He stopped the car and turned on his GPS to record the correct route back to the office.

Luckily for Aaron, he had made the trip to Davies Deli a few dozen times. He knew all the nuances of which turns to take when congestion popped up. He left the paper at 4:40 and was walking up the steps at 4:55—a new record.

The place was much quieter than earlier. The dining area had one or two customers; one was Clarence. He was receiving a refill of coffee and talking with Michael, who looked like a giant compared to the feeble man. Aaron overheard their conversation as he walked past to his seat.

"Son, do you know if the Davies' plan to be open on Thursday?"

"No, sir. We will be closed for Thanksgiving," Michael said, escorting him out as Deborah had done every day before.

"Oh, okay," Clarence said with obvious disappointment in his voice. "I just come here every day. I just don't know where I will be going."

"There are places around that will be open. I can ask for you. Maybe Mr. or Mrs. Davies will know." Michael locked the doors and headed back to Clarence's table to begin bussing.

Aaron was suddenly reminded of his conversation with Deborah about Mom and Pop wanting to do just that—to open their doors to those with nowhere to go. They saw the need of those like Clarence and quite frankly of those like himself. But they were unable to afford it. An idea hit him, and he pulled Michael aside before he went back to Mom and Pop.

After a lengthy discussion, they shook hands, went to the back room and called Mom and Pop over. They all sat in the break area. Aaron laid out an idea for them to consider.

"Last week I was talking with Deborah about the different restaurants I was visiting that will offer meals for Thanksgiving. And she had mentioned to me that the three of you had always wanted to do something like that."

"Yes," Mom said. "We have many people ask us every year if we will be open; many of our regulars. And we have considered it. But with so many shelters out there, we would feel guilty charging for a meal."

"And we can't afford to give away food, no matter how worthy the cause. It's just not possible," Pop added.

"What if I told you that there may be a way to do both?"

"What? How?" Pop asked.

"You have wanted to be able to give back to the community who has always given to you. Deborah has said you want to go beyond that to provide for the less fortunate, like Clarence. I know he has never paid for a sandwich, that is why Deborah escorts him out, and why Michael does it now. You care. What if you could provide that for everyone that walked through your door on Thanksgiving Day? Would you be up for opening your doors?"

"Yes, of course," said Mom. "But we would need more than Erica and Michael, here. But what about Deborah? We need to be with her and—"

Aaron interrupted, "Mom, where would Deborah want you on Thanksgiving Day? Sitting at the foot of her bed, throwing a pity party waiting for a test hours away, or out here doing the thing that you love? Think about it. Would you honor her more here or there?"

She was silent a moment. He feared he offended her by interrupting and his tone. "Forgive me," he said. "I did not mean to cut you off so abruptly."

"You are right to, son. No need to apologize. Our DeeDee would want us to do this," she said, patting Pop's hand.

"But we still don't understand how?" Pop said.

Michael stepped in. "I think this is where I come in. Aaron just asked me about the school sponsorship programs. He remembered that when he attended, that school had money that funded extracurricular activities for volunteer work. This is especially true around the holiday seasons like Christmas and Thanksgiving. They sponsor soup kitchens and provide them with food or the funds to purchase the food to feed a certain amount of people.

"These funds often go unused because they are unadvertised. I am sure that many are available, even this late. I can make a couple of inquiries. My uncle is on the coaching staff and can get me a quick answer."

"Well, we have the food, what about the staffing issue?"

Michael laughed. "That too is my department. Many of the guys on the wrestling team are local, and the volunteer program helps earn credits toward graduation. I can have at least six of them front and center here on Thursday morning, easy."

Mom and Pop looked at each other. A spark of hope ignited between the two of them.

"What do you think, Poppa?"

He furrowed his brows, looked at Aaron, then at Michael. "We would need to act quickly, however, since we are on a tight schedule. We would need to contact your supplier immediately, or the school may know of other means of getting food quicker if need be." Pop smiled, "Alright, let's do it."

Deborah knew she would have some explaining to do if her doctors found out she was eating a meatloaf sandwich, but she was tired of the petrified food they were dishing her. One meal wouldn't hurt anyhow. She listened intently as Aaron gave her every detail of Mom and Pop's Thanksgiving Day endeavor. She was genuinely excited for them. They had always talked about it. It was amazing to her that the inspiration behind it was the very one who helped make it possible.

"I wish I could be there," she said.

"I know. So do they. They were almost ready not to do it because you couldn't be there."

"Oh no, you tell them—" she said.

Aaron cut her off with a laugh, "Relax, I did. I told them that you would want them to. To be honest, I was rather firm about it. I hope I didn't offend your mom."

"You snapped at Mom?"

Aaron's face turned red. "I may have," he held up his fingers, "just a little."

"What did she do?"

"She said that I was right."

Deborah nodded. Mom was the type to admit when she needed chastisement. She was willing to take medicine given to her. He must have said something right. She wouldn't say it to his face, but he scored some major points with his parents today.

"So, the new guy is working out well then, I suppose?" she asked.

"For such a big guy, he moves as graceful as a swan. It is quite a sight."

"And he is a wrestler?"

"Yes."

"Hmm. I missed that on his application. I saw the two years of experience and the college student, though."

"But it worked out to your parent's benefit. Again, God works all things out for the good of those who love Him. Think about it. If you hadn't found him, Pop would not have hired him. Then he would not have been in the restaurant that day to be available to help out with the need presented. God worked it out even before we thought about it. He was working in the little things like a job application to help feed the possible hundreds that will walk into your parent's deli come Thanksgiving."

Deborah smiled. She was still trying to grasp the whole concept of the little things, but there was no denying that it was a domino effect: one thing was leading to another, and that led to another, that ultimately led to another. For the last several years she had been convinced that life was a series of coincidences, and that she controlled her destiny. Now she knew coincidence was the explanation people gave to situations when they didn't want to give credit to God. She knew God was out there, but the little things were still hard for her to believe to be something He would care about, but she was learning.

"So, what happens next?"

"Michael called his uncle, and it seems there is funding, but how much is not fully known. That will be determined in the morning. Then Pop will call the distributor in the morning and get what is needed—"

"I can make that call," Deborah said. "I think I could do a better job of getting a response. I can be a bit firmer than he could."

"I don't doubt that, but do you think you are up to it?"

"I need to do something. I'm just lying here. I feel helpless, plus this is my dream too. I would love to be part of it, and if my head-strong demeanor can get us anywhere, this will be it." She smiled.

Aaron laughed. "Yes, ma'am. I will let Pop know and tell Michael to call you with the donation info."

"Is there anything else I can do?" she asked, feeling a bit of life being given some responsibility.

"Relax and get rest. Read your Bible and focus on getting better." Aaron said.

"I do plenty of that." Deborah sat back a bit deflated.

"So, you are still reading?"

"Mmmhmm," Deborah said. She had, but there were times when it was difficult. Talks of prayers and blessings that were meant to encourage seemed to give her some doubt, given her current condition. She knew God was there, but Deborah could not understand why she was going through all of this. Was it punishment for denying Him all those years?

"What's wrong?" Aaron asked. He must have sensed her struggle. "And don't say *nothing*. We are both above those childish games."

"I think God is mad at me," she said. It was the basic summary of how she felt.

"How so?"

"You already know from Mom and Pop that lately I have

been rather blunt in my feelings about God. Even to the point where I have told them that I didn't believe He existed. I am just wondering if this illness is a result of God punishing me for denying Him."

"I am sure that God does allow illnesses into our lives as a means of grabbing our attention, but I don't believe He uses sickness as a form of punishment. I can't say why you are going through this illness. But God has a plan even when we don't see it," Aaron empathized.

"I guess I know that. I have always known that. But it's just hard to understand, if that makes sense," she said still battling the voices of disbelief in her head. The voice told her all of this was her fault. It shamed her for putting God in a box and packing Him away like mementos from her past.

"God had a plan when He created the world. He had a plan when Adam and Eve sinned, and He had a plan when the men and women in history completely fouled up their lives. And you know something, you are not alone. You are forgetting something, or should I say someone."

"Who?"

"Who was the biggest denier of them all?"

Deborah had to really think. She knew about Adam and Eve giving in to sin, and that the Bible was loaded with story after story of people doing whatever they wanted to do instead of following God. They would screw things up, then get right with Him and end up doing the very thing that God had planned for them to do in the first place. She knew the story of Jonah, who refused to do something God sent him to do and ended up inside a whale. He repented and went on to do what God sent him to do. That was all Old Testament.

In the New Testament, there was Paul who had mistreated and even was behind the killing of those who believed in Jesus. But he was turned around by God himself, and he became one of the most famous of missionaries to the world. But the biggest denier? The one who takes the cake, Deborah thought, that would have to go to, "Peter," she said.

"Exactly. He flat out denied Jesus. *And* he was with him, walked beside him, saw him, talked to him, slept beside him, saw him perform miracles, witnessed him glorified, and still, he was able to deny him. And look at what happened with Peter? He became what Jesus called 'the Rock' that the church would be built on. If it were not for Peter's boldness, none of us would have known about Jesus today.

"So, don't go thinking for a moment that your denying him would put you under any form of punishment. I won't say you aren't in the belly of the whale, but even then, God had a plan. If He had a plan then, He has a plan now. If He was God then, He is God now. And because of that, He will be God tomorrow.

"Just like one of your favorite verses says," he said and nodded to her Bible on the nightstand.

She realized he must have peeked. She knew the one he was referring to. Revelation 1:8—"*I am the Alpha and the Omega," says the Lord God, "who is and who was and who is to come, the Almighty.*"

"So, what does that mean to you, and how does it apply to your situation?"

She thought about it for a moment. While she still struggled with the why, it didn't seem to matter as much. She understood the point Aaron was trying to make. She understood what Carter had been telling her. She understood the message God had been trying to get her to see. She took a breath and answered.

"It means that He is both the beginning and end of all things. And it means that He is everything in between. It also means that He has always been there. Even when I did not believe in Him, He was there. Our belief in Him does not change the fact that He believes in us." She looked up at Aaron, but she could tell he was looking for something more.

"And for you personally?" He raised his eyebrows.

She looked down at herself in the multi-colored scribbled gown and crumpled bedsheet. She looked around the room, at the monitors that were reading her heart rate and pressure.

"If God was God before my illness, then He is God during my illness. And if He is God during my illness, then He will be God after my illness."

Aaron reached into his pocket and pulled out a gift-wrapped box. It was red with a silver bow. He placed it on her lap and sat back down. She sat half-frozen, not sure what to do.

"I didn't intend on wrapping it, but I had found something for your mom and had some wrap left over. Figured it would add to the suspense. The moment I saw this, I knew I had to get it for you."

She looked at him, then at the package, then back at him. He gave her a go-ahead nod. She carefully pulled on the string and meticulously unwrapped the paper. Aaron laughed at how delicately she was handling the gift. She gave him an *oh-hush* look—it was how she did things. Especially with how exquisite it seemed to be. Under the wrapping was a silver, plush box, identical to the ribbon.

The world stopped for a moment; she was almost afraid

to open the box. She knew it wasn't a ring, so that wasn't her fear. It was the nervousness of not knowing what to expect. Which was in itself an odd thing, because all she had to do was open the box to dispel that feeling. She just stared at it suspended in this feeling.

It must have been making Aaron uncomfortable because he eventually said, "Well?"

"Okay," Deborah said. Her heart was thumping as she slowly opened the case. It stopped when she saw the white gold pendant on a chain. "Where did you find this?"

"In a store that I happened upon," he said in a way that sounded mischievous.

"There is more to that, isn't there?" she laughed.

"Yes. One day I will tell you about it," he said and left it at that.

"Help me put it on," she said, sitting up pulling her ponytail above her head.

Aaron clasped the necklace, gave her a kiss behind the ear, and whispered, "I love you." He sat on the edge of the bed and held her hand.

With her other hand, she caressed the pendant, reminded that God will always be there for her. A constant reminder that The Beginning and The End was close to her heart.

Chapter
THIRTY-ONE

No, that is not what I asked for. I will say this one more time, Mr. Reynolds, I need enough to cover 200 plates, no less… Yes, by Wednesday evening… I will leave the sides up to you. Whatever is readily available, I understand the lateness of our request; however, the dressing is a must. Outside of that, shake the tree, and whatever falls out will be acceptable." Deborah was fiddling her new trinket while negotiating the Thanksgiving deal of a lifetime. And she was doing an excellent job at it. Aaron was amazed at her technique. While negotiating was not her cup of tea, stating her case most definitely was right up her alley.

She finalized the information on a notepad that had been sitting by the water pitcher. She thanked Mr. Reynolds after confirming a 'no later than' 8:00 PM delivery for Wednesday evening. She hung up, and Pop smiled at her.

"That's my girl."

Deborah explained that back in the day that Pop could throw his weight around with the best of them. He was never below stating his case and getting what he wanted. It wasn't that he was bossy or a bully; he was firm in getting what he expected out of people, which was usually the job that *they*

253

were expected to do. She had been paying attention. Now that he was getting older, the next generation was starting to get the best of him, and now his daughter was handling the relations part of the business.

And handling it quite well, Aaron mused.

"Well, it is all set. Food is on its way," she said, handing the notepad to Mom.

Pop slapped his hands together and rubbed them. Aaron hadn't known him long, but he would guess from the look on Deborah and Mom's faces that it was the happiest he had been in a long time.

"And Michael said that he has spoken to half of the team, and they are all for it. So, we have six yeses so far, he should know about the others by the morning, and will let you know by lunchtime."

"Oh, DeeDee, this is so exciting. We have talked about this for such a long time." Pop looked over at Aaron and then back to Deborah. "Did you tell him?"

"Not in so many words." She turned to Aaron. "You already know of their desire to do this, but what you don't know is that it was your review piece that got Pop to open up about his desire to do something for the community. The first year his comments were simply in passing, then last year it was a bit more passionate, but discouraging because he knew that it was impossible to do financially."

Aaron looked to the ground with disappointment. "If only I had thought of this a week ago, I could have gotten it in the paper this week. I have already submitted this year's Thanksgiving piece."

"And that is okay," Deborah said. "It is His timing. The final piece of the puzzle had yet to be put into place—Michael.

Without him, that memory may not have been triggered, those resources would not have been accessible, and the volunteer staff would not have been available."

Aaron nodded. She was learning, or remembering, quickly. He felt slightly embarrassed by letting his thinking become like that of Ethan Chadwick. His name would not make the people come. God would. It was the same reason God allowed Abraham to raise his knife to Isaac, the same reason Lazarus remained in the grave for three days, and the same reason the disciples rode through a storm as Jesus slept; it was to push each to the point where the only answer was a miracle provided by the Lord. A goat in the thicket, a voice in the darkness, a hushed word for silence. All occurred not in man's timing, but in God's timing.

"You're right," he said. "If I preach it, I have to live it. Thank you for the reminder." He looked at her and winked.

Then he turned to Mom and Pop. "Well, I better get going. I will let you have some time together. As for me, I have a lunch date with a BBLT tomorrow and need my rest." He kissed Deborah on the forehead and whispered "I love you" in her ear.

"Good night Mom. Good night Pop," he said on his way out the door.

"So, Michael is working out for you, I hear," Deborah said with a hint of *I told you so* in her tone.

Pop did not pick up on it, which was understandable. Pop was never sarcastically minded. "He is fabulous. I would not say he is as good as Josh, but he is pretty darn close, right Momma?"

"Dee, he did not need much training. He understood the shorthand we use and the ones we have just between us, he picked up fast. He must have some sort of genius memory, because I never had to tell him twice."

Deborah had not meant to open the floodgates, and hearing them praise Michael made her feel somewhat intimidated. She had been in the family business her whole life, and even now, she needed the occasional reminder of some of the shorthand Mom and Pop used behind the counter. But she was happy for them. It was what she wanted all along, someone to fill in the gap that Josh left behind so she could get back to her job at the agency. Then why did she feel like she was missing out?

"What is that?" Mom asked.

She had not realized it, but she had been absent-mindedly stroking the pendant around her neck. She blushed. "It was a gift from Aaron. It is an Alpha Omega pendant. From the book of Revelation."

"It's lovely," Mom said, taking it her fingers. "He must be in a gift-giving mood. I got something as well."

"He said something about that."

"You know those old-time booth jukeboxes? Straight from the 60s, and it's beautiful."

Deborah laughed. It was just like Aaron, always thinking of others, making the ladies in his life smile.

"I'm glad he found it for you, Mom." She pressed the button for the nurse. "Nature calls. I wish I could do all of this myself. I'm not a child. It seems ridiculous that I need to have my hand held each time I need to tinkle."

"Yes, Miss Davies?" the nurse said.

"Nature calling," said Deborah.

"Okay, let's get you disconnected." Velcro armband, finger monitor, side rail. Same routine as always. Deborah got up, holding onto the nurse's arm, feeling a bit silly. "Are you sure I can't do this by myself?"

"I'm sorry, Miss Davies. Doctor's orders. If anything should happen—"

"—you could get into trouble, and I could hurt myself. My apologies. Please, lead on my lady."

The nurse led her in, and after Deborah sat, and the nurse was satisfied she gave her some privacy. She did her business, but something wasn't right. The ringing had suddenly stopped, and the swollen feeling tightened around to the back of her neck. As the world went black, and before she got out the word, *Nurse*, she realized why the buddy system was so important to them.

Aaron tossed his keys on the table, making the familiar echo in the single room. He poured a glass of water and sat in his recliner. The end of a long day. A long but eventful day. He was thankful for every moment. From the first fresh bear claw to the final kiss goodbye, and everything in between. He could not picture a better orchestrated day. "Thank you, Lord. You sure do know what you are doing. I am always amazed at how you can make many little things through our day add up to the big picture showing that you are there among us. I just can't see how people miss it and doubt who you are."

He did not realize how tired he was until he laid back. The fifth gear he had been driving in all day suddenly slipped into neutral, and he cruised to a stop. His eyes grew heavy, and he was asleep before he knew it.

He must have been dreaming of working in a clock factory because moments later, he was surrounded by bells and whistles. Stirring around trying to find the source he ran down hallways and corridors then suddenly tripped. As he fell, he woke up, realizing it was his cell phone ringing. The grogginess that only comes with being wakened in a dream state overwhelmed him, and he fumbled with the answer key.

"Hello," he managed to mumble.

He was greeted with panicked sobbing. He could barely make out what the voice was saying. It was Mom. Her crying got worse, and he heard Pop in the background and then other clicks and muffled sounds. Pop comes on the line, "Aaron, you better get down here. Deborah had another spell. They are talking about emergency surgery, and it doesn't look good. The neurosurgeon is less than an hour away. You need to get here before they take her back."

"I'm on my way," Aaron said, and without another word he hung up.

He had not bothered to undress earlier; that was to his benefit. He threw on his shoes and was out the door.

"Miss Davies? Deborah, can you hear me?" the nurse said.

"What did you give her?" Pop asked.

"Something to help with the swelling. The surgeon is on his way, Dr. Krauss gave orders to administer this to see if she would regain consciousness," she said. Then back to Deborah. "Deborah, can you hear me?"

Deborah's eyes began to flutter, and her breathing deepened. Her eyes slowly opened but were vacant. "I can't see," she whispered. "What happened?"

"You had another episode, Miss Davies. We called Dr. Krauss, and she informed Dr. Thompson. He is on his way for emergency surgery."

"But the MRI is schedule—" Deborah tried to say.

"None of that matters now, Miss Davies," the nurse says.

"Why can't I see?" Deborah said, starting to panic.

"Relax, Deborah. You are just going to aggravate your symptoms. Please, try and stay calm, or we will have to sedate you."

Deborah took a breath. "Mom, Pop, are you here?"

"Yes, DeeDee, we are here," said Pop. The nurse moved over, and he moved in and took her hand.

"Do you remember anything?" the nurse asked.

Deborah thought hard, but it hurt. Her whole head hurt. It was quiet though, and that triggered her memory, "I remember going to the bathroom, and when I had finished I noticed the ringing in my ears had stopped, but my head felt thick, like a balloon being blown up. Then I guess I passed out."

"I will note that, it will help the doctor," the nurse said. Deborah could hear her tapping on her tablet. "I will let you know when Dr. Thompson arrives. Emily is getting you something for the pain. She just needed approval from Dr. Krauss since we already administered an anti-inflammatory."

Deborah heard the door open and the nurse's shoes squeak on the linoleum. Emily, she assumed, spoke nurse code to Sarah, and Deborah felt warmth enter her body and a taste in the back of her throat. It was then she realized she had been fitted with an IV. Just as quickly, the pain in her head began to subside, but the dull ringing made a slow return. She informed the nurses; they took note of it.

"Okay, Miss Davies, that is all we can do for now. Dr. Thompson will be here shortly, and he will speak with you on where we go from here. We will be outside if you need us." Deborah could tell they left by the squeak of leather on linoleum fading.

"How are you feeling, Dee?" Mom asked softly.

"I don't know, Mom," Deborah said. "I'm scared. I have never not been able to see before. It is an odd feeling. I can tell my eyes are open, but I just don't see anything."

"Just keep them closed, Deborah. Pretend you are resting. It will calm you," suggested Pop. Deborah did so.

Then it occurred to her: *Aaron*. She sat up. "Aaron. I need to call him."

"Deborah, lie down," Pop said, easing her back into the bed. "We called him already. He is on his way."

"Thank you." Deborah rested her eyes again. "I'm glad you are here. I don't know what I would do without the two of you. I have taken all you have shown me for granted. I never knew what I had until I saw what Aaron didn't have. He never had a loving family growing up. I did, and I never once showed you appreciation for it. I'm sorry. I love both of you. Thank you for never giving up on me. And once this is all over, yes, I will go with you to church on Sunday. I should have gone all along. Forgive me."

"Oh, DeeDee," Pop said, "We forgive you. We always have. You are our little girl. We will always chase after you, no matter where you may wander off to. It is our job, right, Momma?"

"Right, Poppa. Whether it's under the counter of the kitchen, in the halls of a college campus, or in the offices of an insurance company, we will keep our eyes and prayers on you. I am excited to introduce you to our pastor. He has been looking forward to meeting you."

"Now hush. Close your eyes and rest. I don't want you to

overwork yourself. Just relax, we are here and are not going anywhere," Pop said. He had one of her hands, and Mom had the other. They rested there in silence, their prayers answered, their daughter had returned to them, and to the Lord.

B ut you have to wait," Deborah heard her Mom say to the doctor. "He will be here any second."

Deborah was now under the care of two different orderlies. She did not recognize their voices.

"Ma'am, we need to take your daughter now," the closer orderly said. "Dr. Thompson's orders. We need to get her up to the O.R. now."

"Momma, let them go. He will see her when she gets out of surgery," Pop said, taking her hand off of Deborah's arm.

"Mom, it's fine. Let them take me up. Tell the nurses where we are going and to send him up, they still need to prep me anyway."

Mom sighed, and Deborah heard her shuffle her feet back, the orderlies unlocked the bed.

"We can follow, yes?" Pop asked.

"Stay close. But you will have to wait in the waiting area upstairs. Once we get her prepped, you will be able to speak with her briefly before we sedate her and take her into the surgical room," the other voice said.

Without another word, Deborah sensed movement out of the room, through a hall, and into an elevator.

"Mom? Pop? You with me?" she asked.

"Yes, DeeDee, we are here," Pop said.

"Miss Davies, we're taking you up to the neurology wing where Dr. Thompson will go over the procedure with you. How are you feeling right now?" one of the voices asked.

"A bit disoriented," Deborah said weakly. "I can hear the ringing again, but it is faint. My head is still stopped up too."

"Okay," said one of the orderlies. Deborah could hear the tapping of the tablet and again thought of Dr. Thompson getting the instant update and planning his course of action, ready for her arrival. "When we exit the elevator, Mr. and Mrs. Davies, there is a waiting area just to the left. We will come and get you as soon as we have her prepped."

The elevator *binged*, and she was moving around a couple of turns, then through a door where it was much cooler. She found it odd how much the body made up for the loss of one sense. She would never have picked up a temperature difference like this. Or maybe since touch was the most active right now, it was the most sensitive. Either way, she began to shiver. One of the orderlies noticed. "Do you need a blanket, Miss Davies?"

"Yes, please," Deborah said with her jaw nearly chattering.

Moments later, she was covered by a warm blanket. It must have been in some type of warming cabinet. Within a minute, she was comfortable again. But she was feeling weaker and the pressure was building again. She informed the orderlies asking them if they could do something about it. They conferred with her chart, looked at the time and called in the nurse. She administered another dose of anti-inflammatory. Within 10 minutes the ringing had begun again, but the pressure was more manageable.

"Thank you. Where is the doctor?"

"He is reviewing your last MRI with Dr. Krauss. He will be in shortly. There will be another nurse in shortly to shave your head."

"Shave? My head?" Deborah said, not having really considered the part of brain surgery where they have to prepare the area that they have to cut open.

"Not the whole head. Just the lower half of the base of the skull to just above the ear on the left side."

"Oh, okay," she said. "Has anyone heard from my fiancé? Is he here yet?"

"I will check with your parents," the nurse said, and Deborah heard her scrubs swish as she left the room.

"Deborah Davies!" Aaron demanded. "Where is she?" He had come to her room, but she was not there.

The unfamiliar nurse at the station looked up at him, head tilted, "Who? I don't know." She began to look through a stack of charts on the desk in front of her.

"Please, I need to know where she is. I got a call that she was about to go into—"

"Mr. Stephenson," a familiar voice called out. It was Deborah's regular evening nurse. "She was just sent up for emergency surgery. She had another episode. She is on the seventh floor. You better get up there fast. Dr. Thompson was going to get her in the O.R. as soon as she arrived."

"Thank you," Aaron said and headed for the elevator. He pushed the button and waited while his heart roamed every dark thought. Worry and fear flooded his mind. He was taken back to the panic of finding Deborah on the floor and the paralyzing terror of not knowing what to do. He pushed the button again, even though he knew it would do nothing in getting the car to his floor faster. Through the hurried slow motion of panicked time, the elevator eventually arrived and took him to the seventh floor, where he met Mom and Pop.

"Where is she?" Aaron asked.

"Thank God you made it," Mom said. She stood and met him with a hug. "They just took her back. That way, if you hurry, maybe—"

Aaron ran in the direction that Mom had pointed. He turned the corner where the sign said Operating Rooms. Then through a door with two big red 'X's' on them. He saw two gray scrubbed orderlies wheeling a bed down the hallway.

"Hey," he called to them. "Is that Deborah Davies?"

They stopped.

"Aaron," a soft well-known voice called back. He ran to it.

"Sorry, sir. You will have to go back to the waiting area. This area is restricted. She is going into surgery, STAT."

"Yes, I know. And I will. I just want to speak with her just a second."

They both looked at each other. The taller on shrugged, and they both take a step back.

"Thank you," said Aaron. He took her hand and kissed it.

"You're late," she said.

"Yes, I know. Harden was on fire, couldn't turn the game off."

Deborah laughed dryly, then cringed.

"Sorry," he said. "Does it hurt much?"

"Yes. No. I don't know. I want this to be over. I just want to get on with my life. With our life, seeing that we are engaged and all."

They both laughed. She cringed. Aaron teared up.

"I wish I could help you."

"You can. Pray for me while I am in surgery. Think happy thoughts. Think of all the little things that have made the time we have spent together special. I am so thankful for you, Aaron. I am grateful that I can go into this with a clear mind and heart. I know that no matter what, God will work in this. If it weren't for you, Carter, and all of God's little reminders, I would be bitter, discouraged, and lost."

"Carter? The homeless man?" Aaron asked, a little puzzled, thinking of the last encounter with the vagabond.

"Yes, I will have to tell you all about him later. There is so much to tell. He's an angel, you know."

"An ang—"

"Sir," the orderly said over his shoulder. "We need to go now. We have already given you more than enough time. The doctor is waiting. We can't wait any longer. She needs to get into surgery now."

"Okay," Aaron said.

The orderlies got on either side of her and started to take her away.

"Aaron!" Deborah called out.

Aaron stopped the bed and leaned in to kiss her.

"I love you," she said.

Aaron started to chuckle.

"I tell you I love you, and you laugh?"

"You do the math," he said. "Between the two of us, that's our thirteenth I love you."

"Our lucky number," Deborah said.

"Well, not to screw up the math, but I love you too, DeeDee," Aaron said without thought.

Neither he nor she said anything in correction. Maybe because to both of them, at that moment, it just felt right.

Aaron breathed a sigh of relief. He was grateful he got to see her. He wanted her to know that he was there. Although she would be out like a light, somehow, he felt she would rest much easier knowing he was there. And he would relax knowing that she was resting much easier because she knew that he was there.

Aaron returned to the waiting area where Mom and Pop were. She was sitting, twisting the straps of her purse, and Pop was wearing the carpet thin beneath his feet. He explained that he was able to see her just before they took her back. They looked just as relieved as he felt.

"So, what happened?"

Mom explained how it was much different than the time in his apartment. She told him about the doctors being able to use medication to reduce the swelling so they could get her ready to do surgery. This helped her regain consciousness. But the symptoms had grown worse, and the doctors felt immediate surgery was needed. "So here we are," she concluded.

The three of them sat there for what seemed like an eternity. The clock would move 10 minutes forward only to move five minutes backward. The clock itself seem to fight an internal battle. Aaron and Pop took turns pacing and asking questions and receiving no updates. Two hours turned into three. After the fourth hour, the nurse said that Deborah was still in surgery, and they had no update on her condition, but that the doctor was still at work.

Two hours later, Mom was on her third box of tissue, and Pop on his second roll of antacid.

"You know Momma. This reminds me of when DeeDee

had her appendix out when she was 12. You remember that?"

"Remember? How could I forget? You were a nervous wreck."

"Me? You were the one who had to get a sedative from the doctor."

Mom looked at the floor and gave a small grin. "Yes, I suppose you got me there. That was a long time ago."

"Yes. Yes, it was. Remember what the doctor told us?"

"That if we had waited another hour, she could have died," Mom said matter-of-factly.

"This is no different, no?"

"I don't know, Poppa. That 12-year-old girl is a grown woman now. You can't go thinking you should have made her go see a doctor sooner."

"But I should have insisted," Pop said.

"It would have only pushed her away, and we would have seen less of her. We were pushing her enough about church, Poppa."

"She's right, Pop," Aaron said. "One of the reasons me and my dad don't speak is because of how much he thought he could control my life. I am not saying that is how you would be with Deborah, but it could come off that way. You did what you thought was best at the time. And that is all you can do. You are an amazing father. I should be so blessed to have you in that position in my life. Deborah is a lucky woman. So, listen to Mom when she says that Deborah can make her own decisions. To love is your job. Good or bad. And you do a pretty good job of that."

Pop seemed to accept that with a nod and a *Hmmph* grunt. He stopped his pacing and sat, leaned back, and closed his eyes. *Praying*, Aaron supposed. He had done that quite a bit the last several hours. Thinking back to what Deborah had said about how she had a clear heart and mind going into this. He prayed for her, the doctors, the staff, the hospital, and everything in between. He also felt the need to pray for the unthinkable, the acceptance if things took a turn for the worse.

The thoughts turned his stomach, but he knew he needed to pray through such things so his heart would be prepared if such things came to pass. He knew that only prayer could bring peace to any storm. And if this storm should drift his way, he knew that his boat was not the only boat on the water. He looked over at Mom and Pop, who were seated together now, hand in hand. He prayed for the strength that they exemplified together.

Aaron leaned his back just as they had theirs and closed his eyes. All three of them waiting for answers. Answers that were about to be given with a soft but authoritative voice.

"Mr. and Mrs. Davies." Everyone looked up. A man in his late 30s stood before them in dark blue scrubs, a face mask dangling around his neck, sweat-soaked through his cap and the scrub top around his neck. He did not have the smile of good news on his face. "I'm sorry. We lost her. There was nothing we could do."

No one said a word. It was like the doctor had spoken a foreign language, and they were waiting for the translation. Mom was the first to react, bursting into tears. Pop stood, his face turning pale, his eyes burning red. Aaron's reaction was at first shock. He did not know how to react. His stomach was tight, he felt dizzy, then like he was about to be sick, but he remembered his prayer. He needed to remain strong. He took a deep breath and spoke to God again, asking for help to keep it together for the sake of Mom and Pop.

God answered his prayer—mostly. He recalled their last

moment together, expressing their love. And he bawled like a baby. But he cried in the arms of the family of the ones who loved Deborah the most. Then he realized that mourning together is a source of strength. Strength is not about having the power not to let emotion overcome you. It's about allowing the emotions to strengthen you through shared release. Together, they were growing stronger.

Dr. Thompson took them into a private area and explained what had happened. Apparently, even though the tumor was non-cancerous, it had done extensive damage. It had grown into a generally inoperable area. The previous MRI had not revealed the reality of the situation or the severity. He went on to give details about how sensitive the brain stem is, and that once anything invades certain spaces, it is nearly impossible to separate it. The scan just simply did not pick up on the tumor's depth. There was nothing that could be done. Even if she had not experienced the latest episode and had the MRI as scheduled, the same prognosis would have been reached.

Aaron was comforted that he got a decent goodbye; he was not so sure Mom and Pop had. He watched them as the doctor tried to simplify the complicated medical jargon as to why their young daughter was no longer going to eat another Thanksgiving meal with them. Strong as they were, this was as devastating news as a parent could get. He couldn't imagine much that could be worse.

Now, instead of turkey and stuffing, they would be planning a funeral and eulogy. And Thanksgiving would be, at least for quite some time, a painful memory. Just as the Fourth of July did not go by without the pain of his parent's separation, even though it had been over 14 years, it still pained him to think about it. Maybe that was part of the reason he enjoyed being around the Davies so much, why he spent so much time in the diner, why he fell in love with their daughter.

Mom asked Dr. Thompson if they could see her. He said that it would take some time, but once they cleaned her up, she would be prepared for them to see before they took her body to be prepared for the family's final wishes. They would have to discuss that soon as well. It made Mom break down again. The doctor apologized and excused himself pointing them back to the waiting area.

Aaron stood for a moment, feeling like he was watching a movie of someone else's tragedy; wanting to change the channel or hoping for a commercial break, but knowing he would get neither luxury. He went and sat beside Mom. He placed his hand on her shoulder. She grasped his hand and held it tightly. "Thank you for coming back."

"Where else would I be?" Aaron said. She grabbed tighter and cried harder.

"You got to say good-bye?" Pop asked.

Aaron was nervous at how to respond. He knew honesty was always best.

"Yes, sir. I did. Not those exact words. But I would call it closure."

He felt a tinge of guilt in the last part of his statement.

"Good. I'm glad," Pop said. That was all he said.

They sat in silence, each with their own thoughts, their own points of reflection of the life of the loved one that was lost. The only disturbance was the occasional *ping* of the elevator or sniffle into a tissue. Time was lost, but it didn't matter much at that moment—their hearts were empty within their shared grief. Then a nurse came into the waiting area and escorted them into a room to say goodbye to Deborah Ann Davies.

When Aaron woke up, he had no clue what day it was. The sun was either rising or setting. The disorientation made him nauseous, or was it the emptiness once again reminding him of recent events? Either way, he just wanted to close his eyes and go back to sleep. Not much mattered at that moment. But his phone, buzzing from the other room, claimed a level of urgency that made him get up to answer its call.

"Hello?"

"Aaron, my boy," Pop said with unexpected pep in his voice. "Are you working today?"

This statement must mean its morning. He had not even considered work. "Um, I am just waking up. I am not sure at this point. If today is Wednesday, then the publication came out yesterday, so I need to get ready for this week's visits, but that can wait. Why what's up?"

"Big plans, Aaron. Big plans, for my DeeDee," he said with jubilant cheer. "How soon can you be here? The trucks are already arriving?"

Trucks? Aaron looked at the clock, calculated a relaxing shower, felt his face, and added a shave, "An hour?"

"Well, make it quick. We have lots of work to do before tomorrow!"

"Why? What's tomorrow?" Aaron asked.

"It's Thanksgiving, silly boy?" Pop said. "Now, get over here and help Momma and me."

Aaron could hear Mom calling out to him in the same tone.

He was confused, but their energy was infectious. He was in and out of the shower in record time and on the road even quicker. He stopped only for a cup of coffee and to pick up a copy of the *Houston Gazette*. The shop owner wished him a Happy Thanksgiving, and Aaron echoed the sentiment. He also informed the shopkeeper to keep his ear out. There may be something special going on in the neighborhood.

Aaron pulled into the deli's lot as one truck was pulling out and another was backing in. "Wow, Deb. You really know… *knew* what you were doing. Awesome job, babe. I'm proud of you," Aaron said.

He met Mom and Pop on the back dock as the beeping truck released his air brakes. "What has gotten here so far?"

"Vegetables and the ingredients for the dressing. This must be the turkeys."

"That is an awfully big truck for turkey for 200 people."

"Maybe he has more than one delivery, no?" Mom said.

The driver heard them as he approached them, "Yes, ma'am. I have about 50 of these deliveries today. The sooner I drop off these turkeys, the sooner I get home." Then he gave a hearty belly laugh. "Happy Thanksgiving. I have 10 25-pounders for you. Now, the best thing with these puppies is that the location they came from has taken all the precautions with them in getting them prepped for the customer. The temp in my cooler here is 34 degrees, but rest assured, they are thawed and oven ready."

He stacked five crates on a hand truck and wheeled it in through the back entrance. He dropped it into the cooler, obtained signatures, and left with a tip of his hat.

"We better get started, or we'll be late," Mom said, looking at the clock. "It's gonna be a long day and night." She walked away with a joyous smile and almost a skip in her step.

"Pop, what is going on?" Aaron asked, nearly dumbfounded.

"It is really simple, Aaron," Pop said. "There are two things we can do over our DeeDee's passing. We can go home and cry our eyes out, blame God for taking our little girl, and shut the world out. *Or,* we can wipe our eyes, put on a clean apron, and rejoice in the life she had. And the best way we can do that, to shout that out to the world? To finish what she started. We are going to have this Thanksgiving Feast. In honor of our DeeDee.

"You said it yourself. Where would she want us on Thanksgiving Day? If she did not want us at the foot of her bed, she sure would not want us home mourning her. Same for you, boy. She would want us to cook. She would want you to write. What, I don't know. God has something for you. I know that much. You know it too; I can see it in your eyes. I have seen it every time I've seen you seated in my place. We have it handled here. Go. Go to wherever it is that gives you your inspiration, and write. Make my... make *your* DeeDee proud."

Aaron did as he was told. There was no response required. He headed to his jeep, pulled out of the parking lot, and headed down the street then slammed on his brakes. He sat there for a moment; engine idling, then came to a realization. He turned around and headed back to the deli. He pulled back into the parking lot, grabbed his bag into the crazy 60s-themed dining experience, and to his well-molded seat. He set his bag on the seat next to him, pulled out his laptop, and set himself up to write. *Where else could I go to where I would be more inspired than where it all began.*

By the time Aaron was halfway through his review of Davies Deli, the kitchen was a giant cacophony of noises. Chopping and mixing and loud burly voices of boys that were almost men challenging each other to celery chopping contests and who could go the longest mincing onion without tearing up. He could not help but laugh. Of course, Michael was trying to be the voice of reason, asking them to calm down, but he could also hear Pop telling him to let them live, reminding him that life must be lived every day, never missing an opportunity to enjoy it.

He looked around, forgetting that the restaurant was closed today in preparation for the grand adventure for tomorrow. Luckily none the tables were anchored to any of the walls, so they were easily moveable to enable additional seating. Somewhere along the line Michael had secured several folding tables and folding chairs. Erica and Miguel along with a couple of girls, probably from Erica's circle, maybe girlfriends of the master chefs in the kitchen, were setting those up.

Aaron penned a few more words. Mom brought him tea in a to-go cup. She swung around and gave him a hug and went to talk to Erica. He thought about the first moment in this chair, his first glimpse of that purple scrunchie, the first smile, and realized that this review would be more than just a review of the deli that fed an outskirt Houston suburb, or an establishment that would host a Thanksgiving Feast for souls like Clarence who had little. It would be a tribute to an amazing woman, daughter, and lover.

He looked over what he had just written. He highlighted the entire document and hit delete.

He began again:

"Davies Deli is not your normal sandwich shop. Not normal in that Mr. and Mrs. Davies use real bread instead of traditional premade submarine rolls. It is the polar opposite of what you see in the chain restaurants, but that is what makes Mom and Pop unique. To me? What makes, or made, this place extra special was Deborah Davies. Deborah was Mr. and Mrs. Davies daughter. She worked behind the counter, and the reason I had engaged faithful patronage of this amazing establishment…"

He wrote for the next two hours, fingers never leaving the keyboard, tears never leaving his eyes.

THIRTY-FOUR

Steam was pouring from every pot and container throughout the kitchen while oversized men in undersized aprons maneuvered around, stirring the one that was shaking or gurgling the most. Aaron stood in a corner in amusement. It indeed was a long day and night. He had managed to get three or four hours of sleep. Most of the crew did it in shifts using Mom and Pop's home, Aaron's apartment, and the closest student residence. They were now four hours away from service. Six of the turkeys were completely cooked, four were in the ovens. Two of the completed were carved and in rented warmers that Michael was able to get from a contact his parents had in cafeteria services. Another little blessing of God, Aaron reminded himself.

He stepped away from the pandemonium for a bit and hid in the back office where he would always see Deborah steal away. The air still carried the smell of her perfume. As Aaron sat at the desk, the chair gave a creak that he figured would be familiar to her. He looked over the room and tried to see what she would see from day to day; the cookbooks, the stacks of file folders, more cookbooks, and a pair of bright silver objects caught his eye. He followed their glow and saw they were a set of cookie cutters in the shape of crosses. He loved stories and would love to have known the story behind these. He reached out as if touching them would give him insight. A voice did speak, but it wasn't from the cutters.

"They belonged to my mother," Pop said. "Grandmom, Dee used to call her. This was her place before it was mine. She would bake cookies, and DeeDee would help her."

"These are the cutters?"

"You know about them?"

"Deborah told me about growing up and the stories her Grandmom would tell her about Jesus. One of the stories she told, she used cookie cutters as an illustration."

"Those are them," Pop said.

"May I?"

"Please," Pop said.

Aaron picked them up and gave them a thorough examination, as if they were going to transport him back 20 years. "These have been well kept. Your family takes pride in what they do."

"Thank you. It means a lot that someone notices. Not many do. We do, from time to time, take a short cut or two, like the baskets, for instance…"

Aaron laughed. "Yes, Dee told me about those too. But financially frugal is just as much benefit as taking pride in what you do. People couldn't care less about a crooked serving basket. A crooked cookie on the other hand… well, more would notice those things." Aaron said setting the cutters down gently as if handling a crystal vase.

"Are you ready?" Pop asked.

"As I will ever be? Are you sure you want me to do this?"

"As I will ever be," Pop replied.

"I had Nate, my boss, call someone he knows at the newspaper. They said they would try to get something out in the morning edition," Aaron said, partially to give Pop some assurance that people would come, partially to give himself the same hope.

Pop shrugged and puckered his lips as he was known for doing. "They come; they don't come. It's in God's hands. We do this for Him and our DeeDee." He patted Aaron on the shoulder and headed back into the kitchen. Aaron sat back in the chair.

A moment later, Erica stepped in with his bag, "Hey Aaron. Sorry, we were making final adjustments. I did not want anything to happen to this. Thought it would be safer in here."

"Thank you, Erica. I was about to go get this anyhow. Saved me a trip."

"Not a problem," she smiled and darted back out.

Aaron took out his computer, flipped it around to tablet mode, and read through what was now a speech. He had started out with a simple review, but it was no good without the reason behind his passion. And the reason behind his passion was nothing without the person that was within that passion. So, in a little over three hours, he would pour his heart and soul out to a room full of strangers who may not know or understand, but he knew God had a purpose behind it all. Maybe his speech would be someone else's little reminder of what God can do through people who are willing to be used, who are eager to listen, who are determined to be changed.

He sat in that chair where he knew that the woman he loved spent countless hours, struggling with who God was, and he prayed that he would be precise with his words. He envisioned Deborah somewhere, cheering him on, encouraging him to continue on. He needed to remember never to let pain, loss, or doubt get in the way of a relationship of the One who knew what was best for him. Even when he couldn't see it, God could. And even though Aaron didn't fully see why he lost Deborah so soon, he still trusted that God had a plan in it. And that God would reveal that plan in His time.

Aaron must have either lost track of time or dozed off because he was startled when Mom came in and informed him it was almost time.

The room was half full of faces unfamiliar to him, which was a good thing; the word had been spread about what Davies Deli was doing. He did not grab the paper, so he wasn't sure if Nate's buddy came through or not, and his periodical had already been printed. Aaron did see Clarence sitting in his usual area. He was surrounded by four men he was friendly with—could be folk he brought with him, could be others he met on the way—all sharing a common plight. *The holidays tend to erase some lines amongst demographics,* Aaron thought.

"Over here, Aaron," Michael called out from an area set up next to the register that was a bit higher. The young wrestler ran through what Pop wanted to happen. Pop was going to thank everyone for coming and give a brief summary of how the day came to be and why the meal was free. Then he would explain what happened to Deborah and how this meal will be taking place every year from now on in her honor.

"Then he will pass it onto you," Michael said. "At the end,

he asks that you pray over the food, then introduce the wrestling team, and we will begin serving."

"Got it," Aaron said.

"T-minus 30 minutes," Michael said, then disappeared.

Right on schedule, right on cue, Pop began. He had a strong speaking voice that did not falter or break, even when speaking of the loss of his daughter, although Mom did make use of the tissue box that was near her. There was applause with the thanks to those who made the meal possible, shared tears for the loss of a beloved woman even if she were just a name to some, and cheers that this was more than a one-time event, that Deborah's legacy would live on. Nervous that he would pale in comparison to what Pop just delivered, Aaron stood where Pop just did and felt the weight of his shoes.

"Good Afternoon. I am Aaron Stephenson. Some of you may know me as Food Columnist from the *Houston Gazette.* Others know me as Davies Deli regular who sits right over there," Aaron said, pointing to his seat. "I have only known the Davies for a little over three months. But for me, that was a lifetime—a lifetime that has taken me on a roller coaster ride, not only on a culinary scale but an emotional one as well. I have a story to tell you, and it begins in that seat over there.

"Davies Deli is not your normal sandwich shop. Not normal in that Mr. and Mrs. Davies use real bread instead of traditional premade submarine rolls. It is the polar opposite of what you see in the chain restaurants, but that is what makes Mom and Pop unique. To me? What makes, or made, this place extra special was Deborah Davies.

"Deborah was Mr. and Mrs. Davies, daughter. She worked

behind the counter, and the reason I had engaged faithful patronage of this amazing establishment. She wore a purple V-neck t-shirt and a matching scrunchie that Monday, and the craziest thing I had ever heard of was on the menu, Meatloaf Sandwich. I don't know which I carried away with me more, the memory of her ponytail bouncing around or the moistest, well-seasoned meatloaf presented in the most unique fashion that I have ever seen.

"You have always heard that a way to a man's heart is through his stomach. Well, I was definitely torn. But I do not write this so you visit Davies Deli for the eye candy; they have an extraordinary menu and are always pushing the envelope to develop new approaches to food that make your taste buds beg for more—all with a sandwich undertone. From the Caesar Salad Sub to the new and exciting must-try Spaghetti Sub, you have to stop by and have lunch or early supper at their southeast Houston location.

"As for the eye candy, well, she is spoken for. For a short period of time she was on loan to yours truly. We shared nearly three months together. Now she belongs to the Lord. We do not know why God takes those who are the most precious to us, but we always trust that He knows what is best. But in the midst of tragedy, she leaves behind a legacy. The legacy of the meal you are about to eat.

"You see, she—along with her parents—had a dream of being able to feed the multitudes on this Thanksgiving Day. And in her final moments of life, she was making phone calls and through the grace of God and her determination, organized all of this for you. And in case you are wondering, she was wearing an orange scrunchie to match one of the stripes in the gown she was wearing.

"Even lying down, Deborah Davies chose to stand. It was the type of person she was. It was the type of daughter she was. She was the type of woman I fell in love with. May her legacy live on through this meal for years to come."

Aaron watched through tear-filled eyes that many were moved. As he prayed over the meal, he hoped that people would understand who Deborah Davies was. He hoped they would understand what this meal meant to her. He prayed for those in the room and each situation, for the lost souls who had doubts, that they would be reminded of who God is through Deborah's life, that broken families would be reunited through the examples like the Davies family. He prayed for the healing of broken spirits like himself, those who believed that true love was non-existent. He prayed that God would send each of them an angel, even if they were for only thirteen minutes.

One Month Later
EPILOGUEX

I heard you frequent this place," a voice familiar to Aaron sneered from behind him.

Aaron turned to see Ethan Chadwick.

"How in the world could your little column bump a central piece like mine? Especially a piece over a month old?"

"Merry Christmas, Ethan. Won't you sit down?" Aaron motioned to the swivel chair next to his. "Have a scoop of cobbler, on me."

"I bet you think that I will say no. Well, I will in fact impose on your time, Stephenson."

Aaron could not help but chuckle. He had the *Houston Chronicle* neatly folded in front of him. The *Chronicle* was the leading news source for the city. The leading paper with the most circulation. The leading paper with the most readers that recently noticed a gigantic boost in sales of a small local publication due to a recent review of a local deli. The review was written by a small-time column writer named Aaron Stephenson. The lead editor of the *Chronicle* was so moved by the piece that she bumped the normal foodie piece written by his now neighbor to rerun his piece.

Aaron waved Erica over and ordered two bowls of

cobbler. Erica smiled at him and greeted the new arrival. "Anything else?"

"Hmmph," was all Ethan could say.

Aaron laughed. "Put it on my tab, Erica. Ethan here is with me. He is a fellow writer."

"Writer? You call yourself a writer with that dribble you put out?"

Again, Aaron was forced to laugh at Ethan's candor.

"Please, I did nothing to influence the *Chronicle* to print my article. It was as much of a surprise to me as it was for you. I only got the call last night from my editor that your paper was going to run my piece. I don't even know why it matters anymore. It is over a month old. So, insulting me will get neither of us anywhere. We are both professionals here. You were once just getting started yourself. And I am sure you remember your big break. Just look at it this way, you are helping me get mine, just as someone way back when gave you yours. For that, I thank you."

With that, Ethan was silent. Aaron figured he came here for a verbal fight. When he realized he wasn't going to get it, he lowered his shoulders and relaxed. He looked around and took in the surroundings for the first time. "Doesn't seem like much."

"That is the greatest part," Aaron said. "You should have a sandwich."

"Who could eat spaghetti on a sandwich? That's preposterous."

"Again, that is the greatest part, Ethan," Aaron began. "See, I heard you once say that we need to enter an establishment and look for the little things. But you began to look for what was *wrong* and forgot to look for what was *right*." Aaron paused a second, then continued. "Do something for me. Look around you and tell me what you see."

Ethan looked over his right shoulder toward the register and swiveled in his chair as far as it would turn, then turned back and looked at Aaron. "Outdated booths, broken down tinker toys, and dirty old men."

"Okay," said Aaron. "Now, do it again. This time let go of the analytical part of your mind."

Ethan pursed his lips.

Aaron stared at him until he rolled his eyes and closed them. "Now, for once, let go of the negative. Remember what you once knew. Don't look for the wrong, Ethan. See what is *right* with this place."

Ethan breathed in and out and repeated the process, much slower this time. He opened his eyes and looked around the room, then he looked at Aaron, only with a much different look on his face.

"I remember eating ice cream with my grandfather sitting in a booth just like that one. We would play old music using the selector like the one upon the wall. We would drink fountain drinks from coke glasses like the ones near each of the windows," Ethan said with what Aaron would swear were tears in his eye.

"Now, do you understand?"

Ethan said nothing.

"*That* is what I do, Ethan. I can understand what you do to an extent. You appeal to an upper echelon of society. But me? I speak to the common folk, like the dirty older man you spoke of. His name is Clarence, by the way. He is a regular here and a pretty nice guy."

They sat in silence as they both enjoyed their cobbler. For

a moment, even Ethan Chadwick agreed that it was on a different level than he had enjoyed in a long time. They spoke as professionals for the first time and enjoyed each other's company on a professional level for the first time. He still passed on the thought of spaghetti in the form of a sandwich, however.

Your loss, Aaron thought.

"You don't have to spend every evening here, Aaron," Pop said.

"I know. I just enjoy it here. I feel closer to her. It has been a few weeks since the funeral, and I still miss her just as much. I really loved your daughter, Pop. Even if we only knew each other so briefly."

"And she loved you the same, son," Pop assured him.

Aaron smiled and went for his wallet. Pop stopped him. "Pop, I need to pay. I haven't paid you for weeks. I do not like being a freeloader, nor do I like the feeling of being in anyone's debt. Deborah wouldn't like it either. So, I begin paying today." Pop pursed his lips, shrugged his shoulders in surrender. Aaron paid, hugged Mom, and left just behind Clarence.

Near his vehicle, on a bench, sat a lone figure. Aaron stopped and looked around. "Clarence?"

"No, my name is not Clarence," said a voice that Aaron had heard before. He walked toward the bench, and as the lamp cast its light on the figure, he could make out the tweed hat and coat the man wore. "The name is Carter."

"You're the vaga… Deborah's friend," Aaron corrected.

Carter laughed, catching his mistake. "No, I am not home-less. Well, not in that respect. Please, sit."

Aaron sat on the edge of the bench away from Carter, not sure what to expect.

"I'm not going to hurt you, Aaron. I'm here to help. So, to speak."

"How's that?"

"You say Deborah spoke of me? What did she say?" Carter asked.

Aaron recalled his and Deborah's final conversation. He shook his head and leaned into his knees. "She called you an angel. Are you an angel, Carter?"

Carter smiled. "Some would say that."

"She said that you were in places that you shouldn't have been, known things you couldn't have known, and did things that were not possible."

"I do get around," Carter said.

"She thought you put the sand dollar in her car. She said you were the only possible answer to how it could have gotten there, and she didn't understand why until I had given her the Bible. But I had no idea about the sand dollar other than the story she told me about her and Pop on the beach. She told me about the connection of those two items bringing her back to the Lord. And looking at it now, it brought her back before it was too late."

Carter just nodded. Aaron saw a friendly ear listening, but also saw a hint of pride in the twinkle of his eyes. "So, you believe Deborah is in the arms of her Savior right now?"

"No doubt," Aaron said. "But if you are an angel sent by God to save her, then why did she have to die? Why wasn't she saved?"

Carter turned his head, his gray eyes looked deeply into Aaron's.

"Wasn't she?"

Aaron thought about it. He knew that the word of God teaches that to be apart from the body is to be present with Christ. He also knew that the human mind was so earthly focused that people somehow felt cheated if God chose to not prolong a life. He remembered a sermon his pastor preached that the world was not home; heaven was. So, going to heaven was the greatest gift anyone could receive. It was actually an honor to die. *Each person has a job to accomplish here on earth,* he recalled the preacher's words, *a God-given task that we were assigned even before we were born. Then, once that assignment is finished, we are taken home. That job can be completed as a 95-year-old saint with miles on the odometer, a ten-minute old infant with only a few breaths...* "or a 24-year-old restaurateur and recently repentant soul with an inoperable tumor," Aaron added is a whisper.

"I suppose she was. I just don't understand it," Aaron said.

"No one can explain it, Aaron. Nor is anyone supposed to understand it. But God does, and He has a purpose behind it all. I don't even understand it," Carter responded.

"So, you *are* an angel?" Aaron asked again.

Carter again smiled. "Some would say that."

Aaron exhaled into his palms and placed them onto his knees. "I just don't understand about Deborah."

"You think all of this was for her, Aaron?" Carter was boring holes through him.

"What do you mean?"

"This was for you, just as much as it was for her. Both of you discovered something about who God is."

"What did I learn?"

"You tell me. What has been the biggest struggle in your

life? What was the one thing you did not think existed in your life?"

Aaron looked over his shoulder. The glow from the neon lights from the deli reflected off his jeep. Carter nodded in approval. "I learned about family. That there are families that love each other. That moms and dads do get along; that they do love and care for their children. I learned that they would be willing to do whatever needed to be done for them."

"Exactly," Carter said, clapping his hands together. "The Davies have adopted you into their family. Accepted you as their own. You are now witnessing the love of a mother and a father you once believed did not exist. And that love goes beyond Deborah. So, cherish it."

"I plan to," Aaron said.

"What else?"

Aaron thought for a moment but came up empty.

"Something you learned about 30 minutes ago," Carter said, nudging his shoulder.

Aaron scrunched his brows, "Ethan?"

"Go on," Carter urged.

Aaron had once thought poorly of Ethan Chadwick. But through his experience this afternoon, he learned that he was just as human as he was. That Ethan had the same connections to his own past as those he wrote to, he was just blinded by the spotlight that he forgot there was once something about the job that ignited a passion.

"I guess I have learned that God can use us to reach those who have forgotten what it was once like to be who they once were. And that there is common ground, even amongst those whom we feel are the enemy."

"There you go." Carter gave Aaron a fatherly pat on the knee.

Both men sat in silence with just the warm wind blowing. The kind that let you know that a norther was on its way.

"I should let you get going. Wouldn't want you to get home too late and oversleep for church tomorrow," Carter said, standing. He walked along the path headed toward the business complex across the lot. Aaron got in his jeep and headed to his studio and recliner. Tip-off was in thirty minutes and Harden was on another streak.

Carter walked around the corner of the last apartment structure and into the city park. The sun was rising, casting its beam across the grass, setting a plume of steam off the chilled ground. He continued across a path and through a bank of trees when a voice drew his attention.

"Impressive, Carter. You performed above and beyond expectations. He is grateful for your hard work," Gabriel said. He then added with a smile, "I knew I could count on you for this."

"Was there ever a doubt?" Carter said humorously.

"Never," says Gabriel, returning the jest. They both laughed.

Carter walked on a little farther. Gabriel followed. A short distance later, they sat on a bench that overlooked the city.

"People amaze me. They go about living their lives in a rush, and they seem to ignore the very reason they are rushing around for. I don't understand how they can be so preoccupied with nothing at all. It just doesn't seem like it's worth it when you consider the big picture, of course. If I had a nervous bone in my body, it would be very unnerved."

"That's why we are here," Gabriel reassured him. "To remind them."

The two angels sat and watched men and women from each walk of life begin their day, oblivious to their people-watching activity.

"It's going to be a nice day," Gabriel observed.

"That's what they say," Carter replied.

"So," Gabriel said, standing and looking down at Carter. "Are you ready for your next assignment?"

Carter looked up and into Gabriel's blazing blue eyes and smiled.

ACKNOWLEDGMENTS

First, I want to thank Wordcrafts Press and Mike Parker for partnering with me on this adventure. It was a departure from what *The Five Barred Gate* was and new territory for me as a writer. I hope it serves both of us well. I look forward to our next project.

A special thanks to the doctors and nurses with UT Medical Center who have treated me over the past two years dealing with my seizure disorder. From the doctor's office visits to the inpatient hospital tests, I have always felt that I was a priority, and I am grateful for your service. I also learned a great deal through my stays and have incorporated each experience into Little Reminders.

Thank you to Bonniejean Alford. As always, your steady voice of telling me to get back to it has paid off with yet another completed work. Thank you for your continued accountability. Your friendship is appreciated.

To my fellow Weekend Writing Warriors. I discovered you guys this past year and have grown appreciative of our small family. I have enjoyed your feedback through the snippets we've shared. Hearing from fellow writers, learning, and growing is what this is all about. And now you get to see the final product. Thank you for your input in making this work that much better.

And to the one who lives within every female character I write, my wife, Carolyn. Much like Aaron in this novel, when I consider you, I can barely find two words to put together. Know that I love you and that I could not do this without your support and inspiration. Thank you for lending your talents to the painting on the cover. Your gifts will go down in history.

And most of all, I must thank my Lord and Savior for the gift He has entrusted me. I never want to accept any accolades or praise for the success of this or any book I may write. The glory always goes to Him. *Little Reminders* is His message. If you feel drawn to Him through it, it is the power of the Holy Spirit, not through anything I have done. Give Him the praise for that.

Finally, thank you, my friend, the reader. I pray this journey was a special one for you. I hope you enjoyed reading it as much as I enjoyed writing it. From the looks of things, this could be just the beginning for Carter. There are many others out there who need a gentle reminder of the little things that matter in life—the little things that we tend to forget about that matter so much to us. For now, take a moment and look around and don't take those little things for granted.

God Bless all of you.

In His Exciting Service,

Jeff S. Bray

ABOUT THE AUTHOR

Jeff S. Bray lives in a small town in South Central Texas with his wife Carolyn and two of their five children. They are members of the local First Baptist Church, serving in several capacities, including teaching Sunday School, working with Men's Ministry, and managing the church's online presence.

Jeff's passion for writing began in elementary school with a short story about a lost kitten. His circuitous literary career started with his personal blog, *Moments for the Heart*, which led to small paid assignments before expanding into magazine articles in national publications.

Jeff is the author of the contemporary thriller, *The Five Barred Gate*, and the *Elissa the Curious Snail* series of whimsical children's picture books which help parents introduce basic faith concepts like prayer, even in the face of adversity, into their teachings in a fun and entertaining way.

Connect with Jeff online at:

jeffsbrayauthor.com